The Sword of Argall
The Last Days of Atlantis - 2

The Sword of Argall
The Last Days of Atlantis - 2

by
Frank Schildiner

based on the novel
The Last Days of Atlantis
by
Charles Lomon & P.-B. Gheusi

A Black Coat Press Book

ISBN 978-1-64932-121-3. First Printing. July 2022. Published
by Black Coat Press, an imprint of Hollywood Comics.com,
LLC, P.O. Box 17270, Encino, CA 91416. All rights reserved.
Except for review purposes, no part of this book may be re-
produced or transmitted in any form or by any means, elec-
tronic or mechanical, including photocopying, recording, or by
any information storage and retrieval system, without permis-
sion in writing from the publisher. The stories and characters
depicted in this novel are entirely fictional. Printed in the
United States of America.

Introduction

As its predecessor, *The Soul of Soroe*, this novel—the second in a trilogy—is based on *Les Atlantes, Aventures des temps légendaires* [The Atlanteans: Adventures in Legendary Times] (1905) by Charles Lomon & Pierre-Barthélemy Gheusi, translated by Brian Stableford and published by Black Coat Press in 2015 as *The Last Days of Atlantis*.

Although *The Last Days of Atlantis* did not attract much attention at the time of its release, it can be seen in hindsight as a significant benchmark in the history of imaginative fiction, for it is the first great epic fantasy novel of the 20th century—and arguably, the first ever penned.

Black Coat Press is proud to resurrect that long forgotten world and its characters through a series of novels written separately by Frank Schildiner and Randy & Jean-Marc Lofficier, grafting new branches on this heretofore unknown classic of fantasy.

Jean-Marc Lofficier

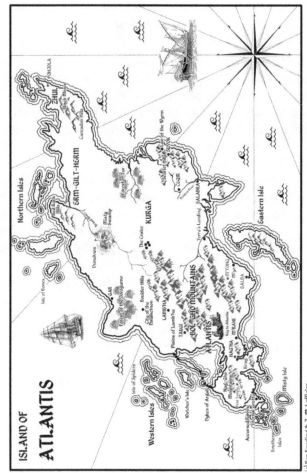

ISLAND OF
ATLANTIS

(c) Ben Spurling & J.-M. Lofficier

"Out of chaos came the light. Out of the will came life."

The Egyptian Book of the Dead

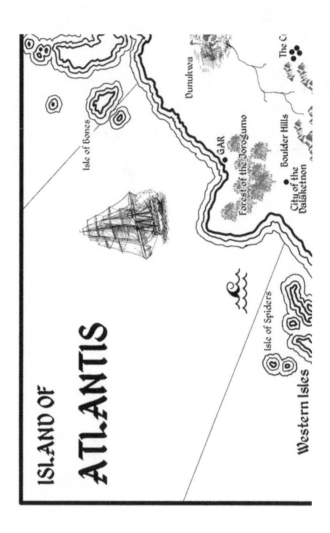

ISLAND OF
ATLANTIS

Isle of Bones

Dunukwa

GAR

Forest of the Jorogumo

Boulder Hills

City of the
Dalaketnon

The C

Isle of Spiders

Western Isles

CHAPTER I

Civil War was impending and there was nothing Argall could do to avert its horrors. His very presence was the cause of the turmoil and anything he did now could bring about the conflagration. Therefore, he followed his nature and listened, learning the identities of the players and the strategies they used in their forthcoming war.

"...looks like the statue! He is the returned Argall, just as she is the returned Soroe!" a noble named Illaz said.

Prince Illaz was a tall, handsome man with deep copper skin and the sculpted sinews of a warrior. The scion of an ancient Atlantean noble family, he was known as an agitator who sought a change in the structure of society.

"We," Ruslem, the high priest of the Temple of Light said, "were fooled for generations by magic surrounding the false immortal queen, Yerra. How can we be certain this has not occurred again?"

The camps were divided into three distinct factions. The first were the military and ancient nobles. Their rage at discovering that their lovely queen, Yerra, was naught, but a series of witches trained by an evil power infuriated them. They would back anyone with a claim against the Crown with the hopes of increasing their power.

The second were the priestly caste, men and women who served the gods in the name of the state. They were also the main bureaucrats of the Atlantean government.

This gave them a great deal of political power, despite having few men under arms.

The final faction was the merchant class. They possessed little actual power, but wielded massive influence over every aspect of the kingdom. They were prosperous men and women, many dressed in greater luxury than the nobles. Additionally, more than a few controlled dangerous mercenary forces that could tip the scale of power in each direction.

"He arrived," Lophan, the one-eyed Admiral of the Atlantean navy said, "on a boat from the north. My ships intercepted the Erm-Gilt-Hermian vessel in the open sea. My sailors and I recognized the man's resemblance to ancient Argall."

Lophan was a tall woman with wildly flowing crimson hair that fell past her shoulders. Attractive in a dangerous way, she was considered the most honest noblewoman in Atlantis.

"How do you know you were not bespelled?" Ruslem asked. "Yerra's master fooled us for generations!"

This was the truth, and few denied that fact. After the death of the original King Argall and Queen Soroe, the saviors of Atlantis, Queen Yerra had assumed power. A lovely, bewitching woman with uncanny magical abilities, she proclaimed herself immortal. After ruling for one hundred years, her subjects had created a monument in her honor, a statue as tall as the palace and equaling that of Soroe and Argall.

It was only thanks to Soroe's modern-day descendent, a priestess of the Temple of Light, that the truth had become known. Yerra was not immortal, but merely one of a series of false queens placed on the throne by a distant unknown mystical force. Her statue held a spell that transformed the stone face and form of the queen into that of the current wearer of the Crown of Yerra.

In a rage, the inhabitants of the city had pulled down the mighty image of Queen Yerra, destroying part of the dwelling of her main supporters, the evil Temple of Gold and Iron. The mob had also driven out the members of that order, realizing that their worship of the demon snake Apophis could destroy their lands.

Argall, the chieftain of his barbaric northern people, had always known that his ancestors had come from Atlantis. An Argall, son of Argall, had always ruled their tribe in the frozen wastes, and were often declared the war chief of all tribes when battle commenced against outsiders. The idea that his ancient ancestor had ruled these lands was one of many surprises.

Soroe, the queen candidate who had overthrown Yerra, stood silently. She, too, had been listening without comment. A stunningly beautiful woman with shoulder-length golden hair, large blue eyes, and silken skin, she was the very image of the ancient queen. What those present also knew was that she had faced terrible dangers in the quest Yerra had recently sent her upon.

Yerra, in the hope of killing a possible claimant to the throne, had sent the young priestess in search of the fabled "Soul of Soroe." This item was a mystic gem possessing unknown powers and was said to have aided the first Queen of Atlantis in her quest towards bringing peace to the kingdom.

Soroe, with the aid of a young thief named Deena, had survived the many trials placed in her path before finding the lost treasure. Few questioned her rights and power upon returning… until Argall had arrived.

"The question of whether the chieftain of the Erm-Gilt-Herm is the heir of Argall can be settled with ease," she said, her voice carrying across the oversized, empty chamber.

"We will not accept the spells of the Temple of Light," Illaz said. "Your uncle is their high priest and greatest supporter."

This caused a roar of protest from the priests, their words flowing together in a terrible, incomprehensible babble. The military and nobles snarled back, and the civil war appeared poised to occur, when Soroe produced the Soul of Soroe.

It was a flawless clear gem that radiated and pulsed with white golden light. Laying atop a golden scepter, the jewel was the symbol of the queen's power in these lands.

The room fell silent again and the gem exuded a warm light that brought peace to all present. Soroe turned in a slow circle, showing again the legendary item that proved her claim.

"The Soul of Soroe reveals the truth in all who live," she said, her voice hushed. "If this man is a pawn of dreaded powers, all shall know."

Turning his direction, she gazed up to his face and asked, "Will you agree to answer the question while standing before the power of the Soul of Soroe?"

"I will," Argall said, and stepped forward.

CHAPTER II

Several miles away from the conference, four figures strode down the gloomy stairs that led to the lowest
level of the ruined Temple of Gold and Iron. The stairs
were made from a dark, smooth stone that shimmered in
the spare light. They did not light any candles, lanterns,
or torches, but strode deeper into the stygian darkness
with purposeful steps.

Arriving at a flat stone wall at the bottom of the
stairs, the hooded figure in the lead placed a red-scaled,
clawed, four-fingered hand upon a lower portion of the
rock and pushed. The wall slid inward, revealing a tunnel leading west, towards the queen's palace.

The four walked down the tunnel, their step perfect-
ly timed with each other. None spoke throughout their
journey through the darkness, and they stopped at the
same moment. The leader climbed upon the shoulders of
the two cloaked figures nearest to him, reached up and
pushed open a circular door hidden in the ceiling. Each
then climbed up, the only sound being that of their nails
scraping across stone.

Within minutes they stopped as a single voice became audible in their hiding spot.

"...I will," they heard, and a look passed between
them beneath their cowls.

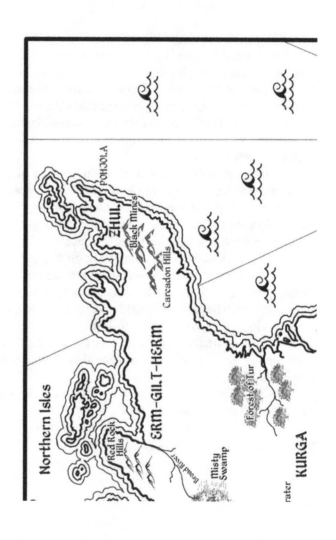

Northern Isles

CRM-GILT-HCRM

Red Rock Hills

Broad River

Misty Swamp

ZHUL

POHJOLA

Black Mines

Carcadon Hills

Forest of Tur

KURGA

rater

CHAPTER III

"Step back, everyone," Soroe replied, sweeping her arm in a circle over her head. "I would not force anyone to reveal their secrets without their consent."

The three factions each backed away, standing outside the luminescent radius of the mystic scepter. Argall alone braved the power of the jewel, his stride unhesitating and relaxed.

A tall, flaxen-haired man with fair skin, grey blue eyes, and the powerful physique of a born athlete and warrior, Argall radiated a confidence that was a force nearly as powerful as the Soul of Soroe. Dressed in the simple cloth of his people, he somehow managed to appear regal among the finery of the Atlantean society.

"State your name," Soroe said as the scepter's radiance grew stronger.

"Argall, son of Argall, Dhu-Hern of my people," Argall said.

"Dhu-Hern... Is that your title? Are you a king among your people?" she asked.

Argall shook his head, "On the Erm-Gilt-Herm wastes, we have no kings. I am merely a tribal leader."

"Are you of Atlantean birth?" Soroe asked, hearing the collective intake of breath from those surrounding.

Argall nodded, "Yes. The eldest son of my line is always Argall, son of Argall. We are Atlantean, though have not been in many lifetimes."

"Did you come with intent to cause the downfall or subjugation of Atlantis?" she asked.

"No," he replied.

Soroe lowered the scepter and said, "One mystery solved. He is who he claims to be. None may lie before the power of the Soul's light."

"That does not mean this barbarian should rule us as our king," Ruslem said. "We just freed our people from the evil of the false Yerra. Must we deliver them to an unknown foreigner?"

From the ranks of the nobles and military stepped and elderly man dressed in the simple robes of a soldier. None were fooled by the modest display, recognizing the ancient Prince and former commander of the Queen's armies, Iztemph.

The narrow-shouldered former general moved with the lithe step of a younger man. His face was a map of deep furrows and his long nose resembled that of the beak of a vast bird of prey.

"In past days," he said, "when such a question arose, an ancient pact was invoked. The Pact of the Oracle. We must consult the Gods for their guidance before bickering like a pack of fishwives at the morning market."

"There is a difficulty in that bond, good Prince Iztemph," Soroe said. "The oracles of Atlantis were the priestesses of the Temple of Gold and Iron. None who served that evil shrine now remain—nor would I trust the word of those terrible men."

A bark of loud, derisive emerged from the rear of the chamber and every head swiveled towards a pillar near the north end of the chamber. Leaning against the smooth, stone support was an odd figure who had arrived with Argall and his Erm-Gilt-Herm barbarians. Shorter than the lofty Northerners, he possessed shoulders wider than any of those powerful men. His arms, legs, and chest held oversized sinews as well as many grey scars.

Oddest of all was the battered steel mask that always covered his face. He never removed the face covering and none had even seen him eat or drink. A few whisps of grey hair fell across the back of his skull and pale, inhuman gray eyes stared out without any form of emotional response.

This was the man known as "The Accursed One" and he made everyone, save Argall, nervous. He rarely spoke, but when he did so, there was an unnerving knowing quality about his words.

"It is almost as if he'd lived so long that he knows everything," Argall's blood-brother, Maghee, had said one day when the Masked Man was away from their sight. "And why does he never remove his mask?"

"I have asked, but his answers are cryptic. I know he practices magic of some type. That alone makes him strange," Argall had answered.

In the present, the Accursed One pushed away from the pillar and continued, "An oracle stands among you, and you squabble. Ask the one with the power. Place the soothsayer with the radiance of your toy and the truth shall emerge."

"Are you claiming you are an oracle, masked one?" Ruslem asked. "You will forgive me if I doubt your claim."

The Masked Man threw back his head and laughed, a sound full of merriment unlike the sardonic sound earlier.

"I? I cannot be an oracle, priest. That is not a power that men can hold! Only women may contact the Goddess and speak her words. She stands right there!" The Accursed One said, pointing towards Soroe.

"Me?" Soroe asked and shook her head. "I have no abilities foretelling the future."

"This is true," Ruslem said. "She has not the power, or it would have emerged many years ago."

The Masked Man's hand did not waver as he replied, "I did not refer to you, child."

Soroe moved to the right, standing beside Argall. The Accursed One's hand did not waver, and only one person now stood in his path.

The recipient of his interest was Deena, the recent companion of Soroe. The girl was tiny, with short scarlet hair, mischievous green eyes, and a delicate, almost childlike, face. A former thief from the worst streets of Atlantis, she had shared Soroe's many tribulations and was said to have been the reason the quest for the gem had succeeded.

"Me?" Deena said, staggering back. "Gold and Iron! Where did you get such rot?"

"You radiate the power, though it lays behind a wall in your mind," the Accursed One said.

Ruslem pushed forward and asked, "The only men who can find an Oracle possess the Eyes of Darkness!"

The Masked Man nodded once and bowed, "My powers come from darkness and cold. Not the demon snake your people sought to appease, but the primordial night that lay over the universe before the light emerged."

"Such power vanished from our lands before the Kings and Queens of Atlantis arose," Ruslem said, tugging at the white whiskers that lay across his chin. "This explains much…"

"It explains what, priest?" Illaz asked, his face flushing with anger. "Are you suborning the crown with this outsider who has not the courage to reveal his face?"

"If you believe you can remove my mask," the Accursed One said, "do try. You will find it as unmoving as your mightiest mountain. As to your first statement, do you believe I care a wit about the politics of your land?"

"Liar!" Illaz said throwing his glove to the ground. "You seek the power of Gold and Iron to stand behind the throne of Atlantis!"

Those present started and inhaled in shock, knowing these words were a clear challenge for a duel. Prince Illaz was one of the premier swordsmen in the kingdom and he invoked this demand when he flew into a passion.

"Outlander," Ruslem said, "Prince Illaz challenges your words. You need not accept since these are not your lands. However, if you refuse, you shall be escorted to the harbor and placed on the first ship leaving Atlantis."

"I accept the challenge," the Masked Man said. "Let us be about this immediately and stop wasting time."

A roar filled the great chamber and the three factions backed away, leaving a clear space in the center of the room. The possible civil war was on hold as everyone present watched as the two combatants moved towards each other.

CHAPTER IV

The two men were clear contrasts, absolute opposites. Illaz was the very picture of ancient nobility, well-groomed, erect, proud, and handsome. A slim blade lay at his hip, a worn weapon used in many battles, both for the crown and his personal honor.

The Accursed One was shorter, wider, dressed in tattered, poorly made clothing that barely contained sinews that appeared oversized for his frame. Leather bracers wrapped in silver chains encircled his forearms and a pair of axes lay across broad back.

"A duel of honor demands noble weapons," Illaz said while eyeing the wicked weapons bore by the masked man.

"Weapons possess no nobility," the Accursed One said. "It is the hand that wields the blade that determines its dignity."

"I believe," Soroe said as a titter of laughter rippled across the room, "that Prince Illaz is hinting that the duel should be performed with swords."

"Then he should have said so instead of preening," the Masked One replied.

He pulled his axes from his back in a pair of smooth motions. Without ceremony, he handed them to Argall and Maghee before returning to an empty space. He then rejected two blades offered by nobles before taking one used by Lophan.

"Are you done?" Illaz asked. "I would like this completed before the winter festival commences next year."

Another ripple of amusement spread through those present, this time favoring the noble Atlantean. The outlander did not reply, but simply raised his weapon and waited.

Illaz saluted briefly and attacked. His blade flashed like silver lightning. His assault was impressive and purposeful; no moves were performed with flashy excess, nor without purpose. His every attack was a demonstration of the perfection of the swordmaster, and Atlantean nobles, military leaders, priests, and merchants gazed with awe.

"Your friend is losing," Soroe said to Argall.

"The Prince has not landed a single attack," Argall said smiling and clapping his hands. "He has no notion of whom he faces."

Soroe glanced at the handsome barbarian chief, "Oh? You know something that is not apparent from his odd demeanor?"

Argall nodded, never taking his eyes from the duel, "You will see. Illaz is a fine swordsman, but he is like a man hoping he can chop down an oak with a blade of grass."

Illaz, sweat pouring down his face and neck, found himself growing desperate. His opponent's sword barely moved, simply appeared before a thrust or a slash cut. Feeling a little desperate, he attempted his favorite trick, a hand switch of his sword performed after a parry.

He was about to smile in triumph, when the outlander's sword kicked out, striking the blade in mid-air. The weapon spiraled upward and the Accursed One caught its hilt in one leathery palm. Glancing at the weapon for a moment, the Masked Man tossed it back into Illaz's fumbling hands.

"Have we finished?" he asked, lowering his sword.

"Duels are not complete until one party dies," Illaz said.

"Then our duel shall never end because I have no need for your death, youth," the Accursed One said. "Consider yourself dead and returned because you have not enough lifetimes in which to defeat me in a duel."

Padhoum, the curly-haired, fluty-voiced, ochre-skinned eunuch majordomo of the palace hovered into view. Dressed in the finest gold and red gown available in the kingdom, he was like a vast ship gliding across the waves when he appeared before the others. Bowing deeply, he cleared his voice for several seconds.

"There is a precedent for such a decision. Viceroy Elim of the lost House Ruskia once granted life to one he defeated in a duel. The loser of the duel, one Prince Hus, was to devote his every moment protecting the kingdom. You will find their statues on the first floor of the hall of heroes, third room, left side, rows five and eight. Do you agree to these terms, Prince Illaz?"

"I do," Illaz said without hesitation.

"A question," the Accursed One asked. "Were the followers of Gold and Iron human?"

"Yes," Padhoum said. "Of course!"

"Why do you ask?" Soroe asked, stepping forward again.

"Because I smell a scent, I hoped I would never face again," he said, turning towards the south side of the chamber and pointing towards a blank wall.

"Masked friend," Argall said, "there is nothing there save a blank wall."

The Accursed One sighed and continued pointing, "Beyond the wall hide four Children of Dimme-kur. I recognize their damned stink."

CHAPTER V

Argall strode forward, drawing the Atlantean blade while barking orders to everyone present.

"Erm-Gilt-Herm, to me! Guards, forward! Priests, nobles, and other unarmed citizens, back away... Not you!" he said, pointing towards Padhoum. "Now, open the hidden door!"

The Atlanteans ran to obey the chieftain's commands, with royal guards and bodyguards stationing themselves in a tight, armed, line between the wall and those retreating. There were twitters of fear from some of the nobles and prosperous merchants as they pressed themselves against the far walls.

"Sir," Padhoum said, his high-pitched voice more whine than words. "I know of no such secret door."

A beam of white light struck him in the eyes, staggering the obese majordomo briefly. The energy flowed between Soroe's open palm as she slowly whispered words of power in an unknown tongue.

"Tell the truth, Padhoum," Soroe said. "You may not speak untruths before the holy light of the Heavens."

The ochre-colored eunuch shook and murmured, "Press the small black dot on the right-side edge."

Padhoum need not have bothered as the wall slowly slid backwards before dropping into the floor.

Four robed figures emerged from the dusty, gloomy corridor behind the walls. They each stood approximately five feet-tall, and their faces were hidden within the depths of their hoods.

Each held their arms folded within their voluminous sleeves and they stopped after stepping into the chamber.

One of the quartets broke from the group, moving one step forward and bowing deeply.

"Dread King," the hooded one said in a lovely, soft tenor tone, "Luminous Queen... I am Akhkhazu, high priestess of Gold and Iron. I greet you and request the return of our temple and its rights."

"No," Soroe said. "Your priests sought the murder of infants to satisfy your demon snake master. They are expelled."

The priestess shifted direction towards Argall, "What of you, Argall, son of Argall? Do you hold with the rulings of the queen?"

"I do," Argall said. "She speaks wisdom. The worship of evil never brings good."

"Apophis, He Who Encircles the World, is not evil. He simply is, and must be appeased with lives. What are a few unimportant souls compared to the lives of millions?" the creature asked.

"Those who ask that question never volunteer to be the sacrifice," Argall said. "You have your answer. Leave now."

The speaker of the foursome shook an unseen head, "No, I think not... If you are intractable, you shall be replaced. There are always humans who are more compliant."

A taloned four-fingered hand emerged from the folds of the cloak, the scarlet scales shimmering in the sunlight.

"Kill them," the speaker said. "Kill them all!"

The four cloaked figures threw off their outer coverings, revealing themselves. A series of gasps and shrieks escaped the lips of many present as these bizarre beings stood exposed in their full, frightening forms.

The creatures the Masked Man had referred to as the "Children of Dimme-kur" were female, with flowing ebony hair that fell just above their knees. Their figures with shapely and might have been impressive and pleasing to the eye. However, that detail was lost in the chimerical horror that transformed them into living nightmares.

Their skin was the scaly hide of a serpent, yet a layer of greenish yellow feathers covered their torsos. Their legs were hairy and twisted like that of a she-goat, but their feet were the splayed talons of vast birds of prey. Sinewy prehensile tails extruded from their spines with ivory-colored stingers on the end.

However, these details were secondary to their faces. Their eyes were multifaceted jewels that shimmered with a pulsing, sickly, yellow luminescence. Their mouths were astonishingly long, with plumb, pink, human-shaped lips that spread wide, revealing oversized, serrated teeth. Long pink tongues lolled across their enormous maws, dripping fluid across their pointed chins.

"Give up now, humans," the lead Dimme-kur said in that same pleasant voice. "Your kind fear bloodshed."

"Not all of us," Argall said, pointing his sword towards the horror. "Leave at once—or die!"

"As you wish," Akhkhazu replied. "Kill the warriors first, my sisters. Then we shall see which of the survivors will agree to our terms."

The three horrors, who had remained still and silent until now, straightened, and hissed. They flexed their hands, and their talons grew several inches longer.

CHAPTER VI

"Do these beasts practice magic?" Argall asked as the Accursed One and Maghee appeared at his left and right sides.

The masked warrior bore his axes while Maghee held his Atlantean blade. The remaining Erm-Gilt-Herm warriors spread out in a line around them, each armed and crouching in their familiar fighting stances.

"No," the Accursed One said. "They don't need to."

That was when Akhkhazu leaped into the air, sailing straight upwards and clinging to the ceiling. The horror scurried across the stone ceiling, hand and foot talons scrabbling and moving across the surface at an astonishing speed.

The second Dimme-kur leaped backwards, crouching on the wall several feet above the ground. The monster's terrible tail lashed out, snapping like a whip as its terrible edge sliced through the air.

The remaining pair remained in their position, standing low and barely moving. Their insectoid eyes flashed as they ran over the warriors in the front rows, their expressions blank.

"Do not let their tails strike you," the masked man said. "They contain a poison that will kill you almost instantly."

"Then how do we kill these things?" Maghee asked.

Argall laughed and swung his sword through the air. "The same way we do any enemy. Take their heads off! My brother Atlanteans, are you with me?"

Shouts of confirmation came from the military men and bodyguards. The barbarians of the frozen north who had anointed him as their leader a year earlier, roared and beat their shields and weapons together, horrified and enraged by these threatening demons.

Only the Accursed One appeared unmoved. He held his axes in his massive hands, blades whistling as they sliced through the air.

"Then ready yourselves!" Argall said. "Let us see if they bleed red!"

The Erm-Gilt-Herm barbarians charged in three groups. The first launched as a body towards the Dimme-kur who clung to the wall like some monstrous, oversized scorpion. The remaining groups charged the pair on the ground, weapons seeking the horror's inhuman bodies.

Only Argall and the Masked One remained in place, their eyes upon the one called Akhkhazu who lurked over their heads.

"Can you bring it down with your magic?" Argall asked.

"No," the Accursed One replied. "If I attack Akhkhazu with my powers, the roof will crumble and kill everyone in this room."

"You had no such concerns when we faced the Dalaketnon!" Argall said.

"Because I did not care if every one of those insane fae fell. Here, I would endanger innocents," he said.

"Can you get me up there?" the chieftain asked.

"No," the Accursed One said, "but you have greater concerns now."

As he finished his sentence, a Dimme-kur landed before Argall. The warrior ducked as the tail slashed through the air, spattering clear fluid across the floor. Sizzling sounds, like that of oil in burning pan, filled the air.

Argall slashed after the tail, missing by inches as the appendage withdrew. The Dimme-kur sliced across the barbarian's chest, leaving four wounds across his torso. The warrior moved to the right, but the monster blocked his line of retreat, and swung an arm out in a blurring motion. The chieftain barely avoided another injury as the other hand sought his throat.

"Do not slash," the Accursed One said, his eyes never leaving Akhkhazu. "Your edge shall never penetrate their skin."

Argall absorbed this information just as the tail and hands barely missed him again. Remembering his training as a gladiator, the barbarian changed his style in an instant.

As the tail pulled back for another attack, Argall lunged, the point of his sword extended. The blade stabbed into the Dimme-kur's palm. The monster shrieked, leaping back ten feet, spattering black ichor across the surface of the smooth stone floor. The wail was horrific, resembling that of a tortured animal screaming as a predator slowly tore it to pieces.

The creature attacking Argall launched itself forward, four sets of talons and one stinger aiming for the warrior. If even one claw penetrated, it would render him incapable of attack, or defense.

Rather than accepting that fate, Argall dove forward, rolling beneath the Dimme-kur and coming back to his feet behind the monster. Lunging again, the chieftain's blade bit deep into the stinger-ladened tail. The appendage drooped and fell to the floor with a meaty splat. The demon screamed again, with a note of despair now.

As the beast leaped again, Argall stabbed out, catching the creature in the leg. The motion ripped the

Atlantean blade from his grasp. He reached for the dagger at his waist when a sword fell at his feet. It was also an Atlantean weapon, though newer in design.

Argall snatched it from the ground, lifting the point ahead of his body. The Dimme-kur, moving far slower now with a sword protruding from one of his legs, reached for the warrior's neck with his unhurt hand. But the barbarian chief smiled, moved to his right, and pressed the point of the new blade through his enemy's neck.

The demon's cries of agony and fury vanished a moment later as the point exploded through the rear of the creature's throat.

An axe clattered to the ground at his feet. The Masked One, still watching the ceiling where Akhkhazu was creeping, held his remaining weapon in one hand.

"Use that to remove its head," he said, adding, "It may take a few swings."

CHAPTER VII

In point-of-fact, it took Argall five swings of the huge axe to remove the demon's head. By then, the other three creatures had also fallen; however, nine warriors lay dead upon the floor, and five more appeared gravely wounded.

"You are both more and less than I believed," Akhkhazu said. "I shall return and eat your still beating heart before your eyes."

Argall laughed while pointing the axe towards the distant monster. "I have heard that threat many times before, yet here I stand. Who sent you, monster? Who dares face the might of Atlantis?"

"You shall find out!" Akhkhazu replied.

An opening appeared in the roof. A moment later, the creature had vanished into the open air.

"Did anyone know a door lay upon that roof?" Soroe asked, looking pointedly at Padhoum.

"Yes, of course I did," Padhoum replied. "I could have told anyone, had I been asked. Nobody considered consulting me regarding the arrangements for this gathering, such as it is…"

"Be that as it may," Soroe said, "you shall now reveal every secret you know about this palace. We cannot risk the lives of more Atlanteans, nor that of their rulers."

"Are you going to let her issue commands like that?" Illaz asked of Argall.

Argall shrugged as he retrieved and cleaned his blade. "Why would I object?" he said. "Her order was exactly as I would have done it. The Queen-elect and I have no true dispute."

"Yes, you do," Ruslem said, stepping forward. "Your presence divides our people. Before the terrible assault upon this room by those demons, we were planning a consultation with an oracle. Or potential oracle, such as she is…"

Deena, who stood near Soroe, shook her head. "I am no oracle or magical person. I was a thief before I met Soroe!"

"When you lived on the streets," The Accursed One asked, "did you always know who to trust, who was dangerous, and the best moment when to steal? Tell the truth now!"

Deena frowned and nodded slowly. "Yes, but that is because I knew how to survive. Everyone learns that when they have no other choice."

Soroe shook her head. "Not really," she said. "You saved me multiple times because of your instincts. Perhaps the outlander speaks the truth."

Ruslem bowed slightly and said, "The ceremony where light joins dark will reveal if this is so. The outlander, if he does not lie, can summon the primordial darkness while I do the same with the light of creation. The intermingling will awaken the power within the child Deena—if she is indeed an oracle.

"And what if I'm not? What happens then? I boil away or crumble into ash or something?" Deena asked while shaking her head.

The masked man chuckled as he replied, "Nothing shall happen to you, save that you shall have a headache for several minutes. The power we call upon can awaken an oracle, nothing else. It will dazzle the eyes and mind for a short time."

"He tells the truth," Ruslem said. "However, we cannot and will not force the power upon you. It must be your choice, child."

Deena thought for a few seconds, then said, "What happens if I say yes? I have to go into some nunnery and pray all day? Give up wearing decent clothing and drinking wine? Gold and Iron! I'd rather go back to fighting rats for food scraps!"

The room exploded into laughter, but the young former thief appeared defiant and serious. She ignored the amusement and watched the priest and the man in the metal mask as the merriment died down.

"The Temple of Gold and Iron no longer exist," Soroe said. "A new direction would be determined for you."

Argall shook his head. "No, I disagree," he said. "If she has the power of an oracle, we should not dictate her destiny. Among the Erm-Gilt-Herm, the witches who see the future have the rights to choose their lives. Even the basest chieftains of the wastes do not deny them a place in their tribes."

"That is unprecedented!" Ruslem said. "Oracles must be contained for fear they will tell all to anyone who asks!"

"Then you would imprison her in a life of misery because of her birth?" Argall asked. "I would reject the power too, if that were to be my fate."

"I agree," Soroe said. "Deena is neither above nor below the law. The rules that bind the rulers of Atlantis are subject to all who reside within our kingdom. Otherwise, we risk returning to the days of the false queen, Yerra."

A ripple of whispers ran across the chamber and the high priest of the temple of light bowed deeply.

"I stand corrected by you both, Soroe and Argall. Should the power of the oracle fall upon this child, she shall hold the same rights that any Atlantean holds," Ruslem said. "Is this agreed, priests and nobles? Merchants who supply our people?"

A roar of acclamation shook the large room and Deena blushed and rolled her eyes at the response. She looked very young at that moment, but she shook off the shyness as the yells died out.

"Fine," she said. "Let's get this over with. What do we need to do? Wait for you two to put on robes and dance about in circles?"

The Accursed One laughed and replied, "No, simply cut off some flesh from your skin. Which finger do you think you can spare?"

Deena snorted and rolled her eyes again. "You're making fun of me!" she said.

"Yes, but I do that to everyone," he replied. "Just stand where you are and allow my colleague and myself a moment of concentration."

"What will happen if someone makes a noise, my friend?" Argall asked.

"All life on the planet shall die," the masked one said and snorted. "No, nothing will happen except you may slow down our incantations. This is a complex summonsing, yet quite simple."

"That makes no sense," Soroe said. "How can an incantation be complex and simple at the same time?"

"How can the air be unseen yet move mountains?" The Accursed One asked in return. "You ask questions that are the very basis of life upon this world."

"Is it wrong that I ask?" Soroe said, tilting her head and studying the odd figure.

The Accursed One laughed and shook his head, "Never in life! Question everything! Accepting every word of the wise as truth leads to foolish choices."

"Even from you?" Soroe asked, smiling slightly.

"Especially from me," the masked man replied.

The Queen-elect's smile grew broader and she, at the fussy gesture of her uncle Ruslem, backed away from Deena. She found herself near Argall, who sheathed his sword and watched the pair with unfeigned interest. The priest and the outlander stood on opposite sides from Deena, Ruslem on her right, and the Accursed One on her left.

"Your friend is very strange," she said as the masked man and the high priest of light each bowed their heads and murmured words in bizarre tongues.

"Wait until you know him better," Argall said.

He grinned and crossed his arms before his broad, deep chest.

CHAPTER VIII

A tense hush fell across the chamber, with those present standing still as each moment slowly passed. Eventually, the whispering pair shifted, with Ruslem raising his hands high above his head. The masked man extended his arms to his sides at shoulder level at the same instant.

Without ceremony or sound, a pair of spheres appeared before them. Ruslem's was a fiery, shifting ball of white light and fire that hovered like a miniature sun. Beams of golden radiance emerged from the tiny globe, and anyone struck by the beam felt a gentle warmth that grew hotter with each passing second.

The sphere before the Accursed One was the same size, yet completely different. This ball was a writhing circle of pure darkness. Simply looking at its stygian surface sent chills down the spines of those present. The chamber felt cooler by the very presence of this orb and many people present looked away.

A heartbeat passed and then two opposing forces flew forward, meeting just above the head of Deena. The orbs mixed and merged, forming a larger sphere that appeared comprised of both light and darkness. A moment later, the energy from this new creation plunged into the head of the young girl, vanishing instantly.

Deena dropped to her knees, grasping her head while moaning softly. Soroe started forward but stopped as her friend stood a moment later.

"King and Queen," Deena said, her voice somehow sounding stronger and older, "the stars and the fates weave the tapestries of your lives. One who live as two, uncrowned and ruling the lands. Find the sword whose heat shall destroy the Wyrm. Extinguish the Prince of Poison or the dark god shall rise and consume the land…"

Deena collapsed to her knees and Soroe rushed to his side, shocked by the blood that dripped from her nose. Pulling a silk cloth from her sleeve, she dabbed the young oracle's damp face while staring daggers at her uncle and the Accursed One.

"You never warned her the cost of this power!" she said.

"Each oracle," the masked man said, "feels the power differently. I have heard the first is always the worst for those discovering their power."

"This is true, daughter of my heart," Ruslem said. "The mysteries of the soothsayer are beyond my knowledge."

"I am fine," Deena said in a strangled voice, "Just thirsty… and I feel like someone is stomping on my skull… I know the rest…"

"The rest of what?" Soroe asked. "You spoke your prophecy."

"Somehow," she said, "I know more… Can some-one get me a drink?"

"Clear the hall," Argall said. "Go home, people of Atlantis! There are too many of us here and we must determine the truth of her words."

Oddly, the priest, princes, military leaders, and merchants obeyed. Within a few minutes, a spare few remained in the chamber. Argall and Soroe stood next to each other with Maghee, the Accursed One, Ruslem, Padhoum, and Lophan as the only persons remaining. Only Deena sat, the others standing or leaning nearby though none crowded the young oracle.

"Before we continue," Argall said, "someone must look to the warriors killed and wounded this day."

"Prince Iztemph and your man Framm are heading there directly," Lophan said, fingering the saber that lay across her slim hip. "Prince Illaz is seeing to a search of the city for those monsters. He does so with the aid of the high priestess Nestatha."

Soroe turned to Argall. "Nestatha represents Manungal, the Goddess of Punishment. She seeks those who violate the law of the universe, not that of humanity. A terrible woman, whose goddess is feared by anyone with good sense."

"We call that goddess Skaði the Huntress amongst the Erm-Gilt-Herm. She is respected and her attendants are fierce," Argall noted.

"That aside," Ruslem said, "I would learn more of this prophecy our new oracle spoke. You said there is more?"

Deena shook her head, "No, I said I know the rest. I didn't hide anything; I just understand some portions better."

"I fail to see the difference," Ruslem said, twisting some of the fine hairs of his beard in obvious frustration.

Deena accepted a cup of wine from Padhoum with a small nod and weak smile. "That's too bad for you, priest. I'm the one who had my head broken by this power I have in me. If you want to debate about it, wait until I can explain it."

"She's an oracle," the masked one said. "They each have similar answers upon achieving their purpose."

Ruslem's eyes narrowed, "You have spoken to oracles in the past? When?"

"Yes, to your first question," the Accursed One said. "One day you may learn the second."

The high priest of the temple of light appeared poised to commence with a debate, one of his favorite activities, when Soroe intervened. She stepped forward and placed a hand on Deena's shoulder, shaking her head.

"This shall not degenerate into a debate upon mystic issues. Let her speak and then we shall discuss the words," she said.

Deena squeezed Soroe's hand in thanks and stood, a little firmer in her stance now. She pointed a finger at Argall and the Accursed One.

"You two must go north. I saw you heading towards a swamp covered in a thick fog. There, you shall battle women who fly in the sky and torment people. That is where your sword is hidden, and it is the only weapon against something I could not see, but feared."

She turned and pointed at Soroe and then tapped her own thin chest. "You and I must go another way, though we will not tell anyone. If I speak the words aloud, the future fractures."

"What does that mean?" Argall asked, which several present echoed.

Deena looked up at him with open defiance, "How should I know? I've been an oracle for less than an hour? I just know that if I explain what Soroe and I do, everything will go wrong."

"What of the rest of us?" Maghee, Argall's foster brother asked.

Deena shrugged and repeated, "How should I know? I saw what was sent my way. If you want, I could make up a story."

Lophan laughed, throwing her long hair back over her shoulders. "I like this little one. She reminds me of me when I got my first command."

"When is the next important moment where we are needed?" Argall asked.

"The ceremony of Gold and Iron occurs 86 days from today," Ruslem said. "If the followers of that demon are intent upon returning, that would be the time."

"On the eve of the last day of the fourth month," Padhoum said, "the red star shines brightest. A sacrifice to the great serpent appeases the demon for another year."

The high priest of the Temple of Light nodded. "It is the time when the underworld opens, and the foulest spirits move through the lands. The Temple of Light is at its weakest, and we must remain in seclusion."

"Then, we must prepare," Argall said. "Maghee and Admiral Lophan, work with the princes of the kingdom and unify their forces."

"Uncle," Soroe said, "convene the temples and determine other means of averting the possible disaster. Who among your ranks would best prevent the priestly gathering from degenerating into eighty-six days of squabbling over seating arrangements and speaking times?"

Ruslem pulled at his beard for a moment as he thought, "Dohety, High Priest of Maat, the Goddess of Justice. He is chief judge of the kingdom and scrupulous in his honesty."

"Argall and I shall sign a proclamation as to his position in this conference. Padhoum, see to the proper and simplistic wording. Where can we afford the holy men and women in comfort, but not too much luxury?" she asked.

"The unused meeting hall of the king and queen. It must be aired but is cleaned weekly. There is a circular table and wooden seats without cushions," he replied.

"Order the servants to supply water and fruits and little else," Argall said. "Keep their fare simple and have them only appear upon emergencies."

"Agreed," Soroe said. "I think we had best disperse and begin our duties."

Everyone bowed to Argall and Soroe, who exchanged a quick fond glance before parting. The Dhu-Hern of the northern barbarians left with Lophan, Maghee, and the Accursed One heading for the former's mansion near the harbor.

Soroe and Deena left as Ruslem and Padhoum began the laborious duty of writing the order in simplistic language. Their haranguing voices echoed through the hallways, sending servants fleeing from the raucous noise.

"Did you notice?" Deena asked, "that you and Argall worked in perfect harmony?"

"Yes," Soroe said. "Very odd. It is as if I knew his mind, and he mine."

Deena snorted and rolled her eyes. "The way he looks at you, I don't need to be an oracle to know what he's thinking."

"Enough," Soroe said, feeling her face grow warm as she blushed. "Where are Argall and his masked friend heading? For that matter, what is our destination?"

"The northerners must travel to the northeast, to a forest near ancient mountains. You and I must find a means of entering the Plains of Lamb'Ha. There, deep in the grasslands, we must find an ancient, ruined, temple."

"Didn't you tell me that shrine was now held by a tribe of cannibals?" Soroe asked.

Deena nodded and sighed. "And from the little I could see, that was the least of our worries."

CHAPTER IX

"Did you understand the oracle's predictions?" Maghee asked the masked man, who lounged on a wooden seat as the others paced the chamber.

They had convened in Lophan's rarely used home, a large dwelling built one hundred or so years ago for the admirals commanding the Atlantean navies. It was a two-story building filled with large bedrooms, a ballroom, and several rooms used for eating or meetings.

Lophan openly despised the place, preferring her small cabin in her flagship, the *Dancing Cloud*. Many of the rooms lay beneath dust covers since she spent most of her time at sea.

"You and your comrades can sleep in any room, save the kitchen," she had said when they arrived in Atlantis. "The cook is good, and I don't want him upset."

Living in such a massive dwelling was odd to the tribe of Erm-Gilt-Hermians, most having resided in long houses in their frozen wastelands. Having servants and people devoted to their luxurious life made little sense to those who fought each day for basic survival.

In the present, the Accursed One shook his head, "No, nor could anyone. Oracles never provide precise answers, only possibilities. I think the young woman shall send word to us later when she understands in greater detail."

"Deena appeared unable to say more," Lophan said.

"That was not the young woman I referred to," the masked man said. "I meant the other, the one your people hail as the queen. Before you ask, no. I know nothing further. I sense her friendship with the new oracle shall

41

prove fruitful. I viewed such a closeness once in the past. More, I cannot say."

"Cannot or will not?" Argall asked.

"Both," the Accursed One said. "You shall lead the way, but I will keep my secrets for many reasons... none of which concern you..."

"I don't understand," Maghee said.

"Good," the masked one said. "That is the beginning of wisdom."

"Let us turn our attention elsewhere," Argall said. "Do you have any maps of the north?"

Lophan shook her head, "My maps are entirely of the shores surrounding the kingdom and some places beyond. I've never had need of overland routes."

"Where do such maps lay?" Argall asked.

"Where else but the Temple of Light?" Lophan said. "They preserve old knowledge and keeps records of events occurring in Atlantis and beyond. Sadly, for you, the former queens of Atlantis suppressed this search for the truth. The priests of Gold and Iron held the true power in the kingdom after Yerra."

"Then you could search fruitlessly for years in this quest," Maghee said. "You cannot do it, Argall. It is one thing to head towards a direction in hope of finding answers. That is understandable. Heading blind into the darkness and hoping you do not fall into a ravine is foolhardy."

Argall nodded slowly. "I do believe Soroe shall provide greater knowledge for our search. More importantly, the kingdom shall have no rulers when the queen and I depart. What shall happen?"

"Nothing for a time," Lophan said. "The queen rarely concerned herself with the minutia of running Atlantis. This, she left to governors, nobles, and the military. You and the new queen must put in place a system that shall act, should a catastrophe occur."

"In our lands," Maghee said, "the chieftains of each tribe have councils that exist as advisors."

"The queen never allowed for such possibility. To do so would mean she was answerable to their rulings," the admiral said as she poured herself a draft of the pale wine she preferred.

Argall chuckled. "Foolish. Every chieftain, king, or priestess answers to the tribe. Power over everything is impossible."

"True," the Accursed One said, "yet there are those who disagree and attempt otherwise."

"You speak from experience," Maghee said.

The man in the metal mask tapped his facial covering, "That is why this covers my face. My rejection of the foolish demands of a ruler were met with unfortunate consequences."

"Did you succeed?" Argall asked.

"Only in saving lives," the Accursed One said. "The tyrant still sits upon her throne of bone, existing in a half-life that tortures the world."

"Why do I find myself mired in darkness every time you speak, masked one?" Lophan asked.

"Because you are very perceptive and know the truth of pain," the masked man said. "Hopefully, your story shall end better than mine."

A silence fell over the room, broken by Maghee who poured himself more wine. He gulped greedily for several seconds before laying down his goblet.

"If you must appoint leaders to this land, brother," he said, "what shall you do with your followers? We are not Atlanteans, but have chosen to make you our chieftain. Do we become mere sell-swords?"

43

Argall shook his head. "Never in life. Illaz told me of an important place in the inner circle of the king. I shall appoint you the master of the royal guards. That is a high place among the Atlanteans."

"Yes," Lophan said, "the last one, a toady whose name I shall not repeat, was as important as a prince and as powerful as a governor. It is a place of honor."

"And the Erm-Gilt-Hermians who came with us shall be your main forces. Those already holding such duties are under your command. You may discharge any not to your liking," Argall said.

Maghee considered the position and smiled slightly in agreement. He and Argall embraced briefly, nothing needed to be said.

"Any you discharge," Lophan said, "send to me. I will make them marines on my ship. They will either serve well, or drown."

Everyone chuckled for a moment and raised a glass in salute of Maghee's new place in Atlantis.

"And you?" Maghee asked the masked man, "do you seek a place in this land?"

"I do not," the Accursed One said. "I shall aid your people for a time, and then I must confront my greatest enemy. The most lethal being in the north."

"What dangerous beast do you face? A demon? A giant?" Argall asked, having viewed the mysterious warrior wizard destroy foes with unmatched skill.

"Worse," the masked man said. "My wife. An army of demons and giants are mere insects compared to the might of the witch queen known as Loviatar, the North Star."

CHAPTER X

Thousands of leagues to the north, the former Queen of Atlantis, once known as Yerra the Beautiful, toiled as she scrubbed floors. The dwelling of the Royal Family of Pohjola was smaller than her former home in the Atlantean kingdom. A simple one-story long house that held the Queen, her mother, and a few servants, was hardly seemed a fitting dwelling for the powerful witches that ruled the northern land of Zhul.

Yet, somehow, the Queen of the terrible lands of Pohjola never required luxury and comfort. Having held power for hundreds, possibly even thousands, of years, the was a powerful majesty within these stone and wood walls.

Having escaped her former kingdom just before her destruction at the hand of Soroe, Yerra cursed her fate each day and night. She had served Louhi, the Dark Witch of Pohjola, and the most powerful witch in the world, for many years. The mistress of the black arts had molded Yerra, transforming her into a lovely, dangerous witch in her own right for one purpose: assuming the crown of Atlantis when the previous Yerra became too aged.

The name Yerra had been one held by dozens over the thousand or so years since the long-dead King and Queen, the first Argall and Soroe, died of old age. Each time, Louhi had secretly provided a replacement, a powerful, beautiful, young woman named Yerra the Immortal.

The truth, unknown to the Atlanteans until recently, was that Yerra was a job, not a person. A series of Yerras appeared, groomed by the witches of Pohjola, for the sole purpose of providing greater power to Louhi and her daughter, Queen Loviatar.

Having lost Atlantis, Yerra had once again become a servant of the horrific, evil pair. Her duties were the same as when she was a mere child, sold by southern slavers to the Pohjolans. She scrubbed the wooden floors with a brush, washed the cooking pots, and occasionally served as a footstool for Louhi when the witch felt the need for greater humiliation.

Right now, she scrubbed, knowing that even a small blemish could result in swift retribution. Yerra was considered lower than the servants in this wooden palace. They received wages and some kindness from the queens and their family. A slave was mere property to the rulers of these dark, frozen wastes. They ignored her, speaking as if she were a dumb beast rather than the former queen of the most powerful kingdom of the South.

"I have scried, my mother," Loviatar said, shaking the snow off her long, silken, platinum hair, "and the signs continue in the same manner. Uncertainty."

Loviatar was beautiful in a distant, cold way that most found fearful. Taller than most men, she possessed long, pale, powerful limbs, blue eyes that were so pale they appeared nearly white, and a sculpted face with high cheekbones and perfect structure.

Yet, for all her loveliness, Queen Loviatar was terrifying to those who gazed upon her countenance. She resembled a magnificent sculpture of a woman chipped entirely from the merciless ice of the North.

Her mother, Louhi, the Witch of the North, was the opposite to her icily perfect daughter. Tiny, wizened, wrinkled, with sparse whisps of grey tendrils for hair, she resembled every nightmare people held about the true face of an evil sorceress. Despite her frail appearance, there was an iron spirit in Louhi that repelled any who sought conflict with her.

"You need not have wasted your time, daughter," Louhi said, her voice resembling the gentle sounds of a young girl. "A battle between beings of power is never clear to fate."

"I wished some hint of how he escaped the clutches of the Dalaketnons. Those bizarre fae possess might even we must acknowledge," Loviatar said.

Louhi giggled, a childish sound that was quite at odds with her withered visage. "Those beings were powerful, child. Sadly, they have fallen into a cycle of decadence. They captured humans and vicious beasts and pitted each in battle for their entertainment."

"Allow me to make a prediction," the queen said, picking up a silver goblet of mead. "The slaves revolted, and the Dalaketnon were forced into hiding."

"Correct," Louhi said. "Power without purpose leads to weakness. I doubt they shall rise again."

"Then how do we discover where my husband hides? Despite the hundreds of years that have passed, I doubt he will have forgiven our treachery," Loviatar said, drinking deeply.

Yerra realized that she had an answer to the Queen's inquiry. Pleasing Loviatar was a means of relieving the daily beatings and near starvation. She had learned that a day after returning to Pohjola when the Queen was about to step into a puddle of dirty water. Yerra lay in the small pool, providing a means for Loviatar of avoiding the filth.

"Well done, slave," the Queen had said with a small nod. "Clean this mess and I shall grant you a full meal and a good night of sleep. Be awake at dawn and resume your duties."

Pleasing the Queen or her witch-mother had been the reason Yerra had survived so far. Though Louhi did not discard her tools easily, she would do so with little concern. Life as a slave was dangerous, harsh, and humiliating. Only a fool would not seek a means of escape.

Pressing her face onto the unyielding wooden floor, Yerra said, "O Dread Queen, Mighty Mistress of Magic, I beg your attention. I may have a solution for you in your search for the one you call Jaska the Gray Wolf, consort of Loviatar, the North Star."

"Do you, child?" Louhi asked. "Then you had best speak your mind and hope you do not waste my dearest daughter's time."

Remaining in her position of subservience, Yerra shivered at the thought of angering the Queen or her witch-mother. Her life would no doubt be short afterwards, though filled with a lifetime of pain in that time.

"Great ones," Yerra said, "when I served as your servant in Atlantis, I learned of a tribe that remain hidden in the Eastern Isle. They were once an army, but are now a religious group that view battle as a means of paying homage to their bloody God. They are powerful, dangerous warriors with an odd code of ethics…"

Loviatar chuckled and asked, "Then why did you not use them on your enemy, the child Soroe?"

"One of their laws is that they shall not seek battle with females," Yerra said. "They consider such a request as unholy."

"Rise and sit upon the floor, child," Louhi said. "We shall feed you as you tell us of these warriors. What are they called, and how do they kill their enemies?"

48

Yerra sat back on her haunches, looking up at Loviatar and Louhi, still fearful of their wrath. She accepted a small glass of mead from the witch's claw-shaped hands, not hiding that she shook with unfeigned terror in their presence.

"Thank you," she said, bowing her head and sipping a little of the sweet blend. "These combatants call themselves the Brotherhood of the Axe and only use those weapons in battle…"

CHAPTER XI

"A tribe of cannibals," Soroe repeated. "Delightful. I believe this quest will be a great deal more dangerous than our search for the Soul of Soroe."

"If you wanted an easy life," Deena said, "you should have become a housewife. Instead, you want to be a priest-queen. Things aren't ever going to be simple for you."

Soroe's eyes narrowed, and she asked, "Is that a prediction from our new oracle?"

Deena rolled her eyes, shook her head and replied, "No, silly, it's basic observation from someone who knows more than you about the world."

Dawne, Soroe's personal attendant as well as one of the lead dancers of the Temple of Light's ceremonies, frowned as she asked, "Why do you let her talk to you that way? It isn't dignified!"

"I'm not dignified," Deena said, dropping into Soroe's personal throne-shaped chair. "No room for it when I was fighting the rats for scraps."

Dawne nodded and touched Deena's arm with a gentle hand. "I understand. My brother and I were not born to the noble families. My dancing and my place in the temple have eased our lives. Though you might learn the ways of the Court so that the high-born cannot sneer and disregard your advice."

"Dawne is right," Soroe said, "though now is not the time for such considerations. Deena and I must leave soon, and I still have many questions."

"Save them," the young oracle said. "I have no idea of what we're going to see. I'm not a book you can read.

I saw stuff and said what was there. What it means isn't something I can tell you. If I knew, I'd have said something already."

"That," the Queen-elect said, "is a little discouraging. Let us return to the temple. We must meditate and plan our path."

The three women did not speak as they left the palace and boarded Soroe's chariot. Her driver, a former soldier name Anu, paid more attention to the horses throughout the drive, clucking his tongue and releasing other odd noises as they road through the busy avenue.

Upon arriving, he merely nodded their direction, waited until they stepped away from the road, and headed off towards the stables. This was characteristic of their rides, the former soldier having been chosen for his disinterest in anything, save his animals.

Soroe led Deena and Dawne through the temple until they reached her private mediation chamber on the lower level. The door was a massive, unengraved stone surface that moved thanks to a lever on the left of the portal. Dawne stood before the metal rod, lowering it with no visible effort after the Queen-elect and her attendant entered the mediation room.

The room was a ten-foot square with two straw mats on the floor, a simple circular brass brazier that lit the chamber, and a ceiling that lay mere inches over their head. An iron bar protruded from the wall near the door, the metal freshly polished and gleaming.

"Well," Deena said, walking around the room twice, "what are we meant to do here? If you say, close our eyes and breathe slowly, I'm pulling that rod now. The whole sitting around thinking business you do every day doesn't work for me."

Soroe laughed and shook her head. "I meditate every morning in the hope of centering myself and getting ready for the day."

"What about around mid-day? Or before you go to sleep?" the young oracle asked.

"Releasing the tensions of the day and bettering myself for better work or sleep. Mediation is not a religious exercise. I've known soldiers and merchants who do it as a way of improving their lives," Soroe replied.

"Good for them," Deena said, clearly disinterested, "Now, answer my question."

"We are leaving for our duties, but doing so before anyone knows," she said, "Remember when we met? I escaped in a similar way. Dawne is now sending word as to where Argall and his masked friend should head. Temple gossip will have us in seclusion for at least three days. If anyone seeks to hinder our mission, we may leave them behind us."

She reached for the iron lever and turned the bar three times. Soroe then removed the rod, stuck the end in an unseen hole in the wall and pressed downwards. A small passage in rocky floor opened up a moment later. The high priestess returned the lever to its original location and smiled.

"The Temple of Light has many passages known only to a select few. Even I do not know every secret. I learned of this yesterday despite having used this room as a meditation chamber many times while growing up," she said.

"Where does it lead?" Deena asked, following the Queen-elect down into a low, dark passageway.

"The last place anyone would look for us," Soroe said and vanished into the gloom.

CHAPTER XII

"Loviatar!" Argall and Maghee said, stepping backwards, their faces blanching, their eyes widening in shock.

Lophan chuckled and fingered her ornate eyepatch, "I believe they've heard of her, outlander."

The Accursed One raised one hand in acceptance. "She has a habit of being quite memorable."

"Memorable?" Argall said. "She is the ice queen who steals babies in the darkness and lures the foolish ones into dying in the depths of the wastes. Anyone who sees her knows true beauty and fear."

"Yes," the Accursed One said. "That sounds like her. Sad to hear that she has not changed in hundreds of years."

"How better to ask why. Why would you marry that evil witch?" Maghee asked.

The pale eyes of the masked sorcerer locked upon Argall's foster brother. The expression in this gaze was one the warrior of the Erm-Gilt-Herm would describe as inhuman to Lophan and the others he trusted.

For now, it felt as if he were being watched by a particularly menacing predator. Maghee felt his warrior spirit arise, though he controlled himself and did not respond with violence borne by fear.

"I had no say in the matter," the masked one said. "Nor did she. The reasons for such a union are a long tale that would not interest you, or make much sense either. Had I been granted a choice, I would have rather wed an ice troll than that witch. I simply hope our children are untainted by her family's blood."

Lophan snapped her fingers and pointed at the Accursed One, "Then that means you are Jas…"

The masked man clapped his hands together quickly, cutting the Atlantean admiral's declaration from finishing.

"Best to never say that name. Louhi, my mate's mother, is a witch of uncanny skill and power. Her subtle arts may have means of knowing when my true name is spoken out loud."

"Is that possible?" Argall said.

The Accursed One shrugged his shoulders broadly, "I have no notion. In certain areas of the ancient arts, her powers far outstrip my own. She always held to the belief that knowledge was the greatest weapon one could use against an enemy."

"I'd choose a sword first," Argall said.

The masked one shook his head, "Then she would happily use you as her puppet. A king who uses his mind as a weapon transforms his subjects into an army that is far more dangerous than the greatest warrior."

Lophan nodded and poured herself another wine. "That is truth. I employ the same tactics at sea. Speaking of which, will you take a ship to your destination?"

"No," Argall said. "I will send one of my people away in the dead of night on one of your smaller vessels. That way, any enemies that seek my death shall turn their attention elsewhere."

"Risking my ship," Lophan said and rubbed her patch. "I have a method of lessening the possible tragedy. I have a young officer who may be brought before the tribunal for piracy charges. I will place him and his toadies aboard the ship and send them upon a quick delivery trip to our base south of the city. The difficulty is, your friend may die from this ruse."

"We accepted that before undertaking this trip," Maghee said. "I will secretly ask for a volunteer. No doubt most will step forward despite the danger."

"I will call a cloak of darkness over us, and we can leave in the night once we have a direction," the Accursed One said. "We have little information from the oracle, which is not unexpected. I doubt that any prophet ever spoke an easily comprehended sentence since the discovery of such gifts."

"You said earlier that only women held such power. Do males have any means of foretelling the future?" Lophan asked.

"Yes," the Accursed One said. "They have no name or title, because they are often called insane or possessed by evil spirits. The male mind cannot handle the visions and the recipient becomes dangerous to himself and those around them in time. In the end, they die badly."

There was an uncomfortable silence, broken by Argall who asked, "You have seen this happen?"

"Yes," the masked one said, "to my brother. We were children when he tried killing me. I slew him and was treated as a murderer by my family from that day forward. Forgive me if I cease explaining any further."

Before any more words could be spoken, a loud hammering on the door caused all those present to start in surprise.

Lophan ran from the room, returning a moment later with a scrap of paper in hand.

"The oracle and the queen have sent you information," she said. "They are more specific about your destination..."

"Where are we headed?" Argall asked.

"North, and east," the Atlantean admiral replied. "Frankly, a location that I would not head into without an army at my back… and even then... I would consider the idea utterly mad… You will travel through the Kurga grasslands to the edge of the Forest of Tur. I have heard of this place. The locals call it the Land of the Ala… The demon women of the skies…"

CHAPTER XIII

Soroe and Deena walked for an hour, the tunnel being straight, square-shaped, cut from the very stone, and completely uninhabited.

The queen-elect spoke a few words and a floating sphere of soft yellow light floated above their heads, illuminating the empty passageway.

"No rats or insects," Deena said. "Never saw a tunnel without them."

"This one," Soroe said, "was sliced from the rock by an ancient power I do not know, or understand. According to my uncle, the one who did this work ensured that it would be safe, should the need for it arise."

The passageway ended abruptly and Soroe probed the surface of the wall for a moment. She depressed a protrusion and the wall silently slid aside, revealing stairs leading up into a heavy, gloomy, darkness.

The scent of mold, charred wood, and rot assailed them as they climbed. Shimmers of weak light emerged from above, revealing dust-stained steps and soot-covered walls.

"Where are we?" Deena asked as they stepped gingerly through a shattered wall into a ruined building.

"The Temple of Gold and Iron," Soroe said, "or at least, its remains. The people destroyed it, looted its wealth, and put it to the torch. There was a lot of anger among the citizens against the priests of this evil place."

"Is it dangerous?" Deena asked, her voice hushed.

"Only if we linger or head into other sections. There is a broken wall to our left that will lead us to a small road that continues through the mountains. I think it is called the Trader's Trail..."

The young oracle stopped in her tracks, looked the lovely Soroe up and down, sighed and shook her head.

"Do you actually think that's an escape? You'll be recognized after two steps. Did you pack any clothing? Food? Water?" she asked.

"Yes to all," Soroe replied. "Upon learning of this tunnel, I hid two packs in case you and I were sent on another insane mission."

Deena smiled and nodded. "At least, I've had some good influence on you. Let's see what you put aside."

Soroe led her companion from the temple to a small pile of shattered timbers and stone that lay near the outer wall that once encircled the area. Wriggling beneath the rubble heap, she retrieved two traveler's packs made from simple leather and hide. They opened both, revealing simple, unadorned clothing, two wooden canteens and dried travel food. Known as Rat Rations, they were created by merchants who had to travel through the dangerous, distant regions of the kingdom. They were barely edible, but provided a full meal with only a few bites of meat and bread.

"Hmm," Deena said, "this will do for now. The trouble is your face and hair."

"What about them?" Soroe asked.

Deena rolled her eyes. "They're too noticeable. We're heading into dangerous territory. Just being women will attract attention. You looking like the first Soroe could get us attacked by every noble and criminal between here and Lamb'Ha."

"Nobles?" Soroe asked. "What do you mean by that?"

"Nobles are just richer criminals, lady," the former thief said. "The young ones especially know they're above the law and can do as they please. A bunch of them together with a little wine in them usually leads to rape and robbery. Not all of them. I've seen a few that seem like good sorts. But there are plenty of the other type all over the place."

Soroe did not hide her shock as she stared at her friend, her mouth agape. She tried speaking for several seconds, but the words died in her throat.

"How can this happen? The laws of Atlantis…"

"…aren't worth a damn if the Queen of the Kingdom doesn't care. Yerra the Beautiful only used the laws as a way of bringing people under thumb. She let them do whatever they liked, but would have her spies keep a record of their crimes. Then, when she needed them, they were offered a deal… Obey or pay for whatever they'd done…" the young oracle explained.

"How do you know this, Deena?" Soroe asked.

The former thief pulled some clothes from her pack and answered, "Saw it happen a dozen or more times growing up. Baron Bucue's son and his friends used to come into the area twice a month or so and grab any women that caught their eye. Then, one day, the Queen's men arrested him and his friends. A few days later, they were seen helping the tax collectors two districts over. Now, I know how we're going to hide your face and hair."

"How?" Soroe asked.

"Like this!" Deena said, smiling wickedly.

She then threw a ball of muck into the Queen-elect's face.

CHAPTER XIV

Argall pulled off the scarf that hid his face, letting the article lay loosely across his shoulders. There was no purpose in a disguise now; they were approaching the legendary Key to Atlantis. This location was a road through the mountains that joined north to south and travelled through the massive Bol-Gho heights. In addition to being of immense military value, this was the main source of trade in Atlantis and was consequently heavily trafficked.

Argall, though tall and handsome to the eye, was otherwise ignored by the northbound travelers. His unimpressive clothing and simple, unadorned weapons made him resemble a mercenary seeking work. There were others of varying degrees of obvious wealth passing through the Key to Atlantis, so few glanced his direction.

The Accursed One wore a heavy hood that covered his metal mask from view. He walked with a stoop and hunched his shoulders, causing him to resemble one of the many pilgrims who walked from temple to temple seeking a cure for their obvious affliction. None of the Atlanteans passing by him openly shuddered at his bizarre gait. Most pretended they did not see him, with a few making warding gestures against the evil eye.

"What is the land of the Ala like?" Argall asked as a heavily laden cart filled with squawking chickens rumbled past.

"How would I know? I've never been there and never heard of it before," the masked one replied. "I passed through the grasslands of the Kurga three hundred or so years ago. I doubt it has changed much in that time."

"Then tell me of that place," the possible future king of Atlantis asked. "What cities are in that vast expanse?"

"None," the Accursed One said, "The people of the Kurga are nomads, who are known as the Horse Tribes. They are a fierce, proud, people who are honorable warriors. They are the best horse warriors I ever encountered and are best left alone. If roused, they will fight and defeat even the mightiest armies."

"Then why don't they rule Atlantis?" Argall asked.

The masked man shook his head. "They have little interest in such encumbrances. They rightly realize a king is a greater slave than the meekest member of their kingdom. I respect them for such wisdom."

"Then you believe I should give up my ambitions for Atlantis?" Argall asked.

"What I believe is unimportant. You made your decision the first moment you gazed upon Soroe, the future Queen," he said. "I know that look, I had the same for my wife when we first met."

Argall frowned and asked, "I thought you despised Loviatar?"

"Didn't mean I didn't feel the need to bed her at any cost," the Accursed One said and barked a little lupine sounding laughter. "For her part, she felt the same way, having seen and chosen me from a distance."

"Then how can you hate each other? Why would she enslave you to those monsters?" the Erm-Gilt-Hermian asked.

"Bedding someone and creating children is simplicity itself," the Accursed One said. "Marriage is a great deal harder. She who is my wife is as beautiful as the legends... but crueler than you can imagine. Our lives fell apart when the attraction became nothing greater than a ram and a ewe rutting in a field."

"I think I understand," Argall said. "I know, you're about to tell me that it is a sign of wisdom."

The Accursed One laughed, his hidden shoulders shaking beneath the heavy robe. "That it is... but only the first step. One must actually experience the pain to full appreciate the scale of it. No matter. What plans do you have to begin our journey?"

"Lophan suggested we travel east to the city of M'Yong first. There is a port a short distance from there and we can take a boat to Salabra," Argall said.

"Salabra? That may be troublesome for us," the masked one said.

"Why?" the future king of Atlantis asked.

"Because Salabra is the city where the demon worshippers of Apophis began their evil religion," the masked sorcerer said. "It is a lovely city of great trade where every shadow contains a thousand knives."

Argal thought for a moment and shook his head. "I looked at the map and I think it is the best way. If we try the overland route, our path will take too long. We must risk the followers of Gold and Iron."

"I assumed you would say as much," the Accursed One said. "Very well. Off we go to Salabra, that city of a hundred minarets. I do say that we may well wish for the torments of Loviatar by the time we leave that cesspit."

CHAPTER XV

Yerra stood, head bowed, behind the simple seats Loviatar and Louhi used as thrones. As a youth, Yerra had looked down on the pair of simple oak seats, unadorned by carvings or precious gems. In her mind, this proved that the Pohjola rulers were little more than barbarians who would never rise about that lower status.

Later, Yerra had learned differently. The witch rulers of the frozen waste were far from uncouth savages who possessed uncanny mystic might. In truth, they were highly sophisticated, viewing such trappings of wealth as unimportant and unnecessary. Crowns, regal thrones, royal guards, and silken robes were mere toys to their ancient, labyrinthian minds.

Take the current event. Most rulers, Yerra included, would have sent ambassadors with gifts and sweet words to the dangerous cult known as the Brotherhood of the Axe. Traveling to the distant Eastern Isle, locating the warriors, and convincing them of to undertake the mission, would take months, if not longer.

Louhi simply waved her withered fingers and the servants appeared, lugging a stone vessel that held a turquoise ball that rippled and quaked without leaving the container. The elderly witch sang an odd sounding song for several seconds and stared into the depths for several moments.

"Ahhh," she said, her black lips creasing into a frightening sneering smirk. "I have located them, my daughter."

"Then, let us sit and speak to these legendary masters of the fighting arts," Loviatar said, seating herself in her chair and gesturing with her left hand.

The world around them melted away, the wooden ceiling, stone walls and ceiling vanishing before Yerra's eyes. The frigid breezes of Pohjola's brutal north wind slowly weakened, replaced by a gentle, sweet, warm, southern breeze.

The air transformed a moment later, lacking any chill bite. Instead, the atmosphere felt heavy, filled with a powerful, moist humidity, and felt sticky and unpleasant upon Yerra's skin. The heady, perfumed scent of flowery growth stung at her nose, and the loud chirping of a universe of insect life emerged from every direction.

The two witches and the former queen appeared in a vast clearing surrounded by leafy green trees overhung with twisted vines. The sward beneath their feet was of a thick, verdant, green grass that felt spongy and strange. There were no people or animal life in evidence, though their eyes could not penetrate far into the bush.

"I see nobody, my mother," Loviatar said, "do they hide from us? Are they fearful of visitors?"

"No," Louhi said as a giggle escaped her lips, "they use a subtle magic that prevents us probing further. They are cautious and watch us from every direction. I do believe our presence has startled them."

"Why do the witches of Pohjola travel to our lands? We have no dealings with the females of the north!" a deep voice said from their right.

"Do you fear facing two of the greatest warriors of the north as well?" Louhi asked and shook her head, "Perhaps the request is too great for any soft southerner."

"We are not children, so easily manipulated by foolish taunts," the voice said from behind them.

"Yet, you play games as we stand here and await a meeting with your leaders. Either appear or vanish into your jungle. We shall not continue exchanging words with men hiding their faces in shame," Louhi said.

The air shimmered for a moment, becoming wavy and unfocused for several seconds. The clearing then returned into view, though this time five men stood before the Pohjola witches and their servant.

These men were warriors, each standing nearly seven feet tall. They possessed monstrously wide shoulders, oversized tanned sinews covered in blue tattooed runes, and heads covered by chipped, worn, iron helmets. Their oversized hands each held great axes, their single bladed edges shimmering in the overpowering sunlight. They wore simple war kilts made from a dark fabric and heavy leather boots studded with metal spikes.

The largest of the pack stepped forward, placing his weapon over his right shoulder, "I will listen to you, witch. Speak your words."

Louhi giggled again and shook her unlovely head, "I said I will speak to your leader. I do not waste my time with servants. Bring forth your master, or flee into the depths of your verdant, green home."

"I am the master of the Brotherhood of the Axe," the giant stated, lifting his axe above his head in one hand.

"You are not," Loviatar said as her blue eyes fell upon the massive warrior. "You are too young and foolish. You are not yet a century old. I feel the presence of greater age in your comrades. Your people would not choose a young warrior for the master of a brotherhood of warriors."

"You are wise, Ice Queen," a softer voice said as a smaller man stepped into view.

He was shorter than the five giants, but no less impressive. A grey beard peaked from beneath his helm and his physique, though aged, was still that of a powerful warrior. Gray scars crisscrossed his torso and legs, and his tattoos were nearly faded into his copper-colored skin. A chipped steel axe rested across his broad back, the handle protruding over one shoulder.

"Forgive the deception, ladies of the north," he said. "Many seek our aid, but few are willing to agree to our terms. The presence of our youngest and fiercest warriors often sends them fleeing back to their boats."

"More fool them," Louhi said. "My daughter and I are not so easily frightened. Shall we discuss terms?"

The unnamed leader clapped his hands twice and a warrior produced a three-legged stool from behind a nearby bush. The master of the Brotherhood of the Axe lowered himself onto the seat and spread his leathery hands wide.

"Tell me what you seek, and I will tell you our price," he said. "I warn you now, we do not negotiate."

"Nor do we," Louhi said, smiling and exchanging a meaningful glance with her daughter.

CHAPTER XVI

"Stop touching your hair," Deena said as they bumped along the road leading to the Bol-Gho mountains. "You'll only call attention to yourself that way."

Deena looked much as she had earlier, her clothing less luxurious and her face a little dirtier. She resembled what she had been before they met; a street thief who survived by her wits alone. Her obvious youth aided in this disguise, and more than a few people held onto their purses and bags when she passed them on the road.

Soroe was also shunned, but for a very different reason. Her clothing, though a little dirtier and with more rips and tears than Deena's, was not particularly bad. No, it was the stench that lay over her now, an earthy scent that exuded from her clothes, hair, and body. Covered in muck and mire, Soroe resembled a beggar who hadn't bathed in months and probably had never truly been clean.

"I can't help it," Soroe said, shifting slightly, "my head itches."

Shrugging, Deena waved towards goats penned behind them on the cart.

"You probably caught some fleas from those mangy beasts. This is good, nobody would expect you to resemble a mucksucker."

"A what?" Soroe asked.

"A mucksucker," Deena said, tilting her head and studying the Queen-elect for a moment. "Some days I forget how little you know about people. When you get dumped on the streets, there's not many choices. You can beg if the guild lets you have a patch of your own.

You can sell yourself and bed men old enough to be your da or granda. You can steal, but that's dangerous if you get caught. Or you become a mucksucker. A mucksucker goes to the dumping areas and walks along the back trails where the smugglers travel to avoid taxes. They look for anything that might be worth a few pennies."

"Sounds horrible," Soroe said, shuddering slightly.

The young former thief nodded, "It ages them. A girl I knew chose that because she was too scared of stealing or whoring. A year or two of that life and she looked old enough to be my ma. Even when they find something big like a gold coin, they can never wash off the smell or the dead look in their eyes."

"That needs to change," Soroe said.

"You can't do it, but I'm happy you want to try," the young oracle said. "There will always be people at the top and mucksuckers at the bottom. It's the way of the world."

"I don't accept that," Soroe said, shaking her head. "I can't let people live like animals while a small group of people live in luxury. It wouldn't be right."

"You can't save everyone, lady," Deena said. "Though you can always try. Just don't get discouraged when crime continues, and people still die of starvation. The world ain't a kind place."

They lapsed into silence as the cart rose higher and higher along the mountain road. The air became thinner as they rolled to the road's summit. The downward trek was a longer route, slowly and gradually winding down the Bol-Gho mighty heights.

"We'll be in Taugi by midday," Deena said as the air grew warmer and easier for their breathing. "There, we can change and stop looking like we just took a dive into a mud puddle. And then, we'll begin searching the plains for that ruined temple."

"I take it that you have no idea where it is located?" Soroe said.

Deena shook her head. "A temple filled with cannibals isn't my idea of a place I should go exploring. I heard it's in there from a few people, but that's all I know. The gangs that live in those lands are deadlier and crazier than anyone knows. There's something bad in those weeds... something that turns bad people into monsters..."

"Then why are you going? It's not that I don't value you at my side, I just wonder why you risk your life for me over and over..." Soroe asked, trailing off and blushing.

Deena shook her head and said, "I could give you some clever joke of an answer, or a spooky one now that I'm considered special. Truth is, I just had a feeling I should. That's the only answer I have. Now don't go all weepy on me. I know you're glad I'm here and will give me anything I ask if we live. Just know that I ain't ever planning on acting like the noble ladies we ran into in the palace. Those cows spend half their time complaining about their hair and dresses rather than important things."

Soroe laughed and nodded, "I know. Males have their own version where they compare scars or expensive items they own. You do know those are tactics for a larger game, right?"

"Huh?" the former thief asked.

"Politics and power positions is the most dangerous art form practiced in Atlantis. Do you know why the baron whose son you mentioned was placed in the tax service?" she asked.

Deena shrugged one shoulder, "Didn't really think about it. I was just glad he wasn't raping and robbing two or three nights a week where I slept."

"Then learn a little from me," Soroe said. "The noble you mentioned was famous for underpaying his taxes. By placing the son with the tax collectors, they were sending the baron a message. Pay fully or your own son will bring about your destruction. This also gave Yerra a test of loyalty for the son. If he obeyed, rewards would follow."

"And if he helped the old man, her spies could have him executed?" Deena asked.

Soroe nodded, "Or sent to serve somewhere lethal like the beaches near the Dykes of Argall... The Watchers on the Threshold eat several nobles each year assigned to guarding that zone..."

Deena openly shuddered, "Those giant things still give me nightmares. Rats the size of giant bears with the tempers of a hungover noble should not exist!"

"Be that as it may," Soroe said, "while you teach me survival in the streets and the grasslands, I intend on helping you understand the violent games played in the palace. I cannot risk you losing your place at my side because of some error you can avoid."

"Fine," the young former thief said, "Right now let's concern ourselves with the alleys of Taugi. The King of Beggars there will see through our disguises in a heartbeat. I only hope he'll be too busy taking on the governor's spies."

"The King of Beggars?" Soroe asked.

Deena smiled and nodded, "The real ruler of the city. You'll see soon enough."

CHAPTER XVII

The road to M'Yong proved a dull, uneventful journey for Argall and the Accursed One. The roads were protected and heavily guarded, with many merchants making use of this safe route between the cities. The cold of the higher ridges had little effect on the Erm-Gilt-Hermian or the former dweller from Pohjola. Both men had resided in frigid lands of the north and found the current chill quite pleasant.

The gates of M'Yong emerged in the distance, a high-walled ancient city that was nearly as old as Atlantis, though far smaller. Neither man had ever visited the location, but Lophan had provided them with a brief explanation as to the land.

"The people of M'Yong are merchants. Nobles have little or no place and the military obeys the Council of Nine. Before you ask, that group are the richest traders in the city, and they accomplish little as a body. Yerra used to create competition between them, seeing which one will rebuild the most roads or finance the repair of the public works. Whatever you do, don't steal anything! You can buy your way out of murder or other crimes, but theft results in a fast trip to the executioners," she had said.

"Any other things to avoid?" Argall had asked.

Lophan had thought for a moment, frowned, nodded and answered, "The people are a touchy lot. Try not to offend anyone."

The masked man had sighed long and loud, "You mean I'd have to fight more duels?"

The Atlantean admiral had laughed, touched her eyepatch and shook her head quickly, "Not a bit, I doubt there are more than three duels a year in M'Yong. The Council of Nine outlawed that practice a long time ago, and placed the offenders under the category of theft. Dueling robs persons of life, so they kill both parties involved. What I was referring to are professional assassins. There are dozens in the city, and each specialize in different ways of killing their enemies. The powerful families keep a few on retainer while the smaller merchants know the means of employing the less skilled ones. I've lost some good crewmen that way."

These warnings remained in their heads as they approached M'Yong along with several long merchant caravans. They blended in with the guards and hangers-on and were ignored by the bored-looking troop of guards near the wide, open metal gates.

"Why don't they collect a tithe for entry?" Argall asked, thinking aloud as the long train of mules, wagons, and people bearing packs entered the busy entryway.

"Merchants," the masked man said, "dislike any form of tax. It lessens the amount of money they can pocket. Coins given to the government are ones not placed in their purses. Oh, and we are being followed."

"Yes," Argall said, "I noticed that an hour ago. A man with a brown beard that curls at the end. He kept ducking behind the wagon filled with grain when I glanced his direction."

"Interesting," the Accursed One said. "However, the one you speak of was not known to me. I refer to the flock of crows that fly past us and kept us under their gaze since we left the high point of the mountain road."

Argall shrugged, "Birds follow large groups of humans, knowing they will find food."

"Yes," the masked man said, "and yet, these never paused and ate in over one day. I doubt they are actually real. They are some forms of magical creatures—or worse."

"Worse?" the Erm-Gilt-Hermian war chief asked. "What could be worse?"

"There are several possibilities, but I expect we shall find out soon enough," the sorcerer replied.

"What can we do?" Argall asked.

The Accursed One glanced up as the flock of black birds circled them once and flew ahead.

"Fleeing is a waste of time. Those creatures are faster than us. We have not weapons to attack them and I doubt my magic is swift enough to disable them in the air. I think we simply continue onward and see what happens."

"I dislike your plan," Argall said.

"Feel free to offer another," the masked man said while lowering his gaze. "I am willing to listen."

That was when an arrow streaked past where his head had been while looking upward. The missile whistled past and stuck into the wooden wall of a wagon several feet to his right. Another whistle sound followed, and an arrow sped with the swiftness of a lightning bolt towards the chest of Argall...

CHAPTER XVIII

"Then we have a proper beginning," the helmeted leader of the Brotherhood of the Axe said. "Speak, witch."

"Two men undermine the future of our plans," Loviatar said. "The first is my husband, Jaska the Gray Wolf."

"Jaska?" the master of the Brotherhood asked. "He is not real. I have been to Pohjola and the people there say he never existed."

"That is because I ordered it such," Louhi said, giggling again. "To violate my demand would mean to become my enemy."

"He is very real and has escaped the imprisonment we placed him in many years past," Loviatar added.

The leader chuckled. "It is said he was a giant who shattered mountains beneath his axe. Each time he blew, the north wind chilled the land."

"Nonsense," Loviatar said. "He is a man, though a dangerous one. He is not as tall as your guards, nor as muscular. His axes cannot break mountains... the thought of such a weapon is ludicrous. Jaska is a master of axes, swords, spears, and bows. He also holds the power of cold and dark because he is of the line of Mielikki, the goddess of the wild. That makes him a sorcerer, but not a giant."

"I thought only the witches of Pohjola held the power of ice and pain," the master of the Brotherhood said.

Louhi nodded, "This is true, but our power is different. Explaining would take too long. Just know that if a magic duel took place, he would lay at my feet, begging for death."

"Tell me of the other," the helmed man said, "then I shall pronounce judgement."

"He is Argall, son of Argall," Louhi said. "A barbarian chief of the Erm-Gilt-Herm. He is a hardy warrior of a dangerous, wild, folk. He thinks more than most of his foul breed. Argall is to be made King of Atlantis."

"They seem unimportant and weak compared to your power," the master of the Brotherhood said. "Why not simply seek them out yourself? You have warriors of your own, as well as supposedly mighty powers."

"We have our reasons," Loviatar said, "ones that we need not share with you. Shall you take the challenge?"

"We shall," the helmed warrior said. "The price being every male child born in your kingdom for five years. Send them with male attendants only. We do not suffer females, except as breeding stock for our youths."

"If you succeed," Loviatar said, "it shall be done. When you have completed your task, gaze into a still pool of water in darkness and say my name three times. I shall know you wish an audience and shall appear."

Louhi clapped her hands once and the three women were back in Pohjola, the frigid winds battering the walls of the royal home of the queen. Yerra wondered if they had truly been transported to the Eastern Isle, or if this was some form of magical projection.

I doubt I shall ever know, she thought.

"Girl," Loviatar said, "why do those warriors despise females?"

"They believe," Yerra said, remembering the writings she read upon the subject, "that any form of pleasure weakens their warrior spirit. The Brotherhood of the Axe live in denial of anything save training and combat.

They do not build, till the soil, sing, or drink pleasant food. They each hold a duty to either kidnap a baby boy or impregnate a woman with a male child. Once that is accomplished, they—from what I read—take herbs that promote muscular growth and lessen their capacity for the fathering of children."

Louhi clapped her hands and laughed until tears dripped down her lined cheeks. Her daughter and Yerra watched her, neither speaking, waiting until her uncontrolled hilarity ended.

"I have a thought, my daughter," she said, gasping the words. "Perhaps, after they accomplish our demands, we shall send the beliefs of these men to the Sisters of the Misty Isle, to the south. They believe men are a plague upon humanity, only useful as breeding stock."

Loviatar stared at her mother and fell back into her seat, laughing with equal volume and malice as the withered hag.

"Oh, my mother! You would bring about war between the Sisters and the Brotherhood as a method of avoiding paying either. With the blessings of the dark one, they shall destroy each other and relieve the world of such fools! Oh, my mother, your mind is a delight!"

The two witches howled with laughter as Yerra shivered in fear. She had forgotten the evil machinations of this pair and remembered why she once considered death a better end than servitude in the presence.

CHAPTER XIX

The young oracle did not explain her remark, nor did Soroe begin her lessons in refinement. They simply sat in the goat cart as the tide of humanity flowed around them, none taking heed of either female.

As predicted, they arrived in Taugi by noon, the sun hanging high above their heads and beating down upon them with a powerful intensity. They careful sipped at their water, sitting in silence as the goats occasionally bleated when they hit a particularly violent bump.

Taugi came into view and the sight wasn't inspiring. More a trading outpost than an actual city, the walls were low, the gate was narrow and there were no guards in evidence. Steady streams of men, women, children, horses, oxen, and wagons filed in and out of Taugi and the market appeared to begin about a mile before the actual city proper.

Deena pulled them off the cart about a half-mile from the walls, sighing with relief as they escaped the stench of the goats, they sat among for so many hours. The cart rumbled along ahead as she led Soroe down a row of tents the ran parallel to the nearby city.

"That way leads to the beast market," she explained, "which is a good place to get trampled by an auroch or some other oversized animal. This way leads to the perfumers, who will leave us alone, especially you. We'll circle to the west wall where there's a public bath. There we can clean up, though it'll cost extra for you. They ain't keen on mucksuckers dirtying up their pools."

"You're finding this very funny, aren't you?" Soroe asked as the fleas on her scalp increased their rhythm of biting her flesh.

"You bet I am," the young, former thief said, smiling. "Wouldn't you if the positions were reversed?"

"Probably," Soroe replied while grabbing her own hands to refrain from scratching her head. "I will make you pay for this one day."

"Actually," Deena said and winked, "I happen to know you won't. I get to hold this one over you for a long time… if things go right…"

The Queen-elect merely sighed and kept walking. She hoped the bathhouse would appear soon since even she found herself offensive smelling.

Happily, the young former thief proved as good as her words. They paid three times the rate for Soroe's admittance, but the owner of the business had reluctantly admitted them both.

The owner was an enormously fat woman with the thick, muscular arms of a blacksmith, six hairy chins, and bright yellow hair of a shade that was certainly not one created by nature. Her name was Thulie, and her deep voice boomed with the power of a trumpet's blast.

The business itself was not as she expected. Instead of rows of metal bathtubs with servants filling the vats with buckets of water, old Thulie had a different system. Each tub was a circular stone vessel set in the floor. The water came from a hot spring beneath the building and a clever system of pipes both filled the vessels and flushed them out when the customer completed bathing.

The place itself was otherwise as unadorned and unifamilial as a warehouse. Cloth curtains surrounded the stone baths and there were simple, plain wooden benches next to each location. A total of ten tubs were available, with four currently filled with unseen customers.

"The old cow hints she was the daughter of an important priest and inherited the spot," Deena had explained, "but I'll bet she strangled the owner and claimed it for herself."

"You," old Thulie said while pointing at Soroe, "take tub seven. Those waters hold a special soap that will kill the little visitors that probably live on your body. If you pay old Thulie a penny, she'll have her girl clean, or preferably burn, those rags you wear."

Soroe tossed the coin as she said, "Burning is fine. I have clean clothing."

"Good," Thulie said as she turned her attention on Deena. "You girl, no robbing or starting fights. Old Thulie will toss you out if you cause trouble again. You can have tub six and we'll clean your clothes too. No extra charge since you steered this fake mucksucker into my establishment."

"How did you know she's no mud dweller?" Deena asked.

The massive woman laughed, causing her voluminous flesh to ripple and flow in multiple directions.

"Her voice, girl, her voice. No mucksucker ever talked like a noble. Also, most of them have spots of yellow in their eyes as they get sick from living in the filth. Don't worry, few would know. But old Thulie sees the truth, girl. She knows how things work. Now, off you go before old Thulie changes her mind. Leave the rags outside the curtain so her servants can burn those rags out back."

Both women followed the enormous proprietor's orders, sighing audibly as they sank beneath the sultry, scented depths of their respective tubs. Neither spoke for a long time as they cleansed themselves and felt the layers of grime fall away. Their aching muscles unknotted and soon they relaxed, luxuriating in the warmth.

After a time, Soroe asked, "How did you find this place?"

"She used it as her hidey-hole," a female voice said from beyond the curtains. "The little shadow came in, rob people blind, and relaxed her for hours knowing nobody would enter."

"Gold and Iron," Deena said. "I'd hoped we could avoid you for a little while."

Both curtains parted and a powerfully muscular woman with short, wavy brown hair appeared before Soroe and Deena. She wore the brown leather pants and shirt favored by war scouts and a rapier lay strapped to her hip.

"Lady," Deena said, "meet Nikke the Finder. She's the King of Beggars' favorite hunter."

"A pleasure," Soroe said, nodding her head.

Nikke smiled without parting her lips. "I doubt it. Get dressed, both of you. You have an audience with the master of the city."

"That sounds bad," Soroe said.

Deena rose, reaching for a towel beneath the bench, as she said, "Trials for your life are rarely anything else."

CHAPTER XX

Having already drawn his sword, Argall was already wary and prepared. The Erm-Gilt-Hermian warrior batted the streaking arrow aside, shattering the head and shaft with his blade. He dove behind a post holding upright a large canopy and rolled into the shade of the stall.

"Can you see the archer?" Argall asked.

"No," the masked one replied, having hidden behind a wagon filled with wooden crates. "You?"

"Only that they stood atop a building with a flat roof ahead," Argall said.

"The assassin left," a croaking voice said from the wagon. "You are safe."

The Accursed One and the Erm-Gilt-Hermian warrior rose from their hiding spots, each glancing about for other avenues of attack. Their search halted when they spotted the source of their information.

Seated on the edge of a wooden box was a massive, black winged, ebony-eyed beast. The creature was a crow, a particularly large one whose baleful gazed rested upon each man.

"Be more careful next time," the crow said. "I cannot protect you from every danger."

The animal then cawed raucously for several seconds before flapping its oversized wings and flying away. Nobody in the M'Yong market appeared to notice the odd scene, with the cries of goods for sale echoing every direction.

"Does this often happen to you?" the masked man asked Argall.

"Talking birds? No," he said. "I can comfortably say that this was the first time. You?"

"Yes," the Accursed One said. "This was not my first time speaking to a bird. Only one ever replied before today. I'd been drinking very heavily and a yellow one told me to go stick my head in the snow."

"What did you do?" Argall asked.

The Accursed One shrugged, "Stick my head in the snow. What would you do if a bird commanded that to you?"

"Probably the same," the barbarian warrior admitted. "Who were those birds?"

"Again," the masked man said, "I have no idea. They appear somewhat friendly, though that could be more deception. It matters little since more come and seek our deaths."

He was not wrong as three men and three women charged towards their position. Each carried long knives in their hands and their faces were covered with yellow cloth masks. The residents of M'Yong pointedly ignored the charging figures, stepping to the side as they continued their mercantile activities.

"Who are they?" Argall asked as his companion tossed aside his cloak, revealing his powerful physique.

"I expect," the Accursed One said as he drew twin battle axes, "that they are hired assassins. Beyond that, how would I know?"

No more words came from either man as Argall placed his back to a post and swept his sword swiftly between himself and three attackers. They came in three angles, each moving with coordinated control. A short, precise distance lay between each, preventing him from fleeing or fouling each other.

Skilled and trained together, Argall thought. *Dangerous, but also a disadvantage.*

Reaching into his belt, the Erm-Gilt-Hermian drew his dagger and threw the weapon towards the middle assassin. He then stepped to his left, tossing his canteen at the woman on the right. Neither missile reached their mark but were knocked aside by the killer's swords.

Not that striking them was the goal. There was an old truism when fighting multiple enemies: always try to use one as a shield against the others. By stepping to the left and delaying two of his enemies, Argall effectively lined all three up so he only faced one foe at a time.

Parrying a sword swing and stepping back from a dagger, the warrior of the northern wastes smiled inwardly and stepped to his right. The two assassins to the rear were once again blocked by their fellow.

This time, his attacker reversed the directions of his blades. The sword slashed towards his thighs while the dagger aimed for his neck. Effective, but also a mistake when facing a skilled, swift warrior.

Argall avoided the attacks and lunged, his blade an extension of his arm. The point sunk deep into the assassin's throat, nearly defenestrating the man in one blow. He fell back into his fellows, blood spraying like a fountain from his neck.

The assassin to his rear stumbled as the body fell against him, fouling the woman to his rear. Argall leaped forward, bringing his blade hard down on the skull of the second killer. The man's head split, but then disaster struck.

The Atlantean blade, a relic he had inherited from his father, held fast in the dead man's body, and would not come free. The corpse of the assassin tipped sideways, falling to the left, ripping the hilt from his steely grasp.

The final assassin, a lithely-shaped woman stepped gingerly over the body of her comrade, placing herself between Argall and his blade. She assumed a fighting stance and slowly advanced, her weapons at the ready...

CHAPTER XXI

Nikke the Finder waited politely as both women dressed, never commenting nor touching her weapons. Her eyes never left them as they pulled fresh clothing from their packs and Soroe tied a kerchief over her wet head.

"Don't try running or anything clever," Deena said. "That will only make her mad."

"As you discovered to your cost," Nikke said. "You led me on a merry chance, child, but in the end, you simply wasted your time and energy."

"Yes," Deena said.

"We didn't steal anything," Soroe said. "We just came here and bathed."

"I know," Nikke said. "And His Majesty does not hold your friend's past against her. Your presence is of concern to him... Need I say more?"

The Queen-elect and priestess of the Light shook her head.

"No, your meaning is fully understood."

"That is fine. We shall walk two blocks from here and enter a carriage. The windows will be blacked, and the driver shall change directions many times. Should you look beyond the closed doors or attempt such silly behavior, I shall hurt you. Then I shall tie you up and place you in a drawer beneath the seat. I should prefer simply sitting quietly with you both through the hour or more we spend in the coach. However, I shall not concern or hesitate in retribution myself if you behave poorly," the Finder said.

"I know that," Deena said. "I won't make that mistake again."

"I will meditate, if that is acceptable," Soroe said.

"Very well," Nikke said. "Though I warn you: no use of magic. I will know and knock you unconscious."

"I understand," Soroe said. "I sensed the truth of you from the start and know I cannot prevail under these circumstances."

Nikke smiled again without revealing her teeth. "Then we understand each other. I shall trust you. I know your follower shall not test me again."

Deena frowned, glancing between both women several times as they exited the bathhouse. The gargantuan Old Thulie watched them leave, expressionless as they passed her seat.

"Old Thulie appreciates that you did not struggle and make a mess. You may come back anytime you pay," she said as Deena pulled open the front door.

The carriage that awaited them was a simple wagon with converted seats. The driver, a tiny man with oiled black hair and a thin mustache over his chapped lips, lowered a crude set of stairs and pulled open a rickety door. Soroe and Deena climbed aboard, seating themselves on the hard bench seat within. Just as Nikke dropped into her place, the door slammed shut and they found themselves plunged into the gloom. The only light in the coach were thin beams of sunlight from the edges of the door.

"You may as well make yourself comfortable," Nikke said. "The trip is never less than an hour."

Soroe nodded, leaned back, closed her eyes, and exhaled softly for several seconds. Her body subtly relaxed, as her breathing grew slower and deeper.

For her part, Deena closed her eyes and fell asleep. This was a skill she learned shortly after her mother vanished and the street became a new home. One of the most important skills she had ever learned was the ability to fall asleep quickly and in any location. The reason for this was because thieves needed to be well-rested and calm when they worked. Lack of sleep was as dangerous as not eating or forgetting you should only drink clean water.

Sleep came a moment later and she remained happily dream free. The fearful presence of Nikke seemed to have driven any possible prophetic dreams away, which was a small blessing at least.

After what felt like a few minutes, Deena heard her name mentioned. She came awake a few seconds later, feeling the eyes of both women upon her.

"I'm awake, I'm awake," she said. "Have we arrived?"

"Yes," Nikke said. "Leave your bags and any weapons here. I will search you carefully if you claim you have no knives or other protection."

Soroe place a thin dagger on the top of her travel back and opened her hands in surrender. Deena chuckled, pulled out three daggers, a lockpick kit with two small chisels, a razor blade with an ivory handle in her boot, and a small leather bag.

"Since when do you carry so many of these things?" Soroe asked.

"I used to only carry two knives. Then we met and I decided I needed to be a little more cautious," Deena said, turning her attention to the Finder. "Search me if you like. I'm empty now."

87

"Mmm," Nikke said, "you will now meet the King. Do not genuflect or damn him with faint praise. He will not trust subservient behavior in either of you."

Neither woman spoke, following the woman as she led them out of the cottage and into a doorway three steps away. The street below their feet squished loudly as they stepped, and the scents of garbage and other unmentionable odors permeated the air.

Gratefully, they entered a well-lit entry hall where Nikke stopped and pointed towards the nearby wooden wall.

"Hands on the wall, time for your last search," she said. "Fight me and I will strip you to your bare skin and toss you before the king in the nude."

"No need to threaten," Soroe said as she placed her hands on the wall. "We've complied with your every request."

"And you will keep doing that," Nikke said, "because you know what will happen if you don't."

Soroe looked over her shoulder and smiled. "Do you really believe I listen to you because of threats? You know who I am, correct?"

"Lady…" Deena said, but found herself hushed by gestures from both women.

"Yes," Nikke said, "I know. What of it? A jumped-up priestess doesn't carry water here."

Soroe pushed away from the wall, turned, and faced the Finder. Her expression was neutral, her hands at her side and unmoving.

"Nor does a filthy, mouthy, violent, bounty-hunter with me," she said. "Either stop barking threats in my direction or we settle this right now."

Nikke chuckled and flexed her hands. "Oh good. I haven't whipped a noble in days. You ready, princess?"

"Does she ever stop threatening?" Soroe asked the rapidly retreating Deena, adding, "Yes, Nikke. I was ready for this after your second insult."

Nikke cracked her knuckles and stepped forward, a smile spreading across her attractive features.

"This is going to be fun!" she said, springing forward.

CHAPTER XXII

The female assassin slowly advanced, her weapons at the ready, only to fall over, a long thin dart protruding from the back of her skull.

Behind her now stood a figure dressed in a long, brown, hooded cloak. A thin hand protruded from under the fold of his cloak, vanishing from sight a moment later.

"When a blade gets stuck in a head," a musical feminine voice said from under the darkness of the hood, "you let it go. Otherwise, the next bugger will gut you."

The Accursed One appeared at Argall's left, cleaning one of his axe blades with a cloth that probably came from the bodies of the assassins.

"She is quite correct," he said. "You are too attached to your blade."

"It is the legacy of my father!" Argall said, pulling the weapon free of the corpse.

"It is a piece of metal," the masked man said, tapping the Erm-Gilt-Hermian in the chest. "You are your father's legacy. Weapons are tools. Protect yourself and those around you first."

"Metal face is correct, northern man," the unknown woman said. "You fight like your people. As a man, you are supreme. Against a well-trained force, you fall easily."

"What does that mean?" Argall asked, feeling slightly off-put by this stranger's words.

The Accursed One gestured to the dead bodies at their feet.

"You fought bravely and with incredible skill. Few could stand before you and survive. However, they knew that. The assassins lured you into a location in which they could attack you at a vulnerable point. Had your weapon not gotten caught, the assassin would have thrown a poisoned weapon into your body."

The woman's head swiveled as she asked, "You spotted the poison?"

The masked man shook his head. "No, but I smelled it on her weapons. I was too engaged to intervene."

Argall was used to the odd sense of smell his masked compatriot possessed. The Accursed One never explained why this occurred and only invoked the details when pressed for information.

"I smelled it too," the woman said as she reached up and shoved back her hood.

A tumble of auburn locks spilled from beneath the cowl, revealing a very pale oval face and large green eyes. A wide smile highlighted by very straight white teeth and bright crimson lips followed.

"I am Macha and you're pleased to meet me," she said.

"You said you wouldn't save us a second time," the Accursed One said.

Macha shrugged one shoulder, "I changed my mind. I'm allowed. Now, why would a pair of northern louts be traveling through the treacherous city of M'Yong? And who have you insulted ten seconds after walking through its gates?"

"It does not matter," Argall said, nodding to his left. "The city guard are here to arrest us?"

Macha laughed, shook her head, rolled her eyes, and replied, "Such innocence! This in M'Yong, man."

91

The city guard were four men in red livery, black and gold helmets, and matching halberds. They marched in perfect step, halting after they surrounded Argall, the Accursed One, and Macha. They pointed the tips of their weapons towards the three but did not advance.

"A fight in the street," a man with a long, curling mustache said. "Six corpses. You are herewith fined six crowns for the bodies and cleanup fee. If you cannot pay, you will work off your penalties in the sewage pits. If you wish to dispute the fine, you will be placed under arrest and be tried immediately by the magistrate. How do you plead?"

"Guilty," Macha said as she pulled out six gold coins from within her robe.

The captain accepted the coins, studied each, touched the peak of his helmet, nodded towards his men, and walked away. A moment later, a cart pulled by tow-chained men rolled forward, loaded the dead bodies onto its back, and rolled away.

"Life is cheap in this city," Argall said. "Where do they bury the bodies?"

Macha shook her head. "They don't, northerner. M'Yong doesn't bother with funerary rites. The diseased ones are burned and their ashes are used to cover the cesspits. Murdered or aged are taken away and never seen again."

"That is a dangerous," the Accursed One said, "and an effective method of infuriating the gods of the underworld."

"Why?" Argall asked. "My people simply place the dead in a makeshift boat and burn them."

"You say words of praise before and after, wishing them well and the like?" the masked one asked.

Argall nodded, "Yes, of course."

"That is enough," Macha said. "Spirits don't need you devoting days and nights to mouthing false niceties. Not doing it makes them angry, though it takes them a time to work up a fury."

"How long has this practice been in place?" the Accursed One asked.

"Twenty years tomorrow," Macha said. "The day the immortal Queen agreed to let the merchants and coin counters run the city so that her purse received more money. And her levy of soldiers and miners doubled."

"Twenty years?" the masked man asked before shaking his head. "No wonder this place smells wrong."

"Wrong?" Argall asked. "You never said anything about the city having a bad odor."

"If he told you every time the air about a place is stinking of foul spirits, he'd be talking your ear off, northerner," Macha added. "Most places inhabited by your kind are spiritual cesspits."

"Your kind? You're not human?" Argall asked.

Macha rolled her eyes again. "I think I just said that, child. Like metal face here, I'm a cousin of your kind. Now, are you coming, or will you run screaming for the hills like every other person with some sense?"

"Yes," the masked one said. "Where to first?"

"We'll be following the death cart and see what they do with the poor people," she said. "Keep your eyes open. Someone doesn't want you in this city."

With that said, she grinned, pulled her hood back over her head and melted into the crowd. Without pausing, the Accursed One turned in the direction the corpse cart headed, his step swifter than usual. Argall dashed after him, reaching his comrade's side after a few steps.

"Why are we listening to this woman?" he asked. "We don't know what she wants. Also, we have a mission to save the world!"

The Accursed One never broke stride as he replied, "An entire city falling into the hands of dark powers is often the first step to a greater danger. The lack of respect towards the dead befouls the entire world. We cannot leave this behind."

Argall nodded, realizing the masked man had made a very good point.

"I simply hope we do not spend overlong here. Now, who is that woman? Have you ever met her before?"

"That is the first time I laid eyes upon her," the Accursed One said, his step increasing in speed.

"Yet, you trust her," Argall said, easily keeping up with the shorter sorcerer.

"Not yet," the masked one replied. "However, saving our lives did mean I will listen to her suggestions. There is the cart. Come, we must follow, yet not arouse too much suspicion."

"Says the man wearing an iron mask," Argall said, shaking his head.

CHAPTER XXIII

Nikke sprung forward. Deena closed her eyes, turned her head, and covered her face. Despite that, she caught the edges of a brilliant white light that dazzled her vision momentarily. Bright lights danced before her eyes for several seconds before she slowly opened her lids, momentarily dazzled.

Soroe stood in the same spot as before, the only difference was that Nikke now lay at her feet. The Finder's many weapons lay in a pile by her head as she groaned and slowly sat upright.

"What did you do?" Nikke said, slowly shaking her head.

"Just a little defensive magic," Soroe said. "A minor summonsing of the Light in time of mild need."

"Mild need? I feel like my head is going to explode," Nikke said, groaning and closing her eyes.

Soroe shrugged, "I did warn you. Possibly in your experience, nobles are fat, weak, greedy fools. I was raised as a priestess of the Light. In the temple, I worked from dawn until dusk, washing floors, carrying buckets, polishing brass, and running errands. Lessons on reading and the like were a welcome change from the drudgery of work."

"She's climbed mountains and faced off with them giant rats that live on the beaches. No screams or whimpering. Though she never used that flash," Deena added.

"There was never a need. The Watchers are immune from that cantrip and the other creatures we faced might have gotten angry. A bit of magic on people gives them a quick lesson in manners and a headache cured by some quiet and tea," Soroe concluded with a shrug.

Nikke looked up, her face twisting into a sardonic smirk. "I suppose I deserved that, lady. I apologize. But I have to drink tea? I hate that brew."

Soroe extended a hand to help the Finder up. "Tea is the fastest cure I know; wine or ale just extends the pain. Oh, and you'll find all your knives and weapons behind you in case that is why you're shaking your left arm."

Nikke accepted the hand. "I wasn't; that wouldn't be fair. I was just checking if you found my strangling wire."

"No," Soroe said. "I didn't. Are you planning on using it on me?"

Nikke shook her head as she replied, "No. You won our little fight. I was wondering if my final holdout weapon could be found. Glad to see I'll have a tool if I ever get caught unaware."

"You've been caught flat-footed?" Deena asked. "I never thought that was possible."

Nikke flexed her shoulders, blinking slowly while slowly rotating her neck.

"It happens, little girl. Talisal's gang almost had me twice this week. I need to be ready in case one of that bastard's monsters comes a'ripping again."

"Talisal?" Soroe asked as Deena shuddered.

"Let the King explain, OK?" Nikke asked. "Follow me... please. No more threats."

Soroe smiled and they followed the Finder down a narrow corridor and into a small square room with a single wooden table and four chairs. Behind the table sat a man with short white hair, a thin, well-trimmed beard, bony shoulders, and a neck with dozens of tiny folds that resembled waddles on a turkey. He slowly scratched a note with a quill pen into a battered ledger book and gestured towards the seats.

"Sit, sit," he said. "No ceremonies in the courts of the forgotten. I cannot offer you food, drink, or salt. That is reserved for those of us who live beneath the feet of the rest."

"What should we call you?" Soroe asked, sitting in the furthest chair with Nikke between her and Deena.

"My title is King of the Beggars," the elderly fellow said, still writing, "but my born name was Jacob. My people simply call me the Listener. Listener will do if you require a means of address."

He laid down his pen, looked up and revealed a gaping hole where his left eye had once been. His other orb was dark brown, and the gaze pierced the three women he surveyed.

"Horrific, is it not?" he asked, "I was walking down the street when I accidentally bumped into the son of a highly-ranked officer. I begged his pardon, but he was not inclined to forgive. He sliced my eye from my head and threw me into the muck. My family, worshippers of Queen Yerra, cast me out for the imperfection. The beggars took me in, accepted me, gave me a home of sorts."

"Why do you tell us so much?" Soroe asked. "Do not lie and say you spin that tale to each who you summons."

The Listener laughed and bowed his head.

"I am suitably chastened. No, I do not. I thought I would inform you of the world you wish under your rule. The court of the Queen is one of beauty, lack of want, and joy. Those of us below your notice live under a different rule."

"You also assume there is no danger to the place I reside. Violence and intrigue are as much a part of life in the court as it is in the streets. I may not know your world, Listener, but do not assume you know mine," Soroe said.

"Well spoken," he said, "and what I hoped to hear. I then ask you something of importance. Do you know of the cult of Queen Yerra the immortal?"

"Yes," Soroe said. "A small religion she may have secretly supported."

The Listener nodded, "Correct. That cult ruled this city. When you revealed her falsehood, they took to worship a darker power. Their leader, Talisal, seeks control of the streets. He sends monstrosities against those whom he considers to be his rivals. The Assassins' leader, the Death Princess, died last month. We found her head torn from her body. The captain of the street guards died a week ago, as did four smugglers. Soon this city will be an unholy ruin if Talisal has his way."

"Continue," Soroe said. "You want my help."

The Listener nodded, "I can't risk my people; there's nothing we can do if those horrors come for us. I keep killers like Nikke in gold by giving them a piece of our earnings. But all of them but her are mercenaries. They won't risk their necks against those things."

"Gold and Iron," Deena said while rubbing her face, "I don't need to see the future to know she'll do this, and I'll be with her. Where does this Talisal keep?"

The young oracle caught the frightened look on the Listener's face and shuddered, "Not there…"

"Yes," Nikke said, shaking her head.

"Where?" Soroe asked.

"The Abattoir," all three said simultaneously, each looking disgusted by these words.

CHAPTER XXIV

Argall and the Accursed One followed the cart for two hours as it rolled from death site to death site. On each occasion, the guards demanded money, received payment, and left. Only once did someone object, only to be dragged off by another set of constables who were in the vicinity.

It was not difficult following the corpse cart; none impeded the progress of the horrible, foul-smelling vehicle. Flocks of birds circled the transport, occasionally dropping low and pecking a fallen piece of flesh that fell from the growing pile of dead.

"They do this all day long?" Argall asked. "This is foul work."

"The guards probably receive a part of each coin collected," the masked one replied. "The workers are slaves. They will eventually die of some disease and be replaced by those arrested and sentenced to servitude."

"How do you know this?" Argall asked. "You viewed such behavior in the past?"

The Accursed One shook his head. "No, never. Simple observation. They have a full complement of slaves working the cart. The guard said those arrested work now in the cesspits. The information was meant as a possible incentive. Human waste is foul and dangerous, but often less so than carrying the dead for hours at a time."

The Erm-Gilt-Hermian chieftain shook his head, "Disgusting. The system in this city only benefits a few who prize their wealth above others. That cannot stand."

"That is the way people live," the masked one said. "I once felt the same as you. The result was over one hundred years of servitude as a gladiator. You and your Soroe seek a worse fate."

"She is not my anything," Argall replied. "Neither of us are in love. I care for another."

"Keep telling yourself that, youngling. One day you may believe it is true," the Accursed One said with a harsh laugh.

"Just because your love betrayed you does not mean all women are fickle and choose others," Argall said.

The masked man shook his head. "There was no emotions between myself and my mate. We married for reasons of politics. It averted a civil war. In truth, we could not stand spending time with each other for long."

"I thought you once said you fathered sons and daughters," the northern chieftain said.

"That was sex and coupling. Do not mistake it for more. She and I were excellent bedmates. It was only when the act ended that our loathing returned and intensified. The difference is something even my people struggle with comprehending," he said, "Ah...excellent. The cart turns north."

"Which means?" Argall asked.

"The burning fields are that direction," the masked one said. "There we shall encounter any who seek power from the horrors of the despoiled dead."

"You know overmuch of this," the Erm-Gilt-Hermian said. "How?"

"Magic has principles," the Accursed One replied. "One cannot simply point a finger and cause transformations in the world. For every action, there is a reaction. I control darkness and cold. However, these powers do not originate from within me. In this situation, if there are ones who use the dead for power, they could not do so in a place of life. They must live among that which they use."

Argall thought for a moment. "I think I understand. Then explain to me this... a witch from my lands as well as Deena can see the future. Where does that power come from?"

The iron-helmeted sorcerer shrugged his shoulders. "There are many beliefs and theories. Some say those who soothsay may receive their visions from the gods. Others believe they touch the very universe. Me, I have never known and considered it for long. My powers come from the nature of the world. And before you ask, I have only the barest notion of that which Macha can do. But I would walk and talk warily in her presence."

"You know that from a single discussion?" Argall asked.

"Two discussions," the Accursed One said. "Now, silence, we are crossing from the city to the death grounds. Cover your face and mouth. The soot of the burning dead can tarnish your spirit."

CHAPTER XXV

At the words "The Abattoir," Soroe noticed the horrified expressions and asked, "Explain further."

"I shall do so," the Listener said. "Many years ago, a powerful noble family were famed for the beauty of their daughters and the handsome aspects of their men. One day, an over-boastful member of that family compared the girls to Queen Yerra, the false immortal. Angered by these words, the Queen sent her troops, who murdered every member of the family…"

"…and their servants," Nikke added.

"…and every admirer who was rumored to speak well of that family," Deena concluded.

"The scourges of the Temple of Apophis tortured and killed hundreds within the grounds of the family's plush mansion. Screams filled the air for days and blood flowed like a river from the gates. The rats… oh, the rats fell upon the corpses in swarms… Their squeals and chittering were as terrible as the wails of agony from the dead…" the Listener said, sweat beading on his upper lip as he spoke.

"Then they left," Nikke said. "No burial. They left the dead and everyone in the city were forced to carry the body parts to a common grave."

"The mansion was nicknamed the Abattoir because it resembled a slaughterhouse for pigs. The stench was horrible and no amount of prayers or cleansing rituals ever removed the taint. It became a place where only the lowest scum would dwell. And many of them never returned," the Listener added.

"I ran to it when Nikke chased me once," Deena said. "But I didn't enter. It was better risking a beating than heading into that place."

Soroe thought for a moment and nodded. "I understand. Provide me with directions and I will go there alone. This Talisal's work cannot be borne."

Deena looked furiously at Soroe and exclaimed, "You are not leaving me behind! You won't survive without me!"

"I will go too," Nikke interjected. "I promised I would protect these people. This is not possible here, so entering Talisal's lair must follow."

Soroe shook her head. "I cannot ask this of you."

"You didn't ask, lady," Deena said. "We made our own choices."

"I shall not accompany you," the Listener said. "Though I am greater than I appear, I have not the courage to enter those gates a second time. Just the thought of that night... I may not sleep for nights..."

Soroe reached out and squeezed the King of the Beggars' hand for a moment, nodding slowly.

"Leave it to us," she said. "Tell your people to be careful tonight."

After a brief exchange of pleasantries, they left. Nikke led them down the street and into a small inn not far from the non-descript building they had just exited. The tavern, a squat square, stone structure, known as *The Skinny Fiddler*, had a large painted sign above the door displaying a skeletal musician playing a violin.

"We need some sleep," the Finder said. "You two look wrung out and I am feeling the weight of the day. Eat first and we will leave when twilight approaches."

"Do you think it actually matters when we break into the Abattoir?" Deena asked. "The place is haunted!"

"Twilight is when Talisal's monsters are at their furthest points from his lair. It will lessen our chances of being quickly attacked by his followers," Nikke replied as they entered a gloomy room lit by several thin tallow candles.

"What type of monsters shall we face?" Soroe asked.

Nikke dropped into a chair and slapped the table once, summoning a fat man with a gray-streaked beard and eyes that never rose above their feet.

"Three," she said to the tavern-keeper before he scurried off. "What does Talisal send out? Demons, priestess. That's the only way I can describe them. They're nothing from this world, that much I can tell you. Just one look and even the bravest are liable to scream and run as fast as their legs will allow."

CHAPTER XXVI

The scent of soot, charcoal, and burning meat grew stronger and Argall found himself coughing as he covered his face and mouth. The stalls of merchants diminished and soon, the only peddlers in evidence were ones buying and selling rags and meat made from rats and other vermin. The people walked with quick steps, their heads lowered, their behavior furtive and frightened.

Argall found himself walking hunched over, huddling inside his cloak. The sky appeared grey, and a chill wind wafted through the streets. It felt as if the entire world had transformed into a pale reflection of itself.

"You are feeling the dark energies," the Accursed One said in a hushed tone. "It wears upon you and brings a feeling of despair if you linger."

"Then why do some reside nearby?" Argall asked, finding his own voice strangled and weak.

"Poverty for most," the masked one replied. "Some find comfort in the gloom."

"Is that why you do not feel it?" the Erm-Gilt-Hermian asked.

The masked man shook his head. "I feel the weight; I simply ignore its influence. My powers are not based on evil, simply a less beloved part of life. The foulness that lingers here has nothing to do with me."

Argall did not comment, finding even walking more difficult now. It felt as if he were treading through a deep swamp, with each step requiring greater strength.

They turned a corner and stopped, remaining in the shadow of an abandoned stall that smelled of musty clothing and sweat. A short lane lay before them, leading to an unguarded open wooden gate. A series of gray-black rises covered the land behind the fence and curls of dark smoke rose from beyond their sight.

"Gods above and below," the Accursed One said, staggering.

"Those mounds," Argall asked, "are they the ashes of the dead?"

"Yes," the masked man replied. "Yet there are greater horrors beyond. The fires beyond our sight are not enough to consume so many bodies. There must be twenty or more on that cart alone. What are they doing with the other human remains? Perhaps coming here was a mistake after all."

"We will find out," Argall said, loosening his sword. "If necessary, we will fight any who block our path."

"Everything we encounter cannot simply be killed with a blade," the Accursed One replied.

Argall laughed and clapped the sorcerer on his shoulder. "I have yet to encounter a being that cannot be destroyed once its head is removed. Come, I would find out what these merchants brought upon this city."

He led the way, his eyes seeking movement among the ash piles. Nothing stirred as they approached the gate and they entered with nary a sound.

The mounds were nine to ten feet high and four such rises blocked their path. The wind shifted the dust, causing small dust devils swirling in different directions. Choking clouds of ash fell across their hooded heads and shoulders. Their booted feet sunk almost to their knees and each step felt as if they strode through heavy, dry, sand.

Argall spotted the remains of the cart's passage, leading them around the third mound through a path they had not spotted upon entry. Neither spoke; to do so would risk inhaling the choking, gray mist that lingered and shifted through the air.

They passed three more piles, the indentations from the cart's wheels guiding them in a bizarre path that circled around the largest piles. As they vanished behind the tallest rise, they spotted a pair of large bonfires a short distance away. Four slaves tossed a pair of bodies onto the fires as the corpse cart they followed drifted a short distance towards a small ivory colored structure about fifty feet beyond the burning zone.

"This is worse than I imagined," the Accursed One said. "What manner of demon would create such an abomination?"

"The worst type," Macha said, appearing at their side. "Mortals seeking power. Do you see why I sent you here? I can't do it alone. Are you with me?"

"I am," the masked man replied.

"Wait," Argall said. "Why are you two so horrified by these death grounds? My people burn their bodies too."

"You do not pile the ashes up in some great hills," Macha said. "Using minor cantrips to keep it all centered in one place. No, youngling, this is wrong and a corruption at the heart of this very city."

"This is the product of decades, Argall," the Accursed One added. "This is an inconceivable number of forgotten dead."

Macha waved a hand, cutting him off and pointing towards the building.

"That is bad enough. My fears are now all based in that nightmare."

"Agreed," the masked man said, removing his axe from his back.

"Why" Argall asked, drawing his sword.

Macha closed her eyes, sighed and shook her head. "Youth! They have eyes. yet less sight than a mole in sunlight. Look, northerner, do you see the building ahead?"

Argall nodded, "Yes."

"Good," she said. "You do realize that it is made entirely from bones, right?"

CHAPTER XXVII

The gloomy streets grew darker and murkier with each passing block. By the time Soroe, Deena and Nikke approached the neighborhood near the Abattoir, the streets were deserted and stank of refuse. The houses and buildings were large and appeared well-made, bordering on the luxurious. Yet all were deserted and showing signs of disrepair and neglect.

"The families that lived here," Nikke said, "used to ignore the Abattoir. Most thought it was a kind of deterrent against thieves."

"Were they right?" Soroe asked.

"Mostly," Nikke replied. "Some insane and foolish burglars did steal on occasion. Often though this was the safest section in the city."

"Safest when I wasn't around," Deena said. "I could get a year's worth of food from one night's work."

"Then even idiots like this one didn't bother," Nikke continued. "Something in the air drove them away. The beggars wouldn't sleep in the shelter of these homes."

Soroe halted, extending her arms, and stopping her two companions. She then raised her hand, palm extended, and slowly moved left and right. Frowning with concentration, ignoring the puzzled looks from Deena and Nikke. A moment later, she straightened and glanced their direction.

"There were no demons in this area in the last month," she said. "Possibly longer. My senses do not extend that far."

"Then your powers are wrong, princess," Nikke said. "I've seen them and they're demons!"

"Don't talk to her that way!" Deena said, pushing into the Finder's face. "If she says they're not demons, they're not!"

Nikke smiled, but this wasn't an amused expression. There was a glint of anger in her gaze as well as a feral bloodlust that was not quite human.

"Getting a little mouthy, aren't you, little thief? You're really willing to take me on?"

"Enough!" Soroe said, pushing between the pair. "We do not have time for such squabbles. Nikke, a demon is a creature from another world. The sheer power required for bringing such a monster into our world usually involves a great deal of blood and careful magic. Just attempting such an act stains an entire area for years. There is nothing like that in this neighborhood."

"Then what do you call creatures with dozens of eyes, tentacles, and teeth?" Nikke asked, not dropping her gaze from Deena's.

"I have no name to give you," the Queen-elect of Atlantis said, "because I have not seen them in my life. I believe what you describe. I simply know they were not what you said. That doesn't mean they are any less lethal."

"Right," Nikke said, pushing her face a little closer to Deena's. "We'll continue this later, thief."

Deena smiled as she said, "I look forward to it, mercenary."

"The first one of you that attacks the other, I will encircle with the light of truth. You will reveal all your worst secrets and fears for two days to anyone you meet. Do either of you wish to chance such an event?" Soroe asked, raising one golden eyebrow questioningly.

"No," Deena said and shuddered.

"Not I," Nikke said, turning away.

"I thought not," the Light priestess said. "It is a potent and rarely invoked punishment. The last person bespelled ran to the beaches and instead chose death by the fangs and claws of the Watchers on the Threshold."

Neither oracle nor mercenary replied, both stepping back from each other and staring off in different directions. Soroe placed a hand on each's closest shoulder.

"I need you both," she said. "I would only use such a terrible spell if it were the best way of keeping the peace. We need to work together and stop this Talisal before his monsters destroy this city. Show me the way to his foul lair."

Before either Nikke or Deena could reply, a being loped into view that brought and involuntary gasp to the lips of Soroe and Deena. Nikke drew a small crossbow from her back and aimed, cursing volubly.

"We waited too long! They're coming back!" she said, and fired her weapon.

CHAPTER XXVIII

"Made of bones?" Argall asked. "Are you sure? Did they learn that evil art from the Dalaketnon?"

"Probably," Macha said. "Only that pack of hedonistic immortals would devote their time to discovering a means of sculpting bones into common objects. I have heard they often sit on chairs of bones with tables of the same."

"It is true," Argall said. "We have seen it."

Macha tilted her head but did not look his direction. Her gaze lay upon the iron masked Accursed One.

"Is that why the mask? I heard they despise flesh that is not of their people."

"No," the masked one said. "I have other reasons. It is a long story."

"Then swallow it," she said. "Inside we go and death to any who turn their back on the danger."

Argall stepped ahead of the others, striding past the slaves while raising his blade. The workers never raised their heads or even glanced his direction. They simply stepped around the approaching trio and reached for their shovels and barrows as the fire grew in strength.

"Why don't they react?" he asked.

"Why should they?" Macha asked. "The poor scroungers were forced into servitude working a job that would remove the humanity from even the strongest spirit. As far as they're concerned, the whole city could burn."

An open door lay at the center of the building, and they heard the sounds of movement. Chopping sounds as well as other odd noises drifted their direction. Argall warily stepped inside and stood frozen at the sight before his eyes.

A dozen or so men, women and children busily moved about, their heads low, their hands perpetually in motion. Their faces were uniformly blank, and their eyes were the haunted, broken gazes of ones who had lost all connection to their humanity.

"Ukko protect me," the Accursed One said, lowering his axe.

"Balor's Eye!" Macha said, her voice choked with emotion. "It is worse than I feared."

The chamber they stood in was a long square about forty feet long and wide. Across the room lay stone tables, each surrounded by several of the busily working slaves.

At the first table, three men were carefully slicing a dead woman's body into parts. They operated with slow, careful efficiency transforming a corpse into a series of smaller segments. Their cleavers rose and fell with a steady motion that the action appeared almost like that of insects rather than humanity.

Two women at another table received the legs, feet, arms, and hands while tossing the heads into a vast cauldron in the center of the room. The pair sat at their table with smaller knives, slowly stripping the flesh from the corpse. The meat they placed on a tray which rested in the center of their table while the bones were dropped into buckets nears their feet.

A pair of filthy children dressed in a few scraps of clothing grabbed the tray and bucket, carrying both items to separate locations. The bones were poured into a series of vats where two large men with stones slowly ground the contents into a thin powder. They dumped the meat into an enormous trough where the remaining

113

slaves sat and toiled. There, the slaves slowly stuffed the meat and gristle into tubes which they tied off and tossed into a growing pile to their rear.

"Sausages?" Argall asked as he fought back the acidic gorge that rose in his throat.

Macha, her hood pushed back, revealed a flushed face as she replied, "The leaders of this city give them free to the poor. They always boast that nobody goes hungry here."

"This ends today," Argall said. "I will stop this if I have to kill every merchant in this land!"

"Ho, ho, ho!" a voice said from the rear as a door in the floor swung open. "What is this I hear? The boastful oaths of an outlander? No, I think it is just more meat for dinner!"

The being that emerged from the trapdoor was human in shape, possessing two legs, two arms, a head, mouth, eyes, ears, and nose. That was where the similarity ended. The creature towered about Argall and the others, with shoulders as wide as three men, an oversized head with protruding tusks from the massive maw, and green skin. In a hand larger than Argall's head the horror clutched a huge gray stone club almost as large as its body.

"An ogre," the Accused One said. "Yes, that fits the day we're having."

"Amusing," Macha said. "Let's kill it!"

"I'm open to suggestions how," the Accursed One said, stepping back.

CHAPTER XXIX

Nikke's bolt sailed into the gloom, heading directly for the oddly-shaped figure. The shape appeared to retract and shrink for a moment before rising again. Nikke muttered under her breath as she pulled another bolt from the pouch on her back.

The creature seemed to glide in their direction, the movement both silent and sinewy. Deena reached for her blades as Soroe pulled her scepter into view, seemingly from nowhere. A white light pulsed from the massive gem's depths, illuminating the area around them briefly.

They caught a brief image of a being, massive in size, which seemed more like a pile of ropy, gray, vine-shaped tentacles with dozens of tiny mouths visible across the surface. The creature possessed at least three off-center eyes and a nose that appeared quite human in shape. The being reared up to its impressive height, but fell back before the light of the legendary Soul of Soroe.

A bolt struck the monstrosity directly in the eye on the left and a dagger flew directly into the second. The tiny openings that appeared mouthlike in shape released wheezing moans before the being topped over, falling into the dirt with a soft, wet slap. Deena threw another knife into the remaining eye, though the beast did not stir.

"It's already dead, thief," Nikke said.

"I wanted to be certain," the young oracle replied. "You can't be too sure with something this horrible. Now, what was it?"

Soroe knelt closer and studied the dead creature, though she did not approach any closer. After a moment, she shook her head and stepped back.

"I have no idea. This is not a demon, nor one of the near human races. I do not know, but I shall find out."

"Is it just my eyes," Deena asked, stepping back, "or is that thing shrinking?"

It was indeed growing smaller with each passing second. The form of the dead monstrosity was not melting or falling apart but diminished before their eyes. Soroe knelt closer, studying the being as it dissipated into nothingness.

Straightening, she twisted her hand and the Soul of Soroe vanished. Her eyes gazed into the space where the creature once lay, and a frown creased her face.

"This is quite bad," she said. "Worse than I imagined. I have a theory, but I hope I am wrong. Come, take me to the location of this Talisal. Retrieve your weapons before we go. We may need every advantage."

Neither the young oracle nor the dangerous huntress could force another word from her after that statement. Soroe simply shook her head and stared into the gloom, her eyes haunted. The expression upon her lovely face hushed both into silent compliance, and soon they were running through the street, stopping before a ten-foot stone wall surrounding a ramshackle pile that once may have been a sumptuous mansion.

The house itself was a two-story structure whose roof was mostly missing. The windows visible from the street were shattered and long tendrils of weeds ran up the walls. The only sound audible was the skitters and chitters of rats; the number of which sounded as if they were in an abundance.

"The gate is rusted shut," Nikke said, waving her hand vaguely to the left. "Over the wall is the easiest means. Can you fly?"

Soroe's face wrinkled in confusion, "No. Can you?"

Nikke shook her head, "No, do I look like I got wings? I just wondered if it's true you witches could fly or walk through walls."

"I'm not a witch," Soroe said while rolling her eyes, "I'm the high priestess of the Temple of Light. None of us can fly."

"Then we do this the hard way," Deena said, studying the surface of the wall.

Her head tilted left and right for a full minute before she slowly nodded. Touching a spot on the wall, she pulled something for a few seconds before shaking her head.

"The stone is too soft to use as ladder. Put any weight on it and you'll fall. Time to make a human ladder."

"A what?" Nikke and Soroe asked simultaneously.

Deena chuckled and replied, "An old trick a thief name Malvo taught me. He used to be a street performer. Used this as a way of getting into places people thought were safe for storing expensive goods."

"What happened to him?" Nikke asked.

Deena shrugged, "One day he and his partners got into a place only to find that the Queen's guards were waiting. They were handed over to the scourges of the Temple of Gold and Iron. Those bastards whipped them to death publicly before tossing their remains onto the beaches to them giant rat monsters. But until then, the trick worked a treat."

117

CHAPTER XXX

"Don't you have magic powers?" Argall asked ther Accursed One.

"My powers are of darkness and cold. Neither will help us now," the other replied, stepping back again.

"Oh dear," the ogre said between guffaws. "The little man is frightened. How very sad for him. However, I am a friendly man. You may strike me once for free before I crush you beneath my feet and serve you as a meal for the slaves."

The monster released his club, stepping forward and spreading his arms wide. Argall snarled, lunged, and thrust his sword towards the ogre's ample exposed gut. His Atlantean sword struck the creature's flesh and snapped in two, falling to the floor at the Erm-Gilt-Hermian's feet.

"Ogre flesh," Macha said, "is harder than stone. Weapons made by the hand of man cannot pierce their hides."

The ogre laughed again, turning his back on them, and returning to his club. He lifted the weapon up, wielding the stone maul as if it were as light and a willow wand.

"This is true, human female," the ogre said. "We mountain folk are made from the bones of Mother Earth. We are the true children of the Goddess, and we shit your folk into existence."

"Does it believe that ogres…?" Argall asked, only to be waved into silence by the Accursed One and Macha.

"Time enough to discuss the religious beliefs of other races later," the masked one said, "if we survive. Run!"

The Accursed One bolted for the door, one step behind Macha. Argall, who despised fleeing a foe, ran after him and leaped through the open door several steps ahead of the charging monster.

"Run, little flesh bags," the ogre said, "I can smell your fear and track you no matter how far you flee!"

Ahead of them, Macha dropped her cloak behind her. She raised her arms, glanced back their direction, winked, and seemed to explode into a dozen different direction. A second later, Argall realized that where she once stood were now a flock of crows, each flapping, cawing, and crying as they flew in a dozen different directions.

"Ymir's Beard!" Argall said while dropping the hilt of his broken sword.

"Yes," the masked one said between pants, "that power usually has that effect on people the first time you see it."

The ogre roared, having fallen back several steps in shock at the change Macha had wrought. Its stride increased and the creature whirled the massive club through the air.

Argall's mind swiftly considered the creature to their rear and an idea came to him a moment later. He glanced back at the rapidly approaching horror as they ran around one of the huge ash piles.

"Do ogres breathe?" he asked, pulling his masked friend up the slope of a huge mound of burnt human remains.

"Yes, of course they do," the Accursed One replied. "I heard a story of a man who killed one by tripping it into a pond. The monster sunk to the bottom and drowned."

"Good!" Argall said as they reached the top of the ash hill. "I have a way of killing this thing. The trouble is, we will need Macha's help."

"How is that trouble?" Macha asked, pulling him up to the summit. "I spotted the pair of you climbing up. The lovely boy below is getting ready to start hammering this mound and sending you tumbling. Better talk fast."

CHAPTER XXXI

Deena braced herself against the wall, her knees slightly bent. Breathing deeply and closing her eyes, she nodded once and glanced their direction.

"Nikke," she said, "step on my shoulders."

"What?" Nikke asked, "Surely I should…"

"Just do what I tell you!" Deena said, her words harsh and sharp. "Step on my shoulder and grab the top of the wall. Make sure you have a good handhold."

The Finder frowned, shrugged, and gingerly placed one foot on the former thief's leg. She used that as a vault and a few seconds later stood with each foot on Deena's shoulders. Her hands grasped the top of the wall and she secured herself by holding the far end.

"OK, lady," Deena said, her words more gasps than statements, "climb up me and Nikke. Then hold her arms when you're up top. Quickly! I can't hold you and this horse up for long."

"Horse?" Nikke asked. "I am going to break your legs for that one, thief."

"Shut up, you oversized dray!" Deena said.

Soroe rolled her eyes as she quickly scrambled up the back of Nikke. She grabbed both of the powerful woman's arms, securing her hold on the wall. Before she could open her mouth, Deena appeared at her side. Pulling Nikke up, she sat down on the wall, mopping sweat from her face with the back of her hand.

"Down is easier," she said, "you lower yourself down, facing the wall. I'll go first and make sure neither of you break and ankle or something."

Without waiting for responses, the young oracle spun on her rear, grabbed the edge of the wall, and lowered herself as far as she could. She landed softly in a crouch, rolled once, and stood.

"Grass and weeds. A soft landing. You first, lady," Deena said.

Soroe turned far slower than her friend and carefully allowed each leg over the side. The edges of the stone sliced into her palms and felt herself slipping as her fingertips held to the edge of the wall. A moment later, she fell and felt her body shift so that she was heading back first to the ground.

A pair of strong hands arrested her tumble, righting her a second later. Deena shook her head, gently placing her aide and catching Nikke as she landed in a style close to the former thief.

"Lady," she said, "you'll never make a good thief. That was the worst drop I've seen since One-Eye Ling's hanging in the square," she said.

"I heard about that one," Nikke said. "The rope tore his head off."

"Yep," Deena said, "blood squirted all over the place and the bitch who got money from his arrest was soaked head to foot."

"Ugh," Soroe said. "My fall was an accident. The other was probably negligence."

Deena shook her head. "I think old Ling planned it. He had a weird sense of humor. Now, where do we go?"

Soroe tapped her chin with one slim finger for a moment and considered the information from the beggar king, Deena, and Nikke.

"These monsters only come out at night. That means they, and probably this Talisal, spend their time beneath the ground. Whether daylight harms them or they only function during those hours, I cannot say."

Nikke pointed to a shattered window and said, "We can enter that way."

Deena shook her head, "Bad idea. Most of the building has been open to the wind, rain, and snow. Wood or stone floors will be weak and may collapse. Follow me. These places usually have two ways to the basements."

"Two ways? Why more than one?" Nikke asked. "In truth, why even one from the outside?"

"Big houses," Deena said, "need more food and other things to keep the place running. The owners need a place to store the boxes and bottles. That's one way in. The other is made when you have servants. Rich folk don't like servants and slaves using the front door. They make a place for that bunch to live and a way in and out."

"How do you know this?" Nikke asked, her voice lowering as they circled to the left of the ruined structure.

"I once broke into the home of a stable owner. His adder-tongued wife went on endlessly about needing two ways into the basement because she visited Lady Big Nose or whatever her name was. I stole a few things that night and a week later, burglarized Lady Big Nose's mansion that way," Deena said.

Soroe leaned closer and asked, "Were you successful?"

"Nope," the former thief answered. "That lord paid his workers well and they tried killing me when I was caught lifting some jewelry. I bit the bitch holding me by the hair and ran out through the front door. Had to join a traveling carnival for six months to keep from getting caught. But the principle is good."

Nikke and Soroe exchanged a concerned look but did not comment. They stopped when Deena pointed a short distance ahead.

"That is close to the gate. That's the delivery door. I bet all them demons come out of there. Let's go the other way and we'll find the servant's quarters soon," she said, turning and heading back the way they came.

Or at least, she was about to do that when several shadows rose into view blocking the direction Deena planned on heading. She stepped back, turned, and froze in place. More silhouettes emerged from the gloom, massive, oddly-shaped forms rising into their path, yet not approach.

"Doctor Talisal," a voice that sounded as if it was speaking through a throat full of phlegm said from the rear of the pack closest to the house, "invites you to his workshop for a cup of tea. Please do not flee or we will be forced to harm you."

The speaker stepped forward into a beam of the silvery gray light from the stars overhead. The being was taller than all three women, narrower than the slim Soroe, with black tendrils of hair that fell across a grayish skinned body that appeared sexless and sticklike. A single yellow eye gazed their direction through the masses of filthy black hair and a long hand with black nails beckoned their direction.

"Follow me," the bizarre voice said. "The doctor will see you now."

CHAPTER XXXII

Argall explained his plan in two sentences, receiving a smile form Macha and a quick nod from the Accursed One. The attractive sorceress leaped into the air, and it appeared for a moment as if she exploded and a murder of crows flew from where she had appeared.

A moment later, they heard the roar and snarl of the ogre below and Argall leaned over the precipice, gazing downward. The same large black birds circled the massive monster, pecking at the exposed flesh while flapping away when the huge arms swung out in defense.

"She has him busy for the moment," Argall said as the masked man handed him an axe.

"Your strategy is strange, but I hope it works," he said.

Argall climbed down four feet or so on the opposite side of the mound. He began digging quickly with his hands, making a hole large enough to fit the axe blade. Jamming it in, he pushed hard, thrusting the weapon deeper into the ash pile. Within a few seconds, only a handhold remained.

Nearby, the Accursed One performed the same action. Like the Erm-Gilt-Hermian, he then lowered himself beneath the handle of the weapon. Thrusting one powerful arm into the mound, he then placed his shoulder against the axe handle.

"On three," Argall said, One... two... three... push!"

Both men heaved, pitting every sinew in their powerful bodies against the massive mound of human remains. The ashes shifted and slid, but soon the force combined with the instability of the pile sent the upper layer tumbling downward.

A raucous series of caws filled the air as the murder of crows sailed above their heads. The roar of the ogre transformed into a shriek of shock as the hill of human ashes collapsed. The avalanche caused by Argall and the Accursed One increased in volume until almost half the mound collapsed over the massive monster.

A moment later, the impact shook the ground and a large stream of ashes from a nearby hill fell, with a huge portion covering the area near where the ogre once stood. The enormous creature vanished from view and five or more feet or burnt human remains fell over that location.

Both men righted themselves, having fallen as the precarious footholds in which they stood collapsed. The Accursed One rose, having retrieved one of his axes, his head swiveling left and right for the other.

"If you're glancing about looking for your wee axe, it's about four feet to the left and about eight feet down," Macha said. "I saw when you lost it and watched as it vanished beneath the piles."

The masked man shrugged as he placed the weapon across his back, "It's just an axe. No better or worse than any other."

The sorceress nodded, approval visible upon her face. "A wise attitude. My uncle once grew too fond of his spear and cried like a girl on an unwanted wedding day when the head snapped off and fell into a river. His wife left him that night for the town blacksmith."

"That talk aside," Argall said, "we must return to the place where the ogre came from. We must know who is behind this evil."

"Agreed," the Accursed One said, "however, we must deal with these untended bodies first."

"I can send word to the priests of the death god," Macha said, "but that will take two or three days. By then, the bad energies may explode and bring the end of all things upon us."

"Leave that to me," the masked one said. "Get into shelter, I'm going to weaken the power of this unsanctified horror."

"And how would you be doing that?" Macha asked, her eyes narrowing.

The Accursed One clapped his hands together once, rubbing the leathery palms together for several seconds. Turning his back, he balled his hands into fists before stopping and looking to the darkening sky.

"By doing something I haven't done in many years… use the true power that resides in me," he said. "Allow me to reintroduce myself, my name is Jaska the Gray Wolf, former consort of Loviatar the North Star, Queen of Pohjola. I am the son of the North Wind and I bring the cold…"

That said, he raised his hands above his head and deep sonorous note emerged from his lips. Removing his mask, he tossed the battered metal aside and exhaled loudly. A long stream of white mist emerged from his mouth.

Argall stood entranced, still not seeing his friend's face, but amazed by the energies that seemed to leap from his skin. He felt a hand pulling at his arm and spotted Macha yanking him towards the building made from bone.

"Come on, you idiot," she said while yanking harder. "Now is the time to run. Himself is calling on powers we best not witness!"

A harsh chill entered the air and Argall realized that the shapeshifting witch was correct. Not glancing back, he ran into the building and closed the door. The slaves were still working, none looking up or speaking as they went about their grizzly task.

The walls to the bizarre structure shook and the temperature of the chamber fell almost immediately. Macha glanced briefly through the crack in the door and nodded to herself.

"Come on, northerner," she said, "we might as well see what's down below. Himself won't be speaking to us for a time."

"Why?" Argall asked.

Macha shook her head, "Ignorance is not a pretty quality, youngling. You have a lot to learn about magic and other powers. Now, come on, I say!"

CHAPTER XXXIII

"I think we had best follow," Soroe said, stepping into the lead as the monster turned away.

Deena was close upon her heels and Nikke a few steps behind, yet the creature never looked back. It led them down several wooden steps that sagged and groaned beneath their weight. There was no door, but and opening where it once lay was visible as they approached.

A well-lit room filled with foul smelling refuse lay strewn about the chamber they entered a moment later. The chambers lighting derived from several glowing orbs that floated about the low ceiling, each slowly moving in small circles leaving tendril trails of yellowish light in their wake.

An opening on the far wall led them into an even larger location, a room that covered the length and width of the enormous home above. Trash of every type lay in heaps and the stench that exuded from the piles revolted Soroe, Deena, and Nikke. Each covered their noses and mouths, gagging and revolting odors that wafted from every direction.

"There are pieces of dead people in these piles," Nikke said, her voice strangled as she tried speaking.

"The doctor does not need every part," their monster guide said, head swiveling 180 degrees and the gray-skinned feet continued walking forward.

"Um," Deena said, stopping in place, "how... forget it... please stop doing that. It's getting me ill."

"You humans are so limited in your bodily functions. Why should a neck stop turning? Lesser beasts in the wild have greater senses than the best of you. If you ask the doctor, we can use his talents and improve you," the creature said in the same sickening voice.

"Is that what he did to you?" Soroe asked. "Improved you?"

The monstrosity's head snapped back forward as it said, "No. I am not a limited being such as you and your species. My people were ancient when yours had not even crawled from the primordial ocean of chaos. We are ancient and great. You are new and quite unevolved."

"You look close to human," Soroe said.

The creature gurgled and the tendrils of hair shook and quaked. A scent of rot exuded from the monster's very form and droplets of flesh fell across the filthy floor. They realized the horror leading them was laughing and falling apart as it moved.

"This is but a vessel for my true self," the being said. "I am not hampered by the physical. I merely occupy your meat and use it as a method of communication with lower lifeforms who still rely upon flesh."

"Did that thing just call us meat?" Nikke asked.

"More you than me," Deena said and giggled.

"I am going to bust your jaw when we get out of here, thief. That's the only way I know to stop your lips from moving so much," Nikke said.

"Silence," the monster said. "Human prattle is unnecessary for this meeting. The doctor requires your presence for his latest work."

From the far end of the room came a cry of agony, one that cut off almost immediately. Soroe, Deena, and even the normally stoic Nikke jumped at the sound. The monster gurgled again, and more bits of flesh fell along the floor.

130

"Ah," it said, "another success. The sheer agony of the transference is music to my ears."

"That was a success?" Deena asked. "I'm not sure I want to know what a failure sound like."

"I know I don't want to hear it," Nikke said as she glanced over her shoulder. "Oh, and several of those things are following us at a distance."

The monster's head swiveled, but only enough so that one baleful eye gazed their direction. "Oh, it is nothing terrible. Just the sound of meat flying every direction. Quite boring. Your species does not regenerate. Explosions are one moment of flesh and fluids in a cloud, and then a pile of decomposing remains."

"How terrible for you," Deena said.

Nikke elbowed Deena in the side as she said, "Kindly do not annoy the angry rotting corpse. I would like to get through this alive somehow."

"That will not happen," the monster said, stepping over the partially rotting skeleton of what appeared to be a child. "You are meat and shall be used. Your lives will be over shortly. But despair not now. You will have thousands of years to do that in Mugen Jigoku."

"Where?" Nikke asked.

"It translates as The Hell of Uninterrupted Pain," Soroe said, her voice low. "It is said to be the worst place in the underworld, reserved for the most horrific beings in existence."

"Oh joy," Deena said.

CHAPTER XXXIV

"Before we do that, I think I have a right to know something!" Argall said. "If the Accursed... Jaska... Whoever he is... can call snowstorms and the like, why hasn't he done so until now?"

Macha whirled his direction, her face flushed and her dark eyes flashing. She looked murderous for a moment before her body relaxed and she glanced heavenward for a moment.

"Grandfather Airgetlám, give me strength when dealing with these northerners!" she said. "I shall indulge you this time, Erm-Gilt-Hermian. Just don't keep thinking you can make demands upon me. Now, you wish to know a little of the ways of magic, correct?"

"Yes, I guess," Argall said.

"Very well," she said. "Then know that magic is not simply a waving of hands and changing the universe. It comes from three sources... Within a body, from the world, or from the entire universe. When you use the first, you risk your life because a soul only has so much energy before it wears out."

Argall's eyes widened as he asked, "You use your spirits to do magic?"

Macha waved her hand, "Humans use their souls for every feat of strength from within or without. A witch or sorcerer does so with greater knowledge. Now still your tongue so that I can finish. The world is the power of nature, like fire, water, storms, and the like. That is where himself and I do our work. If you call water to your location, you take it from another place. You may save yourself and kill a hundred somewhere else. Do you see the problem?"

"I think so," the northern chieftain said.

"The light of knowledge is not lost on even your head full of rocks then," she said without humor. "Yon man did not call the storms before because it could upset the balance somewhere else in the world."

"A snowstorm? What use are they except to kill life and freeze water?" Argall asked.

Macha shook her head, "I don't have time to explain to that boulder you call a skull a lesson on natural forces. However, that's secondary. Himself knows that his use of power will tell others where he's located... Such as a spouse known to be a terrible, evil witch in the lands of the north..."

"Oh," Argall said, seeing the sense of that part. "Is darkness part of nature?"

"No," Macha answered. "Himself plays with the fundamental forces that existed before everything. Like herself that you're pledged to, that is a part of the universe. How else do you think Himself drove off those long-lived bastards, the Dalaketnon?"

Argall shrugged, "I honestly hadn't thought about it."

Macha turned away with a snort, "No, probably not. Now, your lesson is done and if you ask me one more question, I will show you how fast a crow can remove an eyeball."

Sensing this odd, if alienly attractive woman was not joking, Argall refrained from speaking as they circled around the still working slaves. They strode down two roughhewn stone stairs into an unlit square chamber approximately ten feet long and wide.

Macha muttered a few words and a torch on the wall lit, the orange and red flames dancing as if a light breeze blew across the room. The chamber had no doors and was piled floor to ceiling with random objects as well as the white bones of humans and large animals. The stench was terrible, worst of which came from a pallet of rotten straw on the far wall.

"Ymir's beard, what is that smell?" Argall asked.

Macha appeared undisturbed, shrugging as she answered, "Ogres are not known for being clean creatures. They hate the water because it sinks them to the bottom. Also, the layer of dirt and grime is another type of body protection."

"Then what are these piles of junk? I don't mean the bones... ice trolls in my lands have dens the same way," Argall said, potting a battered, broken helmet, a twisted piece of metal, and a new anvil to his right.

Macha stepped over the stinking pile of straw as she said, "Ogres like hoarding things people like or want. They take it and will only return the stolen item if you give them something more interesting. Look about but don't reach into piles you cannot see. You never know what could be inside. My sister, Badb, once found a pearl the size of an eagle's egg in an old ogre treasure pile. She also came out with a terrible rash from getting scratched by some weed growing around the pretty piece, but she still holds that over my head."

Not spotting anything near his position, Argall moved to the other side of the room, across from Macha. He heard her muttering and tossing items aside, though he didn't understand the odd language she spoke.

Pushing over a rather dusty wagon wheel, his eyes widened as he spotted a sword hilt protruding from the mound of refuse. Pulling it free, he smiled, admiring the balance and clean edges on the weapon. It resembled his broken Atlantean sword, though it appeared slightly newer and finer than his father's blade.

"Ah, now I found it," Macha said. "An idol to the Ancient Darkness. This fits together nicely."

"Does it?" Argall asked, swinging his sword in a slow arc, and getting a feel for the weapon.

"Oh, yes," Macha said. "Now I know why we met. Heading to the north, are you?"

"Yes, but not close to my lands," the Erm-Gilt-Hermian said. "Why?"

Macha chuckled, "Oracles are usually false prophets, but my aunt tells the truth. I'm with you from now until what happens, happens."

Just above them, the door to the room swung open with a bang and a pair of heavy feet stomped across the floor. Argall raised his sword as a heavy shadow blocked the light from above.

CHAPTER XXXV

"Humor," a gentle, soothing man's voice said from the distance. "I remember that from days long past. Humans use those clever words as a means of hiding their terror. You need not disguise your fear, human females. Your very skin exudes terror."

Deena opened her mouth to respond, only to receive an elbow in the side from Nikke followed by a warning look. The young oracle frowned for a moment and then nodded, closing her lips as the inhuman creature led them past more rotting corpses.

A man stepped into the light, bowing deeply their direction. He was tall, lean, dark-haired, and handsome with soft pale skin, thick dark hair and a wide smile that gleamed in the flickering illumination.

"How pleasant to meet you," he said in the same tender tone. "I wondered when you would arrive. Soroe, Queen-Elect of Atlantis, her counselor and oracle, Deena, and the warrior huntress mercenary who calls herself Nikke the Finder. Your coming was known to me before you left your place of rest. As you may have surmised, I am Doctor Talisal."

Nikke pushed next to Soroe, her head violently shaking left and right. "No, you're not. I knew Talisal. He was as tall as you with stooped shoulders like a clerk, a white beard that was always covered in food crumbs, no hair, and a nose that birds could land on. Oh yes, and he also had three warts so large they looked as if they we going to take over his face."

"Yes, yes," Talisal said, his smile slipping some. "I did once look quite unpleasant. This changed when my master gifted me with power. I transformed myself and became more handsome than any in the kingdom."

Soroe shrugged, "Argall is far better looking than you, sir. As are several other men in the Queen's court. How did you know we were coming?"

"I see the future in all it's terrible glory. I dreamed you would come to me and become my willing servants. I see I was correct," Talisal said, licking his lips slowly.

Deena giggled, a high-pitched laugh that soon spread to Nikke and Soroe. Within a few seconds, the three women laughed and chortled as tears trailed down their face.

"Humor? I said nothing that you would consider a jest, humans. Cease those inane sounds emerging from your lips. Why do you laugh, you unevolved pack of primates?" Talisal said.

"I'm only doing it because these two started," Nikke said. "I couldn't help myself. Best laugh I had in years."

"Oh, let me tell him," Deena said, pressing a little closer. "Talisal or whatever your name is, let me tell you a little secret about oracles. Men can't do it. It's a female power only. We learned that from someone smarter than you!"

Talisal's face froze, and he stared at them for several seconds. He was about to speak again when Nikke chimed in first.

"I knew you had a spy in the beggars' guild," she said. "Who it was, I couldn't find out. This little fake magic act tells me there's still one in there. So, thanks."

Talisal straightened and smiled, his grin a rictus smirk that was frankly unnerving and quite inhuman, "This matters not, human females. You shall be vessels for my brethren and your spirits shall enter Mugen Jigoku, the Hell of…"

"…Uninterrupted Pain, where you fall through a pit for two thousand years and if you return, you are perpetually stained by the sins you committed and the horror of a thousand lifetimes in the worst hell it is possible for a human to enter," Soroe said. "Yes, I know the story. The trouble is, you are not the judge of the dead and cannot sentence us to that realm."

"Ah," Talisal said, lifting up one elongated finger theatrically, "you are quite wrong, female. You see, my master, the Dark Prince who is the Primordial Pain of the celestial universe, has found a method. Through a spell, I steal the soul of the tormented and replace them with a human whom my followers snatched. The great master of the dead has not learned of this deception since none have attempted so clever a plan before."

"Ah," Soroe said, tapping her chin, "now I understand. That explains why the one who led us here rotted before our eyes. The soul of those sentenced to Mugen Jigoku are too stained to return in a normal human vessel. Intriguing."

"You understand this maniac?" Deena asked.

Soroe nodded. "It is an interesting theory and explains more to me about the dark prince. It also tells me what these creatures that this false Talisal uses as his soldiers. Primordial creatures connected to chaos, not the pits of Hell."

"I am grateful you are impressed," Talisal said, opening his hands, "because it shall serve as a pleasant memory when I send you to the worst location in the universe."

Between his hands, tendrils of stygian darkness emerged, growing wider by the second. The very sight of this murky energy seemed to cause a chill in all three women, and they recoiled slightly through a combination of fear, disgust, and instinctive loathing...

CHAPTER XXXVI

"Well," Macha said, "don't keep lingering on the front step like a tinkerer plying his trade. Come down, man, come down. Did you get the fury out of your system?"

Jaska the Grey Wolf, also known as the Accursed One, slowly stepped down the stairs into the ogre's lair. Argall realized this was the first time he'd seen the man's face.

He was not what one would have called a handsome man, but he did have an impressive, powerful majesty to him more reminiscent of a force of nature than a human. His hair and beard were iron gray and turning white and his blue eyes still held that feral, lupine, air. There was something more substantial to him now, even though he had not changed his clothing other than removing his mask.

"Yes," Jaska said, "it felt good using my powers once again. I did not unleash everything within me, but this release of energy did cover a small area."

"How small?" Argall asked.

Jaska shrugged. "Half a mile or so. I'm not quite sure. I wanted to focus the storm upon this terrible place and the homes of the wealthy merchants."

"That's good. I'll send word for the death priests and hopefully they can appease some of the ghosts. If not, this whole city will fall into ruin," Macha said. "Oh, and look what I found in this pile."

Both Argall and Jaska followed her pointing finger and gazed upon a black statue, the latter of which started and performed an odd sign with his hand. He tilted his head left and right, breathing deeply through his nose as he examined the idol.

The image was carved from a dark material that could be stone or wood. The surface was almost glassine, yet the light did not reflect off the ebony epidermis. The figure was robed, with each fold of the cloth intricately etched and giving the impression that the individual was in motion. Long skeletal hands protruded from the oversized sleeves and each nail appeared to possess tiny screaming faces across the surface. The head was human shaped yet covered with a thin veil that hid the features beneath.

"I've never seen the like before," Argall said, stepping away from the statue.

He did not know why, but there was something sinister and terrible about the image. The artwork was impressive, yet it revulsed him with greater disgust than he felt when viewing one of the giant ice spiders assaulting their prey.

"Be grateful for that," Macha said. "It's a being whose name could bring about madness. Most call him the Dark Prince, but he has other titles. His followers are insane... More beast than human..."

"A demon?" Argall asked.

Jaska shook his head, "Demons quake in fear at the mere mention of this being and his servants. This is a god whose nature is so bizarre that even the worst monsters will serve at the side of light in battle."

Argall gazed back and forth between the pair and only observed deadly serious expressions in their faces. A chill ran down his spine as a memory from his past, a terrible tribe that came from nowhere and stole children... consumed bodies... fought like madmen...

"Tell me more," he said, "I need to understand."

"There's too much to say in one sitting," Macha said, "or even one lifetime. This is a battle beyond humanity, or even those close to your kind. This affects the entire universe, and we are just a tiny fleck of dust in the whirlwind."

Jaska nodded as he sat down on the steps, his shoulders slumping with obvious exhaustion.

"Poetically put, but she is essentially correct. The reason I opposed my former mate was because she and her hated mother were weakening the critical walls between the worlds in their desire for power. Oh, and I lost my other axe."

"Look around here," Argall said. "I found a fine Atlantean blade among these piles."

"Axe? You hove too hard to your past, man," Macha said. "If you're back in this world, use something better. Axes are for trees, or for those looking for brutal ends to their enemies. Wait, I saw something better..."

She moved to the left of the horrific statue, knelt, and picked up an object with both hands.

"Swords are the weapons of the warrior. Axes are for the barbarian or the killer. Spears are for the hunter. This is old knowledge. There is one weapon that represents the power of the warrior and the power wise. Here is a fine one..."

Macha lifted a massive black metal war mace, one with multiple flared flanges across the surface. The weapon was impressive, if slightly frightening, more so when the former Accursed One accepted it and held the handle easily in one hand.

"Among my people," he said, "such a weapon was not among our articles of war. Metal was scarce and a device with only one use was considered a waste."

142

"Mine too. Swords could be used in ceremonies as well as warfare," Argall said. "Spears and bows were used for hunting."

"Yet you are not among the Pohjolans any longer," Macha said, "and I watched you fight, man. You kill without artifice or joy. It is an act you wish completed as swiftly as possible. I bet you hunt that way too."

"I do," Jaska said. "I am an effective killer, but not one that inspires glory."

"Then, the mace it shall be," she said, smiling as she pulled her hood over her head. "Now, let us get ourselves to the harbor. There's something terrible ahead and we must not waste time chattering like old women."

CHAPTER XXXVII

"Yes," Talisal said, "I bring the power of primordial darkness. It is mine to control!"

A dagger suddenly appeared, hovering several inches from the sorcerer's right eye. It quivered in the air for several seconds before crumbling into dust a moment later.

Deena shrugged and said, "I had to try."

"I am beyond such paltry human toys," Talisal said. "There is no power greater than the darkness."

The Soul of Soroe appeared in the Queen-elect's hand, the gem pulsing briefly with power as her fingers grasped the scepter.

"Except the Light," Soroe said. "The Light can defeat the darkness!"

"Ha!" Talisal said as the threads from the void slowly reached her direction. "My power is ancient and unmatched. In the end, everything returns to chaos!"

The rotting guide that led them into the warlock's presence snarled and shuffled towards Soroe, only to meet a whirling blade held by Nikke. The undead head separated from the neck and bounced away as the body shook and an unpleasant smelling, foul-appearing, green viscous ooze dribble out of the gaping wound.

A cry from their rear sounded and the two shadowy figures to their rear shuffled forward. The massive, unwieldy forms moved with delicate, multi-limbed motions reminiscent of that of a spider rather than a human. Their bodies were covered in ropy tentacles, and each possessed multiple eyes and gaping, fang-filled mouths across their bizarre torsos.

"Hold them back," Soroe said. "I must concentrate."

A circular-shaped shield of pure light lay before her, the energy emerging from the luminescent jewel that lay atop her scepter. Her hand shook and Soroe's face appeared bathed in a thin sheen of sweat as she stared into the eyes of her enemy. She held herself straight and proud, her slim body taut with tension and strain as she strained against Talisal's assaults.

The villain stood hunched and cackling, his hands flexing, fingers stroking the air as if he were playing a tune on an unseen instrument. The tendrils of dark force extended and probed, seeking a weakness in Soroe's shield. Each time light met dark, the impact caused a brief flare of energy. The black tentacle would then wither and vanish, while the shield of light dimmed ever slightly. A moment later, the shield would brighten, as if more power were poured into the defense. An ever-widening cloud of darkness grew before Talisal as Soroe's scepter grew brighter.

"I hear more above us," Nikke said. "Pretty soon we will be overrun."

"Aren't you a little ray of hope and sunshine?" Deena asked, pulling another throwing knife into view. "I've faced worst odds."

"And probably turned tail and ran for your life," Nikke said while raising her crossbow. "If you try and make a dash for it, I'll shoot you myself."

"Gold and Iron, you really don't listen," Deena said as the Finder fired a bolt into the hide of one of the monsters. "I told you, I gave that up."

"Huh," Nikke said as her crossbow had little to no affect upon the monster, "once a thief, always a thief."

"Once an idiot, always an idiot," Deena said while throwing her knife. "Gold and Iron, I have an idea. I need to touch one of these things."

"What?" Nikke asked as she loaded her crossbow again. "Why? Are you insane?"

"Probably," Deena said, "Just keep them from Soroe for a few seconds. If this works, do what I tell you."

She then threw her knife and dove to her right, vanishing amongst the human detritus, leaving Nikke alone with two approaching monsters. Behind the Finder, the battle raged on and Soroe's back bowed slightly as the unrelenting attacks continued.

CHAPTER XXXVIII

"Daughter!" Louhi said in a screech that pierced the ears and sent the dogs in the hall fleeing. "Daughter! He has returned!"

"Yes, mother," Loviatar replied, not rising from her seat.

Today she wore a simple crown of black iron that made her white, blond hair appear even paler. Dressed in a simple woolen gown, she perched upon her wooden throne with the regal air of her queenly rank. At her feet lay a man, his massive, pale-skinned, golden blond form unmoving. He stared up at the ceiling of the hall, his eyes vacant, a thin line of drool falling from his gaping lips.

Louhi glanced down at the man, her ancient gaze roving over his body in the same manner a hungry wolf viewed a fawn.

"Leave some of this one for me when you are done. A little fresh life will warm these old bones."

"Of course," Loviatar said. "You came to me because you felt the power. My husband has returned and used his powers. I am aware of him. I felt the ripples and knew the source immediately."

"Could you say where?" the elder witch of Pohjola asked.

"I have some notion," the ice queen of the north replied. "South, closer to Atlantis than our lands. He did not reach in this direction."

Louhi stepped on the prone man before she sat upon the stool that lay next to her daughter's high seat. Shifting slightly for comfort, she used the unmoving man as a footrest before turning her attention back to Loviatar.

"You think too small, my daughter," she said. "Why would Jaska invoke his power once again? He knows we would discover this action and would react. Why?"

"I do not know," the ice queen answered. "Perhaps he has grown reckless in time."

"Doubtful," the witch said, shaking her skeletal skull slowly. "The Gray Wolf does not act out of foolish pride."

"Then I do not know, mother," Loviatar said.

Yerra, who stood nearby with the Pohjolan Queen's favorite wooden goblet, cleared her throat, bowed, and kept her head low and gazing down upon the stone floor.

"If I may offer a suggestion, great ones?" she asked, "I have some notion of the Gray Wolf's actions based on your teachings and discussions since my childhood."

"Speak, slave," Loviatar said, taking her goblet from the tiny hands.

Yerra cleared her throat and said, "The one you called Jaska opposed your mystical intentions. He believed you accessed powers that were anathema to our world. This is true?"

"Yes," Loviatar said. "Speak swifter slave, or I shall return you to scrubbing floors again."

Yerra's narrow shoulders shook slightly as she continued, "If he uses his own powers, knowing you can feel his actions, he must have had a reason. A strong one. Could the patron you pay tribute to daily have a foothold in the south? If so, then would that not require an expenditure of his might?"

Both Pohjola rulers stared at each other and then their servant for several seconds. Louhi nodded slowly and a slow smile spread across Loviatar's beautiful, frigid face.

"I think you are correct, slave," the ice queen of the north said. "That would cause fury in Jaska the Gray Wolf. However, we must consult the god."

Louhi lifted Yerra's beautiful face upward with two fingers beneath her chin. She gently patted the soft cheek and stroked the former Queen of Atlantis's silken, ebony hair with the same fondness one might use for a favorite pet.

"I am grateful I kept you alive, my child," she said. "You once again proved useful to me, despite your failures."

"Thank you, great one," Yerra said as she stood rigid before the terrible witch.

"Go now," Loviatar said, "and speak on my behalf to the captain of my guards. Tell him to bring ten of the best captives to the forbidden caves. We will meet him there when darkness blankets the land and only the stars light the world."

"They must not be drugged or beaten," Louhi said, "bound and fully aware of everything. Oh, and cover their naked forms in blankets. I would not lose any to the cold and ice."

"Yes," Loviatar said, a slow smile spreading across her pale, pink lips. "They must be alive and feel every cut of the knife that sends them to the god."

Yerra bowed and backed away, turning only when she left the room. The echo of malicious laughter followed her as she ran down the corridor, towards the hall's guardhouse.

CHAPTER XXXIX

The ship was a comfortable trading vessel named the *Wave Rider*, and it cut through the rough surf with an impressive ease. Twenty passengers sat in the hold of the vessel, each squatting in small groups as they listened the creak of the timbers. The gentle rocking of their temporary wooden home created a calming effect, broken only by the occasional crash of waves against the sides.

A fat woman in a gray dress held court in the center of the hold, seated on a barrel as she spun amusing tales of sea creatures and nautical misadventures. She was a squat woman with yellow white hair pulled back in a bun, a jowly bulldog face, and skin pitted with scars from past illnesses. Her hands were rough and her voice slightly screechy, yet her stories had those surrounding her whooping with laughter.

"...and I told him, that may be true, sir, but I'm not the one who just ate from the shit pail," she said, completing another anecdote.

"That story is older than me," Macha said *sotto voce*, "and that's a considerable time."

"She tells it well, at least," Jaska said. "A poor storyteller on a sea voyage can result in a mutiny."

"Speaking of which," Argall said, "what do you make of those men on the far side of the hold?"

"The four warriors who are pointedly looking everywhere but our direction?" Jaska asked, "or the two thieves who keep creeping towards the group around the storyteller?"

"The warriors," Argall said. "Should we be concerned by their behavior?"

"Oh yes," Macha said, "we should be fearful and weep until they approach us and tell us our true fate. Youngling, you soften your language too much. Ask what is truly on your mind."

Argall flushed slightly, stiffening at the mocking words. Macha, unlike the former Accursed One, was very forthright in her amusement at their apparent age difference. Jaska, though apparently equally ancient, possessed a degree of diplomacy in his responses.

"Fine," he said, "are they here to attack us?"

"Yes," Macha said. "They are warriors from the Brotherhood of the Axe. They seek one of us, or possibly all three."

"I never heard of them," Argall said.

"Well," Macha said, "you wouldn't, would you? They keep to themselves and don't mix with your folk. They were once a mighty army that sought power in the East. Now, they are merely a small order of male warriors who seek those whom they believe are evil and a challenge. Yon group are the youths who seek fame by battling a legend."

"How did they find us?" Argall asked.

Macha shrugged and closed her eyes. "They have their ways. Rest easy, they never start battles in enclosed spaces. It adds unnecessary risks."

Argall glanced once at the four men, gaining in the impression of powerful, thick arms knotted with bulging bronze sinews. Massive battle axes lay across their backs, the double edges nearly as wide as their enormous shoulders. None wore mail of any kind and they neither spoke nor demonstrated any other signs of life.

"Before you ask," Jaska said, "we will soon stop for half a day at the port of Yerra's Landing. There, we can lure them away from any crowds and confront them in a place better suited for a fight. Until then, listen to the stories, or sleep."

Argall had no time in which to respond since Macha stood and walked over to the storyteller's group. Jaska, who already had his back against one of the vast wooden ribs that held this vessel together, closed his eyes and fell asleep seconds later.

"Impressive," Argall thought as Macha vanished into the small knot of people as well as Jaska's almost immediate ability in falling asleep. "I wonder if those skills come from being so long lived."

He remained lost in thought upon the life of one who survived more years than even the eldest of the dwellers on the Erm-Gilt-Herm. The very idea filled him with dread and a bit of longing that he barely admitted to himself.

"How do they live for centuries? Is there some gift they receive because of their magic?" he thought after several hours of ruminating on the subject.

"Jaska," he asked as the pitch and roll of the ship changed and he heard the sounds of other boats nearby, "how do you live so many years?"

Never opening his eyes, he said, "You may as well ask the same of a tree. It's something I was born with, like many from my home."

"Not so much with my people," Macha said, dropping to his side. "Those who stop aging are those who learned practice the arts. At a certain point, the years stop affecting you."

"Oh," Argall said, "I'd wondered if there was a spell of a potion that granted you the gift."

"There are, youngling," Macha said, "though they're guarded by them who hold the secret. There is a tribe of the north who eat apples that restore their youth."

"They're dead," Jaska said. "Died battling the giant tribes who were their distant ancestors. It is called the Isle of Bones and nothing lives or grows in that soil."

"I heard of that place," Argall said. "My father and some of the elders of the tribe visited that island once, to see if it might be suitable for crops. They said the soil was ash and everywhere you stepped, your boots broke bones."

"That aside," Macha, "there are ways to keep living, but most are terrible, and you end up worse than when you started. Also, you could not survive it in the end."

"How do you know? We of the Erm-Gilt-Herm are a hardier people than any of the south," Argall said as he felt his face flush.

"Still yourself," Jaska said, "she spoke no insult. Few have the inner strength for a life longer than that granted to most humans."

Macha nodded and smiled in the Pohjolan's direction. "No cruelty intended, youngling. When a human, unused to an extended life is gifted or cursed with that change, it destroys them in their heart. Watching their loved ones and friends die tears them asunder and is slow torture. They usually become unfeeling beasts whose cruelty makes them a mockery of their previous self."

Jaska frowned and looked away, staring into the gloom of the ship's hold as he said, "The student of magic who gains that ability suffers too, but less so since their mind is usually lost in their books and scrolls. The rest of us become distant from those around them, knowing you should not befriend a mayfly. Human life is a season to some of us and we shall go on when the mountains fall, and new lands appear."

"Gloomy, aren't you?" Macha asked and elbowed his side before turning back towards Argall, "I do not mean any offense when I call you a youngling...you are to me. I was a girl back in the days when the tribes of the Erm-Gilt-Herm poured out from their frozen, dark, misty hills and put the Lemurian cities to the sword."

"A good thing that was," Jaska said, "never before or since were a people so tainted by blood and darkness."

"Lemuria?" Argall asked, "I thought that empire was just a myth!"

"A myth? A myth he says!" Macha said, laughing until her pale skin turned crimson. "A myth!"

"What is so funny?" Argall asked, feeling the anger, a defect bred into his people, slowly rising.

"Argall," Jaska said, "who do you think we fight now? The ancient people of Lemuria were the worshippers of the demon snake Apophis and the ancient Gods whose very presence among us would mean the end of life in this world."

"Yes," Macha said, her mood shifting, her lovely face turning as stony as an ancient cliff face. "We speak not just of humans, or our folk. Everything that lives from the most advanced human to the smallest insect sitting on a blade of grass. They would burn the lands and boil away the seas, reducing this world to a vast graveyard. Then, after a few lifetimes, they would seed the lands with their kind and a true horror that would be to the universe."

"How do you know?" Argall asked, his voice hushed.

Macha's eyes fell upon him, and he felt their weight, as if she laid a huge burden across his shoulders. "My sister sees the paths of the future. As we are triplets, she shares her pain with us to ensure she does not go mad when the visions fall upon her. What we saw... It was a horror that almost had her tearing her eyes from her skull."

Just then a loud bell chimed and the ship's bosun called down, "Yerra's Landing! We leave on the next tide! Any not returning before the tide will be left behind!"

"Good," Jaska said, "I could use some food."

"I know a good stall near the market," Macha said. "The wine is poor, but the ale is good. Excellent pigeon pies and pasties."

"Perfect," Jaska said, rising.

Argall followed them out, "What of those four warriors to our rear?"

"They can buy their own ale," Macha said. "Be calm, Erm-Gilt-Hermian. We can eat, rest, and still have time for a scrap before the ship leaves."

CHAPTER XL

"Gold and Iron! I knew you would run!" Nikke said to Deena while stepping back three paces. "Never trust a thief!"

She fired a crossbow bolt at the closest monstrosity, smiling slightly as the twisted creature screeched and fell backwards.

"When in doubt," she said while swiftly reloading, "poke them in the eye. Nobody loves that."

She heard a scream from behind the demonic thing, and Deena stumbled into view, diving over a pile of garbage.

"Gold and Iron... So cold... so cold... the pain..." she said, moaning the words as her hands scrabbled among the bones and bodies.

"Wonderful," Nikke said, firing again. "My only help got her brain broke by touching the demon."

Behind her, Soroe moaned and closed her eyes, the pain of resisting the attacks that assailed from every direction. The antediluvian power of the chaotic darkness appeared overwhelming, closer to an elemental force than that of a mystic attack by a dangerous enemy. Her attempted responses merely delayed the inevitable as the might of Talisal grew with each passing second.

I cannot beat the force before all life, she thought, *I serve the Light, I do not command it*.

"Surrender to me," Talisal said as his smile literally split the skin around his mouth. "None can stand against the Dark."

He is right... but he's also wrong, Soroe thought, realizing a possible means of defeating this enemy.

"Cold," Deena said while digging among the detritus, "cold, cold, cold..."

Nikke sighed as she fired her final bolt, "This is my fault. I trusted you."

The closest creature's shadow rose above them, the inexplicable form of a pustule covered horror with human eyes and an ooze-covered tentacle slithered their direction. A vast gapping maw opened in the center and twisted cilia emerged and extended their direction.

Deena struck something and cried out; her words lost as the malformed fiend rose above them as gelatinous squishing filled the air. The former thief rose, a yellow light emerging from an item in her hand.

"Not so cold now," she said while extending a torch made from bone and rags.

She threw the flame into the newly formed mouth and jumped back. The torch fell upon the waving feelings, which immediately ignited, the tongue of fire spreading across the vestigial maw and spreading with growing ferocity within a heartbeat.

The horror fell backwards as the flames licked and danced across the malformed figure. Charred pieces fell from the oozing flesh as the heat grew more intense by the second. The shadowy figures to the rear halted as their brethren slinked their direction and slowly crumbled into the dust.

Deena fell forward, rising seconds later with another torch. Nikke seized the growing flame and threw it towards one of the beasts in the distance. It struck the being, immediately coating the creature in a growing bonfire formed by its own flesh.

This demoniac horror screamed, a quite human sound, before tumbling sideways. The rubbish piles to the side ignited and fire spread across the basement.

Within seconds, a growing inferno emerged from Talisal's basement lair.

Soroe, her lovely, perspiring face quite serene, said, "Eyes," in a voice that carried across the room.

Deena and Nikke closed the covered their eyes, keeping their back to the high priestess of the Light. Despite their closed lids and turned backs, they were still momentarily dazzled by the flash of light that appeared from the legendary Soul of Soroe.

Talisal shrieked in pain, his hands reaching for his eyes. The terrible darkness that sprang from his hands immediately engulfed his body. He wailed and howled as the threads of primordial power ripped him away, drawing him into their unfathomable depths.

Then he was gone, his screams of terror echoing in their ears. Soroe collapsed to one knee, only to be pulled to her feet by Nikke and Deena. The Finder led them past where Talisal once stood, a harsh chill emerging from that location, before dragging them out a nearby exit.

A moment later, they gulped and coughed as the cool air filled their lungs.

Flames spread upward as the ruined mansion was soon aflame from the conflagration below. Timbers cracked and they heard the inhuman screams of Talisal's creatures as the cleaning flame swept them from the Earth.

"I need a drink and an explanation," Nikke said. "I'm buying."

"I'm drinking," Deena replied. "Something powerful that will knock me out in minutes."

Nikke threw an arm around the former thief's neck while keeping a firm hold on Soroe's arm.

"I know just such a place and a drink that will have you snoring under the table in two swallows. It's a special brew known as Troll's Piss."

"Sounds disgusting," Deena said as they stumbled around the burning house and towards the rusted gates.

"It tastes worse," Nikke said, "but it will knock you out faster than a club to the head and you'll sleep without dreams."

"I'll have three," Soroe said, and the trio laughed weakly as they stumbled towards the sleeping city.

CHAPTER XLI

Yerra tightened the bonds that held a dark-haired woman's hands and feet. The girl, more child than adult, writhed with futile intensity against the leather thongs that prevented her escape. The black stone altar on which she lay was oddly warm to the touch and occasional appeared to pulse with an unseen energy beneath the glassine surface. The captive soon stopped struggling and stared upon Yerra's impassive face, studying the former queen for several seconds.

"You are not of Pohjola," she said, not asking but stating this as a fact. "You are a southerner."

"I was," Yerra said, lifting the wooden bowl and the copper knife, placing both upon the altar near the captive's head.

"Then why would you serve such evil? They are monsters, these witches!" the girl asked. "Why would you assist them in their actions?"

"A good question," Loviatar said as she appeared from the rear of the cave.

The pale-skinned ice queen was a regal sight, erect, proud, a crystalline crown holding still her long, platinum locks. A gray wolfskin cape lay across her broad shoulders and she wore no other clothing despite the frigid wind that howled through the caves.

Yerra dropped to her knees, bowing her head to the floor as the Queen of Pohjola stepped silently towards the obsidian altar in the center of the chamber. Loviatar's long, slim, chilly fingers tangled deep into the former Atlantean's queen's hair and pulled Yerra to her feet.

"And I shall answer," the ice queen said. "Yerra is a slave. She learned as a child at my feet that it is better to live as a prized pet than it is to die in agony beneath the blades of her masters."

"That is wrong," the captive girl said, shaking her head. "I will die soon, this I know. Yet the pain will end in time, and I shall join my parents and the others of my tribe in the fields of joy. It is better to die free than it is to live long as a slave to evil."

Loviatar laughed, a harsh, mocking sound and her eyes glinted with cold, terrible, malice. She lifted the copper knife in one hand as her other gently caressed the face of the unknown girl.

"Such innocence is amusing to me," she said. "Thank you, little worm, your words gave me true joy for a moment. However, you make one mistake. You do not realize that she who is my mother, and I will make every last second of your paltry life feel like an eternity of agony."

The girl shook her head and replied, "I know that. I shall scream and experience your torments. Yet like the winter vanishes and the spring arrives, the season of pain shall eventually cease. Then I shall know peace."

She paused, her head swiveling left and right, her dark eyes meeting that of Loviatar and Yerra.

"Neither of you shall ever know peace. This much I see. You will drive for more of what you seek and, in the end, find it has slipped through your fingers like water in a stream. Now, bring forth your knives," she said, laying back and closing her eyes.

Loviatar did not hesitate and immediately sliced a thin line across the girl's exposed flesh. A gasp of pain emerged, followed by a scream of agony as the torment commenced. The ice queen of Pohjola was an expert in inducing pain, which she performed with a precision guaranteed to draw forth the fullest horror from the flesh.

Slowly, inexorably, the flesh of the captive peeled away, yet the torture continued. Loviatar's smile never waved as she sculpted her victim's pain, raising the sensation to a height unmatched by any who practiced those terrible arts.

The victim's voice became a ragged croak as her screams rent the delicate chords that produced sounds in her throat.

By the end, little more than low, animalistic whimpers emerged from her bloody, ripped lips, finally dying away as the Ice Queen of Pohjola released the final strand of life that held her captive alive.

"Such joy," Loviatar said as she gently played the now dull copper knife about the crimson stained obsidian altar. "That was wonderful. Have the guards place the remains in the pit of sorrows. This one I shall reanimate as a *draugr* who shall haunt the wastes for an eternity."

Yerra bowed deeply in reply, hearing the swish of her mistress's cape as she left to join rites currently being performed by her dreadful mother.

When the sound drifted away, the former queen of Atlantis raised her head, gazing down upon the torn visage of the now-dead unnamed captive. She stepped back in surprise, the sight before her as frightening as the torturous actions of Loviatar.

The face of the dead girl, though ripped and barely recognizable as human, stared upward with empty dead eyes. Yet, the expression upon the face was that of pure, true serenity. Though the child underwent torments unheard of in the civilized world, she was at peace.

This image shook Yerra to her core and she found herself lost in thought for a time. Mechanically, she obeyed the orders of Loviatar, but her mind was contemplating this revelation...

CHAPTER XLII

"They are following us," Argall said, leaning forward and whispering his words. "They stand…"

"…halfway down the street, staring our direction," Jaska replied. "Yes, we know. Stop whispering."

"Only whisper," Macha said, "when you want someone to listen carefully. Hushed words carry more weight than roared ones."

"Also," Jaska added as he placed his now empty ale mug on the scarred wooden table, "when you whisper, people are always positive you plan on some kind of mischief. If you speak calmly, you can plan a robbery before a crowd, and few will realize your intentions."

Argall tilted his head and said, "That is an odd statement. Why would you act in such a manner?"

"War makes one behave strangely," the former masked man replied. "The best means of discovering the schemes of a baron who planned a rebellion was by stealing his maps and other items. To hide our intentions, we robbed his townhome of many goods. Loviatar studied the maps, remade them and we left them behind. The rebellion failed."

"Too bad," Macha said. "Your woman is a monster."

Jaska nodded, "True. The difficulty at the time was that the baron was worse. He was a follower of the Dark Prince and would have led thousands to an altar of blood."

"Which she does now," Argall said. "The raids of the Pohjolans are one of the great dangers of the north. Not that they attack the Erm-Gilt-Herm. The rare times they do, our tribes send few survivors back to their lands."

"Which is purpose of the expedition," Jaska said. "Loviatar and Louhi send any ambitious noble to your lands, knowing the wild, gloomy tribes of your frozen wastes will destroy any forces. Your people serve the Ice Queen and the Dark Witch of Pohjola in the end."

Argall's eyes widened as he learned this information. He sat back in his chair, remembering battles with the skilled warriors of the ancient mystic ice kingdom. The Pohjola warriors fought better than the Atlanteans or any of the southern kingdoms, near equals to the tribesmen of the Erm-Gilt-Herm. The idea that they were sent intentionally to their death shook him to his very core.

"Politics," Macha said after a few minutes of silence, "are a dangerous, treacherous battle of wits and blood, youngling. My people have been engaged in such for generations. Our nearest neighbors would overrun us if we didn't use cleverness as a weapon. Learn it now, otherwise your Atlantis won't last much longer."

"Yes," Argall said, "I see that. That aside, where do we lure the four axe-men?"

"It doesn't matter," Macha said. "They will wait for open, clear ground. If we head to a crowded location, they will wait. They are a patient lot despite their murderous tendencies."

"Interesting," Argall said. "Can they be reasoned with? Such powerful warriors could be very useful in battle."

Both Macha and Jaska smiled his direction with the former shaking her head.

"No, but a very clever notion. Once they agree to a duty, they follow their trail until death."

"Then why did you appear happy?" Argall asked.

This time Jaska answered, "Because that was the thoughts of a ruler of a kingdom. Before that moment, you thought like a warrior and a chieftain. A king or a queen must consider methods of turning an enemy into a friend… or at least a neutral force."

"Did you ever do that?" Argall asked.

The former Accursed One appeared surprised by the question for a moment. He recovered himself and shook his head again.

"I was never a ruler, Argall. I am ill-suited for the control of lives of others. I was an advisor at best."

"I am the same," Macha said. "When the call for battle begins, I am in the front, battling with fury. A queen must inspire love if she wishes to keep her crown for more than a year."

"That aside," Jaska said, "let us lead these men to their doom… or ours. They appear formidable enough."

"That's your plan? Lead them to a clearing and fight?" Argall asked. "Forgive me, but that appears foolish and simple."

"I have no bow or spear," Jaska said, "and cannot kill them at a distance. Nor can I use my powers upon them… I no longer have the selective control for such small actions."

"Also," Macha said, "complex battle tricks often fail. Complexity in a scrap means more thinking, which can slow action. My grandfather, Balor Great Eye, lost few battles in his lifetime because he did not overthink. Come along, this will be a pleasurable one."

They rose, Argall a step behind, and walked from the stall. The lovely shapeshifter led them down the street, past a small row of tinkerers and other lesser workers, before halting near a field beside a fenced field filled with snorting, squealing, pigs.

"This will suit," she said, throwing back her hood, "come along, men, we're waiting for you."

The four axe-men strode from around the corner of the street and walked with purposeful steps in their direction. They appeared taller, thicker, and more formidable than they had in the ship's hold. Each threw aside their capes, their movements precisely timed so that each cloak swirled off and landed at the same moment. Their stride was exactly in time, with each stepping and swinging their arms in tight coordination.

"I wonder how long that took in practice," Jaska said. "It's very pretty."

"Why would they do such a thing? It seems a waste of time," Argall asked.

"It's a method of binding a group," Jaska replied. "You train them together, they begin working even closer and with great attention to details. This band takes it quite seriously."

The quartet stopped ten feet from their position, with the largest of the four taking a half step forward. He nodded once and studied them for several seconds before gripping his massive double-sided axe tighter.

"You are Jaska, called the Gray Wolf," he said in a deep, rich baritone. "Have you abandoned your axes?"

"I am Jaska, and a weapon is naught but metal," he replied. "I use whichever suits me best."

"That is a foolish belief," the warrior said, raising his weapon. "This is the axe of my father, and his father before him. It is a weapon of noble origins. Can you say the same of your club?"

167

"Even if I knew," Jaska said, "I would not say so since that sounds a little silly to me. I have no sentimentality over methods of murder."

The axe-man flushed slightly and shook his head. He studied the white-haired warrior sorcerer for a heartbeat before snorting.

"You will still be honored as a once-great warrior. This we, the Brotherhood of the Axe, pledge to you," he said as he stepped back, joining his fellows.

"Kill the males," the leader of the foursome said, "and save the sow for breeding stock."

Macha's eyes narrowed as she asked, "Did that one just call me a breeding pig?"

"Yes, he did," Argall said.

"Nobody touches that one but me," she said and lifted her arms above her head.

CHAPTER XLIII

The infamous brew known as Troll's Piss, lived up to, or possibly down, to its horrible reputation. A bitter, sour-tasting potion with a strange, unsettling aftertaste, there were no effects for several seconds. Then, the world began tilting and spinning, and Soroe, Deena, and Nikke each collapsed as if they had drained a full keg of beer.

This was already planned, with the price of the Troll's Piss also including a cot for the night, as well as a guard. Though costly, the proprietors were never lacking in customers. A safe, dreamless sleep was a commodity few, rich or poor, could refuse. Happily, several competing merchant houses imported the item, so the price was far from outrageous.

The next day found the three women waking to a bright world of noise. Their shared hangovers were horrific, only soothed after partaking in a steam bath, followed by a short bath in a cold pool. Within two hours, they sat together at a table in a nearby tavern, slowly consuming corn gruel and a gentle red wine that relaxed their admittedly weak stomachs.

"You promised me an explanation," Nikke said. "I would have it now. What did you do?"

The question was addressed to Deena and Soroe, with the former jumping in immediately. She shrugged and lifted her open palms in an almost comical manner.

"Are you ready to listen? I told you, things changed and I'm not a thief anymore."

"After last night?" the Finder asked. "Yes."

"Fine," Deena said. "I found out I'm an oracle now."

She went on to explain the circumstances of meeting Soroe, helping her through her search for the legendary gem, and the strange, masked sorcerer who had identified her as a prophet.

"I didn't ask for it," she said, "but it's how I found out how we could kill those demons."

"They're not demons," Soroe said immediately.

"I know exactly what they are, lady," the young oracle said. "I touched one and knew they were something else. The trouble is, I can't pronounce what they're called. If I try, my throat will probably start bleeding."

"They serve the Dark Prince," Soroe replied. "Telling you more would take a long time. Deena and I must put an end to his servant, a being called the Prince of Poison."

Deena's head swiveled her direction, "You never told me that!"

"You told me," the Queen-elect said, "when you had your prophecy. You mentioned stopping the Prince of Poison."

"Oh," Deena said, "I thought we were fighting the Dark Prince."

Soroe sighed, rolled her eyes, and shook her head.

"That would be like a grain of sand declaring war on the ocean. That being—a horror with a thousand names—is beyond our conception. I doubt that he will even know we exist. Our battle is with his servants, who hold terrible powers indeed."

"Then you two madwomen are heading into the grasslands? You do know there are insane tribes who eat human flesh residing there?" Nikke asked.

"Yes," Deena said. "There's supposed to be a ruined temple in there where they worship their master."

"There is," Nikke said. "I saw it once when I served the crown. My regiment went into the badlands well-equipped and ready for battle. Only fifty or so of us escaped alive. Most of the survivors climbed into a bottle and drank themselves to death afterwards."

"I should have known," Deena said. "Don't mind me, I'll just be under the table crying."

She didn't actually drop beneath the furniture though her hand shook a little as she poured herself more wine.

"Here's what only a few living people know," Nikke said, leaning forward and dropping her volume. "That strange high priest who calls himself the Prince of Poison? He vanished before our eyes."

"Vanished how?" Soroe asked. "And what did he look like?"

"I have no idea," Nikke said. "He wore a robe with a hood, and I couldn't see inside it. His hands were soft, that I saw, before he waved them in the air and a black circle covered him. He vanished and there was nothing there once we got to that spot."

"Interesting," Soroe said, tapping her chin with one finger. "Anything else?"

"We then had to fight our way out since somehow every single cannibal in that place was waiting for us. We could hear them as they got close... They laugh... They always laugh and shake..." Nikke said.

"Interesting," Soroe said, her eyes distant.

"Ready to give up your mad trip?" Nikke asked.

Soroe started, her eyes focusing before she shook her head. "No, of course not. I'm just considering the implications of what you said. The power used in moving a person from one location to the next is enormous. There are stories of stones that serve as portals between realms. If the Prince of Poison uses that as a means of fleeing, there must be a trigger, a key to unlocking its mechanism."

"Which you will try to find, even if a horde of giggling man-eaters are charging your direction," Deena said after downing another mug of wine. "Correction, *we* will try."

"We will need a week's worth of easily carried food," Nikke said. "Water is plentiful at least. Also, knives for cutting the reeds when they get thick, heavy boots, and some black root."

"Is that your way of saying you're coming too? If so, I'm not carrying you if you get tired," the young oracle said, adding, "What's black root?"

"A plant, idiot," the Finder said. "You crush it and squeeze the pulp out. That, you rub on your skin and the insects leave you alone. So would most humans since the smell is foul."

Soroe handed a few coins to Nikke. "Get us what we need. What about the beggars?"

Nikke shrugged, "I work for them as I choose. With Talisal gone, I'll tell them I'm off for a time. Then I'll get any information the Listener has about the tribes. He won't refuse us anything now."

"How much will your services cost?" Soroe asked.

Nikke shook her head as she said, "Nothing. If you have a way of stopping what's happening in the badlands, I'm with you. I lost a friend or three to those laughing lunatics. Some debts need to be paid, and not in cash."

Soroe nodded... "Thank you. We will meet you by the north gates in two hours. Oh, by the Light... This means I will have to roll in filth again..."

"We all will once we hit the grassy plains," Deena said. "You just get a head start on the process."

Soroe shot the young oracle a withering look, which was promptly ignored. They fell into a gloomy silence as the full weight of the coming trials fell upon their shoulders.

CHAPTER XLIV

The three axe-wielders charged forward, their massive weapons raised above their heads. They roared incomprehensible words of challenge as they leaped into battle. A heavily-thewed man with a battle-axe larger than his head was in the lead, his path straight towards Jaska.

It was Argall who reacted first, his Atlantean blade flashing in the sunlight like a silver lightning bolt. The keen point of the sword pierced the lead man's chest, halting him in place. The deep lunge sent the blade through the warrior's heart, emerging and withdrawing from his back a second later.

The axe-man's weapon fell from his grasp as he stared stupidly at the blood spilling across his naked chest like a crimson fountain. His knees gave out on him, and his fellows stopped, staring as their brother fell.

"That wasn't fair," he said and pitched forward on his chest.

Nearby, Macha clapped her hands above her head. Her robe vanished, replaced by an odd dark metal mail that covered her from neck to knees. A long slim spear appeared in her right hand and covering her left arm was a wooden shield painted crimson and black. A bright crown of silver metal with jutting spikes held back her scarlet locks and she crouched in a battle stance.

"That one," she said in a husky voice, pointing at the spokesman of the group, "is mine. Do as you will with the others."

The leader vaulted over his dead comrade, bringing his weapon down towards her. Rather than blocking, she

174

stepped aside, stabbing out with her spear. The massive warrior avoided the attack, somehow turning sideways as he landed. He bared his teeth, snarled, and swung his enormous axe in a swift arc towards her shield.

Macha angled her shield, so the keen edge glanced off the surface. The power of the swing threw the warrior off-balance as his axe only sheered a few splinters off the protection.

Macha's spear pierced the warrior's leg and blood sluiced from the wound. The giant ignored the injury, attacking with increasing force each passing second. Macha continued circling, the point of her weapon stinging her enemy, yet never delivering a killing blow. For his part, the axe-man never wavered, his blows striking her shield with growing force.

White flecks of spittle flew from the warrior's mouth, his eyes grew darker, and his movements became less precise with each passing second. It was as if this man, formerly a normal individual, was now possessed by a bestial creature inhabiting his body. His swings and chops were delivered with terrific power and lightning speed while the many wounds across his oversized torso pumped precious lifeblood without halting.

Nearby, two of the remaining axe-men dashed for Jaska, though one found himself facing Argall instead. This man, a leaner individual with a tan complexion, spun his long-handled axe with unerring skill, each slice and swing an artistic and lovely movement.

The final warrior charged Jaska, his weapon high, his voice yodeling bizarre ululating war cry. The former Accursed One ran towards his opponent, stepping aside at the last minute. His newly gifted mace swung out in a short arc and the gut-wrenching sound of shattering bones cut short the battle yells. A ragged scream of agony rent the air followed by the sound of a body striking the ground.

The warrior who had charged Jaska now lay upon the muddy earth, shrieking and writhing. His axe fell near his fallen form, and he grabbed his leg, howling with even greater volume as his fingers touched the now exposed bones jutting from his left leg.

Argall, who was trading blows with his opponent, spotted the injured warrior and uttered an oath.

"That's a foul blow," he said as he parried a downward swing.

Jaska shrugged, stepping over the twisted leg of his enemy. Bones thrust through the man's leg, the impact of the mace having destroyed the limb in one blow.

"No rules in war, Argall. Only survival," he said as he raised his weapon and crushed the warrior's skull in a downward strike.

The screams cut off immediately and the body of the Brother of the Axe fell sideways upon the bloody sward. A moment later, his axe vanished from where it lay beside his corpse.

"Interesting," Jaska said as Argall dispatched his foe with a single slice across the throat.

The man fell, landing several feet next to his dead brethren. His axe also disappeared without any visible effect.

The crazed leader dropped to his knees, the stinging cuts across his limbs and torso slowly pumping blood from at least seven places. His axe fell from white-knuckled grip and his face slowly transformed from a blood-mad savage to that of a confused child.

"But," he said as he coughed, spraying saliva and vitae across his face, "but... you're.... you're... female..."

176

"You say that as if it's a bad thing, child," Macha said and lunged.

Her spear pierced the warrior's left eye, extending through the back of his skull before being withdrawn.

He then pitched forward, falling upon the blade of his oversized axe. The blade bit deep through his flesh. Several seconds later, his body crumbled to the ground, his weapon disappearing in the same manner as the others.

"Interesting enchantment," Jaska said.

"Foolish," Macha said, wiping clean her spear with a cloth she removed from her glove. "A waste of time preserving their toys. It's weapon worship which is selfish and silly. These silly beggars love their axes and hate everyone else."

"It seems a good means of knowing that the owner died," Jaska said.

"I see your point," Argall said, grabbing some clean blades of grass and wiping his sword.

The blade of his new weapon snapped as he touched the edge. The sheared off portion of the sword pierced the ground near his foot, and he stared at the broken weapon.

"Better you find out now, youngling," Macha said, clapping her hands again.

Her armor, shield, and spear vanished from view, replaced by her hooded cloak. She grinned and pointed at the dead bodies.

"If we dragged yon men over to the pig pen, the squealing bastards will reduce the remains to scraps. Unless you have a need for burial. Then we'll miss the ship."

Argall shook his head as he grabbed a leg. "Not I. My people leave dead enemies for the beasts. Once the

177

vessel is empty, there's no purpose in building a monument."

"Not sure I agree with that," Jaska said, picking up a corpse by the neck. "Right now, however, I will hold back my concerns."

"If you fear ghosts, I'll place a charm around your neck. I have one my niece used to wear when she was afraid of the dark. Then she turned six summers and no longer needed it anymore," Macha said.

Jaska's response was unheard as the beautiful warrior witch and the King-elect of Atlantis shared a laugh. Their merriment lasted through their work and only ceased minutes after they lay down in the ship's gloomy hold again.

CHAPTER XLV

A piercing wail shook the bloody cave as Louhi tossed a penis and a set of testicles into the wooden bowl Yerra held in trembling hands. The screams ended a moment later as the ancient witch ripped through the body of her sacrifice and tore the man's heart from his chest.

The bloody, still pulsing organ landed in the bowl with a meaty, fluid slap and a spray of scarlet blood splashed across the former Queen of Atlantis's face. Her hands, arms, torso, and face held the results of dozens of such moments, with much of the blood dried and exuding a scent of rot.

Louhi dropped her flint knife in the bowl and cackled upon gazing at the filth-stained sight awaiting her commands.

"My, my," she said, giggling girlishly, "you are quite lovely now, child. Do you not feel honored that I appointed you as my assistant in these preliminary rites?" she asked.

"Yes, mistress," Yerra said, hearing the dullness of her tone.

"Liar," Louhi said, gripping the former queen's face with her powerful fingers. "You are revulsed and will cry as you clean the juice from your hair and face. It matters not, the first ceremony has concluded, and you performed well. Not a whimper or a shudder. You accepted the flesh of these cattle without a sound. You will be rewarded. Now, leave me. Take these items to my daughter and assist her in the next stage."

179

"Yes, mistress," Yerra said, curtsying and backing away from the ancient, evil creature.

The caves were sparsely lit, but Yerra knew the way despite her many years away from Pohjola. As a slave of the Ice Queen and the Dark Witch, she served them, knowing full well displeasing either could result in the same terrible death that greeted all their captives.

My sister, she thought, remembering a happy child that even smiled despite their time as slaves under these harsh women.

Yet the day came when she disappeared, only to re-appear as a bound captive placed upon the altar of the Ice Queen. Her unbelieving eyes had stared up at the future Queen of Atlantis, not comprehending why the beautiful, pale ruler of Pohjola cut out her tongue.

The worst part, Yerra thought, *I cannot remember her name. Only her eyes... Her sad, lost eyes...*

CHAPTER XLVI

"You look marvelous," Deena said as Soroe appeared at her side.

"Shut up," Soroe said. "One day I will make you pay for this indignity."

"I will help," Nikke added. "Getting back at former thieves is a good bit of fun."

"Enough," Soroe said, her eyes shifting between her two companions. She suspected they were secretly laughing at her, but neither face expressed amusement.

Once again, the Queen-elect of Atlantis had disguised herself as a mucksucker. Her clothes were filthy rags supplied by the beggars as a gesture of gratitude. The stench that wafted from these ancient, tattered, dirt-brown, garments, was nearly as horrific as the mud and garbage Deena had pushed Soroe in as a means of finalizing the disguise. Other than her crystal blue eyes, which she kept lowered, there was no indication that this was a beautiful priestess who resembled the legendary ancient Queen of Atlantis.

Deena and Nikke were garbed much as they had been earlier, the latter having added a small horn bow and arrows to her arms. A pointed hunter's cap with a single green feather in the crown completed her outfit. She resembled a professional hunter or mercenary and was subsequently ignored by the merchants and pilgrims on the road leaving Taugi.

"Gold and Iron," Deena said, stopping suddenly. "Trouble ahead."

Nikke and Soroe peered down the road, spotting a small train of pack mules approaching as well as several

181

knots of peddlers and men and women walking the road. None appeared threatening nor were the small groups heading towards the Plains of Lamb'Ha.

"I see nothing to be wary of," Nikke said.

"Wait for it," Deena replied, still not advancing but reaching for her dagger.

A clatter of hooves broke through the general noise as ten men on horseback emerged from behind the caravan. They were lightly armored, with each wearing gold sashes around their waists. They held curved blades in their hands, and they blocked the road in both directions.

"Good people!" a man with a huge black mustache and a gray black wolfskin cape said in a very odd lilting accent, "I call for your attention!"

The traffic in both directions halted and the men raised their swords above their heads, whirling the blades in circles and whooping loudly. The blades caused whistling sounds through the air which only halted when the spokesman raised a hand.

"Good people," he repeated, "you ride across the ancient lands of my people, the Lamb'Hai. We never accepted the rule of corrupt, bloody Atlantis and shall maintain our ways, no matter who sits upon its throne!"

"A pretty speech," a fat man seated upon a wagon filled with melons said, "though you only make it when the royal hussars are elsewhere."

The spokesman threw back his head and laughed, riding closer to the merchant. He sheathed his sword, extended a leather gloved hand, and patted the man's cheek.

"You are brave, old fat thing," he said, patting the other's jowly, bearded face. "I like brave. You shall only pay twelve gold coins toll!"

"Twelve!" the merchant asked, standing on his cart. "That is more money than I shall earn in a year!"

The leader of the Lamb'Hai laughed again, snatched the purse in the man's belt and counted out three silver coins. He handed the remainder of the pouch back to the merchant and patted the man's face again.

"You are brave, flabby face," he said. "I shall allow your passage for three silver coins. The rest of you shall pay. My men and I shall charge each of you a small toll for the gift of using our lands."

"And if we don't want to pay?" a large, heavily-built man dressed in silver armor asked.

Three arrows sliced through the air from somewhere to the left of the road. They landed next to the armored man's feet mere inches from his boots.

"Then, my friend," the spokesman said, "my people shall no longer view you as a guest, but as an invader. Would that be your wish?"

The armored man shook his head quickly, raising his hands in a gesture of surrender.

"I know better than to get into a fight with hidden archers. How much do you want?"

"For you," the leader of the Lamb'Hai said, "one silver piece. Wisdom comes with a price."

The warrior slowly tossed a coin towards the bandit leader, who examined the metal, tested it with his teeth, and nodded once.

"This man may pass. The rest of you shall present yourselves to us and we shall levy your toll. I warn you, my new friends, arguing in the home of your host is a most sinful way of behaving. Accept your fate and the Gods shall smile upon you as proper guests in the lands of my people."

The travelers appeared tense as they slowly approached the warriors, though many found their payments were small charges such as a single copper piece. Complaining appeared to anger the Lamb'Hai chieftain and fines grew accordingly. Nobody quite rose to the heights of three pieces of silver, though a woman in a carriage did receive a charge of two.

"Two!" she said. "How dare you! I'll have you know I am the wife of the late Baron General..."

"If you finish that sentence," the bandit leader said, his yellowing teeth flashing, "I will raise your payment to four. Is that your wish, woman?"

The woman dutifully handed over the coins, closed the door of her carriage and pulled down the shade. Her driver barely hid his amusement as they slowly trotted away.

"Ah," the leader said, reining his horse before Soroe, Nikke, and Deena, "now we come to the reason my people and I are here. You females shall come with us. Our *idugan* foresaw your passage and sent us as messengers. She offers you salt, fire, food and shelter until you leave our lands."

Nikke stepped forward, touched her fingers to her brow and bowed deeply to the horseman. She straightened and spread her hands and arms wide in an inviting gesture.

"Then we, as your guests, shall follow the obligations of a visitor among your people. We shall honor your ancestors and commit no offenses while we rest under your yurt."

The bandit leader touched his head with his fingers and bowed in his saddle.

"Your offer is accepted, and we honor you for your proper respect, female. Welcome to Lamb'Ha. Do your silent companions know our ways?"

Nikke shook her head as she replied, "No, they are as ignorant as a city dweller upon the plains. I shall instruct them in proper behavior."

The leader chuckled and said, "Go from the road. Three ponies await. You shall feast in our tents tonight."

Nikke bowed again, took Soroe and Deena's arms, and propelled them away from the road.

"Before you start squealing," she said, "just know we are safe. The *idugan* will protect us with her life if need be."

"What is an *idugan*?" Deena asked, "and how come you know so much about these... um... people..."

"The second is a long story," Nikke said. "As to the first, an *idugan* is a wise woman among the Lamb'Hai. She speaks to the spirits and sees things. Remember me telling you only a few of us made it out of the badlands? The reason we did is an *idugan* knew the proper way out of those mad swamps. She led us out and cured our injuries. Once one of them gives her word, that is their bond. They cannot lie."

"Then you had best begin explaining how we must behave. I do not want us upsetting some taboo and getting us killed," Soroe said, scratching the filth in her hair.

"Yes," Nikke said. "First, you must never ask for their name. The Lamb'Hai believe..."

185

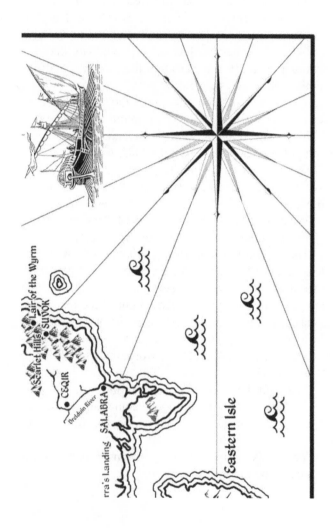

Scarlet Hills • Lair of the Wyrm
SUVOK
CÉQIR
Dryddin River
rra's Landing SALABRA

Eastern Isle

CHAPTER XLVII

The same storyteller squatted upon an upturned bucket, but this time, Macha appeared disinterested in her tales. She dropped between Argall and Jaska though she did not speak to either for several hours. Just after dark, as the storyteller joined a raucous game of dice, she broke the silence by clearing her throat.

"We're being watched again," she said.

"I hadn't noticed," Argall said.

"Nor had I," Jaska said.

Macha shook her head. "Not by eyeballs, fools. Something unseen visited here, lingering above us for a time. It left, but has returned twice more."

"I felt nothing," Jaska said. "Nor could I smell the presence of another."

"Well, you wouldn't, would you?" she asked. "Stealth against you is the point. No need for hiding from the youngling. He couldn't see a spirit if it were dancing before him like yon ghost near the back."

Argall's head snapped the direction she indicated, only to receive a giggle of laughter from Macha.

"Just a tease, youngling. There're no ghosts on the ship that I've noticed. I have a good smell for such intruders and beasts."

"She was joking," Jaska said. "The last ghost I saw was the old woman in the back of that stall we ate at earlier. She just stood there, watching everyone."

Argall shook his head. "It is easy for me to forget you do more than fight."

The former gladiator shrugged his broad shoulders. "It's unimportant, really. Humans accomplish far more destruction of the world without being born upon that path."

Macha snorted and punched his arm. "Stop this gloomy talk, man. I get enough of that rot from my family. Now, tell me the prophecy that sent you on this damned fool errand."

Frowning, Jaska brought his hands together softly. Narrowing his eyes, he pulled them apart, slowly, as if some force held them together. He let his arms then fall to his sides and exhaled loudly. A hush fell across the ship, and it felt as if the entire world stilled for a moment. Even the creak of the wooden walls and the gentle slap of the waves against the sides ceased.

Macha studied him for a moment, the corner of her mouth lifting slightly in a crooked grin.

"Nicely done, very subtle. How long do we have?" she asked.

"Just a few moments," he said. "I veiled us completely."

Argall opened his mouth though the questions died upon his lips. A warning look from the sorcerer stilled his tongue.

Then Deena appeared before them, her form a ghostly image. Nobody in the hold stared in their direction as the young girl's face contorted in pain. Argall realized this was the moment in the throne room when the young girl had spoken her first prophecy:

"King and Queen, the stars and the fates weave the tapestries of your lives. One who live as two, uncrowned and ruling the lands. Find the sword whose heat shall destroy the Wyrm. Extinguish the Prince of Poison or the dark god shall rise and consume the land..."

The image vanished and, a second later, the chatter of those within the hold filled the air again. The ship groaned as if rode a rising wave and landed with a soft crash back into the water.

"I have power," Jaska said, his voice strained, "over darkness. I summoned that force and hid us from prying eyes. For a moment, nobody on or near the ship could see or hear us. Placing that curtain before that many was very taxing on me."

"Ah," Macha said, "but it's enough. You look for a sword that will solve your troubles. How very silly."

"Silly?" Argall said. "Swords, like spears and other weapons, are noble. They are a tool used for the saving of lives."

"And taking them," Macha said. "Sorry, youngling, a sword is like any other instrument. The trouble is, this one does more harm than good. Perhaps we never should have taught the humans how to shape metal."

"They didn't need metal to kill each other. They, like my people, were doing well with wood and stone for generations," Jaska said. "Argall needs a mysterious sword as a means of stopping a dragon or something equally terrible. Then the Atlanteans will make him their king."

"Until the next trouble strikes?" Macha asked. "Do you think stopping one creature will slow the Dark Prince and his minions?"

The formerly masked man shook his head. "The walls have been breaking down for some time. We can only confront one danger at a time."

"Forgive my intrusion," Argall said, leaning forward so both could see his face, "but what are you two talking about?"

"Prophecies, youngling," Macha answered. "The last days of the land. The Dark Prince has slaves everywhere. They will one days break him from his prison

189

and then everything dies. The Wyrm? That was one of his children, a long time ago, just like the Prince of Poison. He was vanquished by Marghael of Ceqir, but if they steal enough power or burn the land to a cinder, that ancient monster will throw off his shackles."

"Do not despair, Argall," Jaska said. "That may be a thousand years from now too. We have no means of knowing. The one who predicted the end was a man who received the power of prophecy from a god or a demon. He could be wrong."

Argall frowned, "I thought you said men cannot possess that power."

Macha shook her head and grinned. "If a great power places that burden upon your shoulders, you will hold it for a time. The one himself speaks of was Nikodemus the Mad. He spoke of his visions for five straight days, clawing his eyes out after the first prophecy appeared in his mind. Each hour he became less sensible."

"Then what happened to him?" Argall asked.

"His head exploded," Macha said. "Disgusting, it was. Ruined my best dress and I couldn't eat flesh for a year after that."

There didn't seem to be any means of following that statement, so they fell into another thoughtful silence. Soon Argall closed his eyes and drifted away, his dreams that of men with skulls that kept flying apart and coming back together a moment later.

CHAPTER XLVIII

"Resew those fingers, little fool," Loviatar said, kicking Yerra's rear and sending her sprawling onto her face.

"Yes, mistress," Yerra replied, lifting the cold flesh upward and running her needle through the thin layer of stiff skin.

If the sacrifices were horrific, the secondary work was equally terrible, if not worse. The requirements of the Ice Queen of Pohjola were even more demanding than before. Every detail must fit her exact specification. Any failure resulted in brutal violence.

Yerra tightened the nearly invisible spider silk that bound the fingers in place. Only a keen eye would spot the infinitesimal threads that tied this creation together. Yerra concentrated only upon her work, busily ensuring that there were no blemishes or poorly sewn areas.

Hours later, she crawled backwards, bowing her head, and awaiting the judgement of her cold mistress. She felt the shadow of Loviatar over her, leaning forward and staring downwards with intense attention.

A soft tapping echoed in the distance and the chilled presence of the terrible ancient witch encompassed the chamber. Yerra felt Louhi's harsh, inhuman, gaze upon her for several seconds before turning elsewhere. The former queen of Atlantis shivered, feeling as if the Dark Witch of these frozen lands were about to tear her apart as she did with the poor captives.

Instead, the withered hands gently stroked Yerra's tangled, odiferous locks. Her claw shaped nails scratched the scalped beneath the thick hair, only slightly painfully. This was as kind as Louhi every managed towards her slaves. A touch of pain disguised as the same fond stroke one would use towards a favored pet.

"Well done, child," she said, "I see your years of comfortable living in a palace did not rob you of the skills you learned at my feet."

"Thank you, mistress," Yerra said, keeping her head lowered.

Loviatar chuckled as she circled the area once again, "She was a bit slow at first, but remember your lessons well, my mother."

Louhi cackled and stroked Yerra's head again, "My best servant in centuries. Perhaps she will serve us again as more than a body slave."

"Plans of that sort are unnecessary, my mother," the ice queen said. "We must begin the encirclement. The hour shall be upon us soon."

"Do not teach me how to steal eggs from a nest, daughter," Louhi replied. "I instructed you in these arts!"

Loviatar laughed and shook her shining platinum hair. "And I discovered sources of power you did not dare approach. Do not speak to me as your student, my mother. You are great and dangerous, but I am queen."

"You grow to bold, daughter," Louhi said. "However, fighting has never assisted either of our causes. Light the candles and we shall begin the spell."

Yerra scuttled back to the filthy heap near the mouth of this cavern and squatted there. She gazed through her unkempt mane as the candles, each made from the fat of human children, ignited at the same instant.

The Ice Queen of Pohjola and the Dark Witch of these terrible frozen lands lifted their hands and began chanting a strange rhythmic song, one in a language that was both musical and painful to Yerra's ears.

Dark specks emerged from their spread fingers, floating of pure void danced through the air. The dots danced and swirled like a whirlwind, their numbers growing with each second.

Sickened, the former Queen of Atlantis looked away. Something repulsed her about the energy the evil pair summonsed, an inner terror that came from the depths of her stained soul. Yerra knew she should flee, yet she did not.

I am tied to these two to the end, she thought, shuddering at the implications of that terrible truth.

CHAPTER XLIX

The Lamb'Hai's camp lay several miles from the road, down several narrow, twisting tails and around a small hill filled with bright yellow and white wildflowers. The smells of cooking meat and horses wafted their direction and soon they heard the laughter of children joining the general tumult.

The camp consisted of twenty or so tents, each made from thick hides and held up with ivory-colored poles. It took Soroe and moment to realize it, but she suddenly recognized the source of these supports.

"Those are the bones of beasts! The giant mammoths and the monstrous lizards!" she said.

"That is so," the leader said, chuckling as he led them through the center of the small village. "We honor the spirit of those great creatures who fed, clothed, and sheltered us for many seasons."

"This is good," Nikke said.

The leader shrugged and said, "This is the proper way, female. If you kill, you must honor the fallen. To fail to do so invites the dark spirits."

He raised a hand up and a massive dark shape fell over his arm. Deena and Soroe started in fear, yet Nikke sat in her horse, a smile upon her face.

"Oh, my," Soroe said, eyes widening, "Is that…?"

"An eagle?" Nikke asked. "Yes. The Lamb'Hai raise and train hunting eagles to be their companions."

"They are our brothers and friends," the bandit leader said as two more massive birds landed upon the arms of other warriors.

The eagles were mighty creatures, each approximately three feet in height with wingspan that appeared far larger. Their feathers were dark brown and the plumage about their heads were a rusty golden color. Each of the enormous talons on the edge of their toes looked capable of tearing the flesh from your body.

However, it was their large, ebony eyes that were the most unnerving. They were deep, inhuman, and unyielding, the orbs of a born predator. These were creatures who were the masters of the air, and they made that clear immediately.

"I never knew such a thing was possible," Deena said, her voice almost childlike as she stared at the great raptors.

"It is," the leader said, stroking his bird's head with evident fondness. "It takes many years and much learning. The bond of hunters ties the pair together forever. This is *Aguu Anchin,* which in your debased tongue means Great Hunter. She has fed well and now shall find my family some meat for the pot. But first, I must take you to the *idugan.*"

"Thank you, male," Deena said, hesitating on the last word.

"You are welcome, female," the leader said, stopping in the center of camp before sliding from his horse.

The camp was a sea of constant movement, with men, women, and children each moving different directions while engaged in various tasks. There were a group of children wrestling, their fellows shouting as a squat woman with gray hair watched and shouted encouragement. Nearby, a group of men and women shaping sticks into arrows, each chatting as their carefully shaped the shafts before fixing feathers and metal points. Near the tents, elderly-looking people stirred pots of various concoctions while a group of similarly aged people played flutes and drums, stopping every few seconds and engaging in short discussions.

"A busy place," Soroe commented.

"We prepare for war, female," the leader said. "The great battle comes, and we would be ready."

"What war?" Soroe asked.

"Speak to the *idugan*," he said, "she knows and shall teach you wisdom. Ah, we arrive!"

A squat man dressed in furs stood outside a tent made from dark, thick furs held up by tusks several heads higher than any present. He held a long, wicked spear in his hands and there was a massive, curved sword pushed through his sash. He stared their direction, his unblinking gaze as unnerving as the monstrous eagle's.

"This is Kharuul," the leader said. "Call him that or male, he will not reply."

"His name means, 'Guard'," Nikke added. "It's a title of honor."

Kharuul stepped aside, lifting a fold of the tent with one hand. Nikke stepped inside first, followed by Soroe and Deena. The tent within was a twenty-foot circle held up by more ancient tusks. A series of fur mats lay upon the ground and a small fire danced in the center of the chamber. There was a drum and a feathered rattle on the other side of the fire and nothing else visible.

Another flap, in the tent wall, lifted, revealing a small chamber within. A tiny, robed figure dressed in furs emerged from the other end and shuffled forward. An odd wooden helmet lay upon its head with a pair of painted eyes on the crest. A thick, beaded veil hid the face beneath.

"You are slow moving, Soroe of Atlantis, Deena of the Spirits, and Nikke the Finder," a soft, gentle voice said. "You tarry and waste time while the road of darkness lays in your path."

"How do you know us?" Soroe asked. "And why do you use our names? I thought that was forbidden by your people."

"I shield you for now from the black spirits that seek your souls, smelly queen," the other replied. "You are in my lands, under my protection. For a time, you are safe. Only a short time since your light would draw the foul one towards my people."

"Then why did you bring us here?" Soroe asked.

The tiny figure giggled, a girlish sound that appeared incongruent with her odd appearance.

"I would teach you wisdom, Soroe," the *idugan* replied. "You could be the first of your kind that learns the truth of the lands of Atlantis. Are you willing to take that journey?"

"Yes," Soroe said, "though I only speak for myself. I cannot answer for Deena or Nikke."

"They were not summoned here by chance, smelly queen," the shaman said. "They have their own destinations. If they deny that truth, they may leave now."

"I'm not leaving," Deena said.

"Nor am I," Nikke said.

"I know," the *idugan* said. "You just needed to say it before I could begin. Sit down near the fire and we shall begin."

They complied and the tiny, hidden woman lowered herself on the other side of the dancing flames. She pulled a pouch from the folds of her robes, reached into the hidden depths, and tossed a handful of small items into the blaze. The flames immediately grew larger, turn-

197

ing a light blue in color and releasing plumes of white smoke.

Oddly, the smoke did not choke them, but felt sweet and pleasant when inhaled. The *idugan* picked up the rattle, shook it several times, and tossed more items into the growing flames. Soon Soroe, Deena, and Nikke found themselves sweating as the tendrils of pale scented vapors obscured sight.

The sound of the rattle grew louder, and the pitch of the jangle transformed from low to high with each passing second. A gentle crooning joined the vibratory noise, adding an unreality to the three women.

"Gaze into the smoke," the *idugan* said, her voice echoing as a deep drum joined the unreal sounds, "look closely and see the truth."

Soroe stared into the smoke as it drifted before her eyes. The mist grew darker, and her eyes widened as she the sounds of howls and shrieks joined the drums. The cries grew louder, madder, and less inhuman as the world transformed into a landscape from her worst nightmares.

"By the Light!" she said as she bit her hand, holding back a scream.

CHAPTER L

"What evil witch did you anger?" Macha asked hours later, having sat upright suddenly as she spoke.

"My wife and her mother," Jaska said. "I told you that much."

"Not you," she said, nodding towards Argall. "You, youngling. What witch did you enrage?"

"None," he said, "I only dealt with one when I lived in the Erm-Gilt-Herm. She was no enemy. Why?"

"Because I feel the weaving of a spell, a dark one," she said, "aimed in our direction."

"I sense nothing," Jaska said, "and I see nothing."

"I believe that was intentional. Did you kill any demons recently?" she asked, frowning.

"Yes," the former Accursed One said. "Children of Dimme-kur. Their leader, Akhkhazu, escaped."

Macha nodded slowly, "Yes, that would fit. A powerful being has her eyes upon the youngling and shall endanger us all shortly."

"Can we prevent it?" Argall asked.

"No," Jaska said. "However, we can trace the source. It will take both of Macha and myself if we are to be successful. You will have to combat the sending."

"Alone?" the Erm-Gilt-Hermian chieftain asked. "It took several of us last time those Dimme-kur attacked."

"You are capable," Jaska said. "Just remember, everything can die, nothing is immortal."

"Even the gods?" Argall asked, rising.

"Especially them, youngling," Macha said. "Gods need us more than we need them."

"Take this," Jaska said, handing Argall his mace. "It may help, it may not. Just do as you must. Every life aboard this ship depends upon you."

Argall rose, thought for a moment, and walked up the stairs. If something terrible would appear soon, he wished the creatures away from the others on the ship. At the top of the stairs, an older man with a gray and black beard, narrow shoulders and hands that appeared too thick for his body looked his direction quizzically. He stopped winding the rope in his hands, cleared his throat and ducked his head quickly.

"Passengers should stay in the hold. No offense, sir, but landsmen are a danger on deck," he said.

"I was just looking for a quiet place for some meditation," Argall said, remembering those words from one of the Atlantean nobles.

"Oh," the sailor said, "then walk down the next companionway and into the pump room. Them pumps is locked, but nobody will bother you down there for a time."

Argall remembered that city people thank each other with coinage. Pulling five of the copper pieces from his pouch, he handed them to the sailor, who smiled a gap-toothed grin and returned to his rope work.

Argall felt the familiar rise and fall of the sea as he crossed the deck towards the nearby set of stairs. He didn't bother correcting the sailor that he wasn't a landsman. Spending time with Admiral Lophan had taught him that those who sail larger ships viewed themselves as the only true pilots of the sea.

Very few of them could survive in our dugout boats for weeks at a time, he thought as he walked down a longer series of steps, *but why bother arguing?*

The pump room was a rectangular-shaped chamber with a series of long iron bars in the center. The bars were chest level and connected to a post of some type, one that was hard to see in the unlit gloom of the hold. The room stank heavily of rotted fish, urine, and other foul scents that assaulted the nose.

"Stinks, doesn't it?" A voice asked from the darkest corner of the room. "The sailors spread vinegar and clean the hole they steak the human cattle in. Here, they just ignore the odors since they're used to the stench."

"Who are you?" Argall asked, gripping the mace tighter as the shadowy figure approached.

"Don't you recognize me, Argall?" the voice asked as a wide smile appeared on the indistinct face. "You should at least recognize my voice."

The dark man drew a long silver sword and stepped fully into view. He was tall, powerfully muscular, handsome, with long blond hair and the pale skin of a north man.

"After all," he said, "we have a lot in common."

Argall gaped at his exact double whose grin widened as the silver Atlantean sword rose...

CHAPTER LI

The song of the Ice Queen and the Dark Witch rose to a height, the notes and bizarre sounds joining into an unreal cacophony that overwhelmed the senses. Yerra covered her face, squeezed her eyes shut and hoped the end would come soon. The unrelenting discordant rhythm shook her fragile nerves and soon she found her body swaying in time with the notes. A mad piping and drumming joined the song and the cavern seemed to vanish beneath the terrible, enrapturing, music.

Then a single note rose above the jangle, a powerful thrumming sound that began as a background addition and slowly encompassed the whole. It resembled the chime of a massive iron bell; one whose echo grew greater rather than fading after achieving a natural height.

Yerra squeezed her eyes tighter and covered her ears, hoping the end would come soon. She felt blood in her mouth as well as the rusty scent of the *vitae* in her nose. The overpowering resonance engulfed her senses, removing any and all thoughts beyond that of hope for blessed silence.

Just when she knew her mind would shatter irrevocably, the sound ceased, and she collapsed to the frigid stone floor. Yerra panted with exertion, unwilling to move or even open her eyes. Slowly her hearing returned and the malicious laughter of Loviatar and Louhi rang in her ears. It took her a few moments, but soon she realized their amusement was not directed towards her fallen form.

"...lives, my mother. I do not think even he could overcome so terrible a foe," said the Ice Queen.

"Of course, he cannot, daughter," Louhi replied. "We wove a spell so mighty, few upon this world could even imagine the implications."

"I have difficulty with such concepts. Have we bound it to our service? If the flesh dies, is it free or does it return to the darkness?" Loviatar asked. Then, she added, "Ahhh. Our favored slave rouses. She survived despite being present at the opening of the gate."

"Let us soon how well," Louhi said, and her rough, withered hands yanked Yerra up by her hair. "Open your eyes, child."

Yerra whimpered at the pain to her scalp, but kept her eyes firmly shut. She felt a chill through her body, a sudden wave of cold that had her body shivering violently. Her teeth chattered and the former Queen of Atlantis hugged herself in hopes of some shred of warmth.

"Open your eyes, child," Louhi repeated, her grip tightening ever so painfully. "Do so now, or I shall slice the lids that you hide behind."

Yerra slowly opened her lids, wincing in pain as the light flooded in. She closed her eyes again briefly and then slowly attempted again. The Dark Witch hovered over her shuddering form, her harsh eyes probing the former Queen for several seconds.

"The light of intelligence, such as it is, still lays within this one," the witch said, releasing Yerra's hair and letting her collapse to the stone floor again. "She has greater fortitude than I imagined."

"We shall see, my mother," the Ice Queen said. "Rouse her and have her gaze upon our miracle. Then we shall see if she is worthy of the mantle, we may place upon her."

"Agreed," Louhi said and pressed a single finger-nail against Yerra's temple. "Listen to me, child. You feel my finger upon your thin skull. I shall count to three. If you do not stand with your eyes open, I shall visit upon you a lifetime of pain with each passing second. The strongest of men grow faint within seconds of this torture. One…"

Yerra's eyes opened, and she saw the dark robes of her mistress before her face. She felt the talon against her head and knew this was no bluff on Louhi's part. Placing both hands upon the ground, she pushed upward, feeling her strength ebbing in an instant.

"…two…"

Yerra rose to her knees and, with a cry that was more a weak, kittenish mewling, rose to her feet. Her left hand steadied herself against the cavern's slick, frigid wall, but she was on her feet as the witch count continued.

"…three… There! I knew you had it within you, child," Louhi said, lowering her hand. "Under my gentle tutelage, you have grown stronger and possess a vitality you previously lacked. Now, turn your head to the right and look upon the genius we've wrought with your servile assistance."

The former Queen of Atlantis slowly turned her head to the read, her eyes barely registering the smirking, Loviatar. The form just beyond the ruler of Pohjola straightened, the full figure stepping into the light, becoming fully visible.

Yerra stared for several seconds, her mouth falling open in shock. A scream ripped from her body, and she fell backwards, shrieking ever louder while her mistresses laughed…

CHAPTER LII

Before Soroe's eyes lay a temple of stone, a ruin lacking doors, roof, and many walls. The remains of elaborately detailed scrollwork lay upon its shattered pillars and floors, fine art from an early epoch of Atlantean history. A scent of burning flesh filled the air and a choking cloud of gray dust rose above the ruins, falling from the sky like a madman's rendition of rain.

Drawn inexorably forward, Soroe spotted dozen, possibly over one hundred men and women kneeling, their arms held above their heads as they raised and lowered themselves in abasement before a distant object that emitted a bright yellow and orange glow.

The men and women were a savage sight, each dressed in filth and gore, their eyes wild, their bodies covered in bizarre brands and tattoos. The sight of which nauseated the high priestess of the Light. Many were missing limbs or seemingly possessing new vestigial body parts whose function appeared flawed.

Before the horrific congregation stood a hooded figure, its face and head hidden from view. The mad howls and shrieks did not move this being, who stood as a silent sentinel among the insane mass of horrific humanity. This individual could be male, female, demon or even a red-cloaked statue.

Behind the caped figure lay a metal construct, a brass-colored object shaped in the image that shook Soroe to the core of her soul. The image possessed the skull of a massive bull with huge red jeweled eyes that appeared nearly human in shape. The body was that of a man and within the depths of the chest of the twisted simulacrum of life lay an enormous red and yellow bonfire. The odor emerging from the terrible furnace was that of charred meat and Soroe spied blacked bones at the heart of the flame.

The unmoving being standing between the crazed savages and the terrible icon stirred slightly. The head lifted a mere inch, though no flesh emerged into sight. From the depths of the dark cowl emerged a single word, one that sent the crazed masses into a riot of ecstasy of howls and shrieks.

"Another," came the whispered word, though it echoed across the dark landscape.

From behind the wall emerged four men, their physiques slightly more robust than their fellows. They were still wild-eyed, crazed, and covered in muck, yet they strode forward with a gait reminiscent of an average human.

Held within their clawed hands lay a man, a merchant based upon the softness and richness of his silken clothing. His face was bruised and battered, his nose flattened and bleeding, his lips puffy and stained with blood.

"No," he said, his voice a mushy slurring sound, "No! Please, please let me go! I'll pay you! Please no!"

The savage men and women that filled this temple of madness, screamed and shrieked, their howls imitating their captive's pleas. The four men stopped before the hooded figure, who did not stir as they waited, but simply stood in the same frozen pose.

"Continue," the unknown voice said.

The overwrought flock ceased their yips and yowls, falling again to their knees. Their raised and lowered their bodies upright and fell face first upon the dusty floor in perfect harmony, their mouths repeating the same chant as the beseeching merchant sought their attention.

The mantra was a single word, one Soroe had never heard before this moment. Yet somehow, in a deeper, hidden part of her mind, she recognized the sound of that name, one best forgotten in the depths of time.

"Moloch! Moloch! Moloch!" the savages screamed, their voices rising to a fever pitch as their fellows tossed the hapless victim into the titanic fire raging within their metallic idol.

Soroe felt an atavistic wave of terror and nausea as the unfortunate man screamed. The wail soon died away, but the inhuman music rose again. The savage denizens of this forbidden, ruined temple rose and writhed, their motions hysterical and insane, repulsing the young Queen-elect as she watched.

The scent smoke crept back into her senses and Soroe heard the rattle and drum that she recalled the *idugan* held when the ceremony had begun. Slowly the horrific scene melted away and she felt the soft fur beneath her legs, and sweat trailing down her face.

"You return," the *idugan* said, her voice piercing the veil which slowly parted. "You return from the now, and wisdom lays upon your soul."

They were back in the Lamb'Hai's tent, the shaman squatting across them as the fire slowly diminished. Soroe found herself panting, her body weakened and wasted. Near her, Deena and Nikke looked similarly exhausted, with the young oracle quickly wiping tear trails from her face with the back of an arm.

"What," Soroe asked, "did you do to us?"

The *idugan* giggled, her face still hidden beneath the odd, dark, veil. She swayed in place while lowering her drum and rattle, squatting in place.

"I did nothing. I asked the *natigai* for aid. They showed you a vision of the now," the shaman said.

Deena's eyes narrowed. "They showed us the future?"

The *idugan* shook her head beneath her headdress as she said, "No, no, no. That is not the way of the *natigai*. I shall instruct you swiftly, so listen and gain wisdom. The *natigai* are the spirit of the land, the mothers of life. The *tngri* are the black and the white, the low and the high. The future is a gift of the *tngri*, but they will only speak to certain persons. I spoke to the *natigai* who showed you the path of the present. They have no interest in the paths of the coming. Do you understand?"

"A little," Soroe said. "Is that the ruined temple within the plains of Lamb'Ha?"

"Yes," the shaman said, standing, "and the reason the land and those within its tall grasses sicken in mind and body. That is one of the *Karaoğlanlar,* the sons of the great evil. You call this one the Prince of Poison... A silly name... We call him, in our tongue, *Kerey Han*, the spirit of discord."

"There are hundreds of those insane creatures near that foul shrine," Nikke said. "I was part of the force that tried cleansing it. Almost none of us escaped!"

The *idugan* pointed a tiny finger at the Finder and said, "You and your warriors went in boldly, moving like Watchers on the Threshold across the grasses. They heard your passage and did not engage you. They picked you apart like a pack of hounds bringing down a bear. Your people were brave, but foolish. Silence is your weapon, not war horns. Now, you must leave. My people will lead you to a secret way into the corrupted lands. If you survive, we shall find you again."

She then turned, walked to the flap in the tent where they entered, opened the gap, and shooed them outside. Her motions were that of an elderly woman waving a fly from her face. A moment later, they stood outside in the blazing sunlight.

The bandit leader was waiting, a long pipe gripped between his teeth. He grinned in their direction and nodded quickly.

"Yes, she always does that. No farewells or even curses. Just, you leave now," he said. "She told me I must take you to the dark lands. Are you sure you wish that? My people avoid those mad plains."

"Yes," all three women said.

"So be it, on your head and all those words of regret," he said. "Come, the horses await, and you must be there before the darkness falls."

"What happens then?" Deena asked. "Though I probably shouldn't ask."

"You shall see, girl, you shall see!" he said and laughed with little humor in that sound.

CHAPTER LIII

It was only his native-born reflexes that saved the Erm-Gilt-Hermian from death in that instant. Without realizing it, Argall had raised his borrowed mace and parried the swing. He swung the heavy weapon at his enemy... himself...

His double danced backwards, smiling savagely while swinging his sword left and right.

"Slow, are you not? I guess soft living in a palace weakens a man."

"Who are you?" Argall asked again, stepping to the side while keeping his weapon between his body and the other.

"Slow of mind too," the double said, making a tsk-tsk sound. "It does not matter. Once I kill you, none shall be the wiser. Your brother and the other barbarians shall be easily dispatched once the crown sits upon my head."

"They will know you instantly!" Argall said, swinging the mace towards his enemy's side.

The double pirouetted gracefully and slice a thin line across the Erm-Gilt-Hermian's chest.

"They will not," he said in the same voice as Argall, "because I am you. I hold your memories, your skills, and your desires. I shall rule kindly for a time. Then, when the time is right, I shall indulge myself."

The double lunged, barely missing Argall's heart and backstepped immediately, avoiding the mace.

"First," he said, "I shall enjoy the pleasures of your virginal queen. She shall learn pleasure and pain in my arms... In time, she shall be little more than a harlot I shall send as a gift to those who support my whims."

Argall heard the words of his double and felt cold. It was as if a wave of frigid water from the icy rivers of the gloomy wastes of the North had suddenly bathed his body. He had only experienced this feeling twice before, both in times of great peril; moments when death was imminent, and he had sought the blood of his enemy, joining him in the dark embrace.

A bestial snarl issued from his chest, and he stepped forward, mace held high. He charged forward, cutting his palm as he batted aside the side point that his double extended. The mace crashed into his enemy's shoulder, shattering the bones beneath.

The double screamed, the sword falling from his grip. He stumbled backwards, barely avoiding two more swings. Circling to the left, he stepped on his sword and smiled.

A loud crackle filled the air and the blade melted away, reappearing in his hands again. The double stretched his shoulder and laughed.

"Painful, but temporary, Argall. I cannot be harmed for long. My body rebuilds itself immediately," he said.

Argall did not pause, he simply charged again, the mace striking the sword, arms, and legs. The double moaned as the Erm-Gilt-Hermian's assaults continued, the huge iron weapon shattering the flesh and bone as fast as they reknitted. Finally, Argall swung the weapon down with such force that the battered being with his face folded in half around the weapon.

With a snarl, Argall grabbed his enemy's writhing legs, dragged him up the stairs, pausing only long enough to stomp on the creature's skull. Arriving on deck, he dragged the false Argall to the rail and, with a single heave, threw his enemy into the ocean.

"What was that you threw?" the sailor who met earlier asked. "Your club?"

"Yes," Argall said, panting.

The sailor snorted with obvious, open contempt.

"You shouldn't throw things into the sea. The captain don't like it. And you're bleeding, landsman. What happened? Trip and fall down the companionway?"

"Yes," Argall said, "sorry."

"Get back down below before you fall overboard," the sailor said with a sigh. "The sharks would tear you apart before we could change course and drop you a line."

Argall didn't answer but touched his brow and returned to the hold. He picked his way through the gloomy depths, dropping next to Macha with a sigh. She and Jaska ignored his presence, seated across from each other, hands linked, eyes closed. They did not speak, twitch, or move. Only the slow inhale and exhale of their breathing, somehow simultaneously timed, indicated they were alive.

Two hours passed, long enough for Argall to apply a poultice to his hand, eat, drink a mug of ale he purchased from the ship's cook, and relax. Just about the time darkness fell, they shifted, unlocked their grip, and opened their eyes.

"Worse than I thought," Jaska said.

"As bad as I figured," Macha said.

"I fought a double of myself," Argall said. "I hit him with the mace and threw him to the sharks."

"We know," Jaska said. "We viewed your fight. Very impressive. Few people defeat a trow with a regular weapon."

"Tossing the beast into the sea was clever," Macha said. "Normally it may have turned into a fish, but the

212

sharks made a meal of it, and I doubt there's more than a handful of it left."

"It may still live," Jaska added. "They don't die easily."

"Can only a piece of a trow live? If they're in pieces, will they reform or try and start new on their own?" Macha asked. "I'll ask my cousin. He is part of the sea and would like such a puzzle."

"How did you... forget I asked, I already know the answer, magic," Argall said. "If you saw me, couldn't you have lent me aid?"

"No," they said simultaneously, grinning.

"We weren't in our bodies," Macha said. "We could see you and much more, but only from a distance."

"We traced the source of the sending, though," Jaska said. "It closer than we intended. The Scarlet Hills are short trek from the city of Ceqir."

"But our destination was the Land of the Ala," Argall said. "I remember that was the prophecy."

"If it is a prophecy," Macha said, "then you shall arrive there soon enough. First, the Scarlet Hills. Unless you desire more magical assaults from whoever doesn't like you there."

Argall thought for a moment and nodded, "You are correct. Tell me, why are they called the Scarlet Hills?"

"Because the stones are red and cover the hills," Jaska said, frowning. "Why?"

"Usually when you mention a location, there's usually a story of terrible battles, murders, and monsters," Argall said. "It is an understandable question."

"The youngling is right, though not this time," Macha said, chuckling. "Let me tell you of how the inn known as the Hopping Harlot received its name... My father Cichol loved a good scrap..."

213

CHAPTER LIV

Closing her eyes and covering her head, Yerra cowered before the terrible miscreation, her wails of fear echoing in her ears as Loviatar and Louhi's mirth continued unabated. Part of her sought oblivion as the image she viewed appeared again in her mind's eye. The rest of her felt lost, broken before the horror which her hands assisted in fashioning.

"Enough, my mother," Loviatar said an eternity later. "The wretch suffered enough. Either end her now or bring some semblance of sanity to her head."

Louhi laughed, a youthful sound of mirth that lacked her previous malice.

"Very well, my daughter. I enjoyed her pain and felt you bathe in the primal fear that engulfed her mind and body. A veritable feast for you, no doubt."

"This is truth, my mother," the Ice Queen said, "yet I have had my fill. I would use this one if she is still able. Revive her or feed her to our visitor."

Louhi shuffled Yerra's direction, her aged voice crooning an odd song whose melody was both sweet and intoxicating. A warmth covered Yerra, and she felt her body calm, her muscles unknot, her mind empty and still. The horrific images she witnessed still existed within her, yet they felt less sinister and terrible.

Opening her eyes, her blurry vision gazed upon the twisted mockery of mankind that stood in the center of the chamber. The three pulsating yellow eyes studied her as an overlong black tongue periodically lolled upon the edges of the serpentine-shaped mouth.

214

Somehow, Yerra did not shriek again, her terror still rising within her yet never to her breaking point. She stood, bowed to the evil witches, and stood silently; her head lowered several inches in submission.

"Tell me, child," Louhi asked, "do you understand who our sorcery has brought to Earth?"

"No mistress," the former Queen of Atlantis said.

"I thought not," the Dark Witch replied. "You wisely knew that tarrying with the dark powers would result in your end. I shall not instruct you, save placing a name upon our ally. Before you stands a prince among the dwellers of the underworld. The name he wishes spoken is that of Hiisi. Do you know that title, child?"

Yerra nodded, her eyes lowered, "Yes, mistress. A son of the great master of the darkness. A feared god called evil by your enemies."

"You taught her well, my mother," Loviatar said. "I admit I am impressed. Hear my commands, wretched one. You shall now serve Hiisi as slave. If you perform well, he shall return you to your marble throne in Atlantis. Would you like that?"

"Yes, mistress," Yerra replied, her voice nearly lifeless.

"Lift your eyes, former ruler of the greatest kingdom on Earth," a gentle voice said. "Look upon me, Yerra. You belong to me now and I shall make you greater than any thought possible."

"Remember your bargain, Prince Hiisi," the Ice Queen said. "Perform as we command and your desires shall be indulged to your heart's content."

"Of course, Loviatar the North Star, Queen of Pohjola," the soft voice of Hiisi replied. "Though I am an ancient demon of the greatest order, I must follow certain rules. Honoring an agreement is the first law of my kind."

Louhi tapped her cane upon the stone floor of the bloody cavern as she strode away from Yerra's side.

"For our part, we shall seek the means of opening the great gate between worlds. Now, take this one and do as we command."

Yerra felt three enormous, cold, moist hands close about her arms and neck. The flesh across these over-sized limbs was green, mottled and covered in warts and leaking pustules. Despite that, she felt no fear as the hands lifted her and stepped sideways into a dark, frigid void. The stygian gloom surrounded her, robbing the former Queen of any bodily sensation, or thought. She smiled, embracing the nothingness, and hoping it would never end.

"I am spent, my mother," Loviatar said, "I must rest and feed. Send word to the villages that a festival shall commence, and their Queen shall provide a day of feasting, drinking, and contests."

"...and you shall consume every drop of envy, fear, sadness, and anger that follows any place where mead quaffing, and contests follow. I taught you well, daughter. Your powers are not as vast as mine, yet in some areas you are my better," Louhi said.

"Praise indeed, my mother," the Ice Queen said. "Sleep well. Soon your dreams of destruction shall become a reality."

CHAPTER LV

The sun hovered dangerously low over the western horizon sending golden trails across the lush Plains of Lamb'Ha. The high grasses, many several feet above that of a normal man, swayed gently in the soft breeze, a gentle rustling sound drifting every direction.

"We have arrived, females," the Lamb'Hai leader said. "Dismount and see your trail."

Soroe, Deena, and Nikke obeyed, dropping to the ground, and pulling their packs across their shoulders. The bandit chieftain trotted aside, revealing a narrow circular opening among the tall reeds.

"That is our path?" Nikke asked. "It looks like an animal trail."

"That it is, female who hunts like a Lamb'Hai," he said with a barking laugh. "*She* told us that this path was once a crossing for many beasts who dwelled across the plains. They abandoned the trail when the mad ones brough the dark spirits into the land."

"Then how does it exist now?" Nikke asked. "The land would cover it with weeds and hide it from view."

The Lamb'Hai leader shrugged as he pulled his pipe out once again.

"That is all I know. Perhaps the *natigai* maintained the trail for the beasts who still live across the plains. Perhaps the *idugan* knows, but I shall not ask her. Accept that she assists you as she is able. This is enough."

Nikke touched her head, lips and chest before bowing her head. "It is enough. Long life and good hunting to you and your people. May the wind always ride at your back."

The bandit leader performed the same gesture, grinned and answered, "I would wish you the same, yet I doubt your chances of receiving such gifts. I shall instead hope the spirits grant you luck in your battle against the dangers ahead."

That said, he and the others rode away, the three borrowed horses trailing in their wake. They vanished from sight a moment later, only the circle enormous birds of prey above them indicating their passage.

"I will go first," Nikke said, removing a long wide bladed knife from her back. "Soroe. you will follow me and you, thief, to the rear. Keep the talking to a minimum since sound echoes across these plains. Just remember that any unnatural sound is probably one of those twisted beasts. If they catch us, we've only three paths. Join them and turn insane, become a sacrifice, or become dinner."

"Can I vote on which I'd prefer?" Deena asked as they stepped into the high rushes.

"Go right ahead," Nikke said. "Split a bottle of wine with them as they start chewing on your liver. Now, shut up."

The sward beneath their feet squished and sunk beneath their every step as the tall grasses swayed in gentle rhythm to the gentle breeze. The chirp and chitter of insects rose and fell as the path wound left and right through the plains.

Within a few minutes, their sense of direction had vanished, with only the diminishing sun as a guide as to which direction was west. There were no actual signs of life, though there were soft rustling noises and shivering stalks as some small animal fled unseen.

The edges of the path grew darker as the light struggled to penetrate the thick vegetation. Within what felt like an hour, the lands outside the path had become murkier and less distinct. The click of insects had grown stronger and there were occasional glimmers of jeweled phosphorescent flashes in the distance.

Darkness fell over the plains, blanketing the sky with a cloudy, stygian gloom. The path was barely visible, with Nikke slowing her pace to a slow walk. She briefly halted, placing one of Deena's hands on Soroe's shoulder and one of the latter upon her broad back. Nikke held a finger to her lips, hushing them from speaking, before resuming their slow march.

Time passed, though the murk and the endless waves of enormous rushes had removed any capacity for following the passage of the minutes or hour. There was a powerful sense of unreality about these lands, as if they had slogged through an endless dreamscape whose end would never be discovered.

Then the sounds came, yips, barks, howls, and yowls. Bestial whines that rose and fell with no sense of timing. There were snaps and crashes as bodies hurled themselves mindlessly through the reeds, the echoes of the charging bodies adding a hallucinatory affect to their already jangled nerves.

Oddly, none of the insane screeches and cries approached the path, though the shivers in the high grasses did suggest a surprising nearness to where they walked. The moon, hidden beneath a heavy layer of clouds, provided just enough shimmering, silvery illumination for their eyes. The path remained always visible, though never more than few feet from where they slogged.

The trail turned left, then right, and an odd reddish glow appeared in the distance. Their vision cleared and, after a walk of twenty or so feet, they stepped free of the grassy sward.

"Gold and Iron," Deena said, her voice a whisper, "that was the reason for the light."

"No need to whisper now," Nikke said. "They see us."

They stood a few steps away from the ruined temple they had viewed in the shaman's tent. It was taller than they had imagined, the shattered cyclopean columns spiraling high above their heads. The metal statue of the taurusian features of the demonic idol was shimmering just as the bonfire within.

Dozens of naked, maddened savages stood between them and the idol, their crazed eyes and twisted features staring their direction. The closest, a pale-skinned man with filth-stained, golden hair, gazed upon them, loud panting sounds emerging from his blistered, fevering lips. Yet, he and his fellows never moved closer; in fact, they stepped aside, creating a path to the temple.

"Approach, Soroe of Atlantis," the heavy voice they heard in their vision said. "They shall only touch you if you flee. If you run, they shall pull you down and consume you as food."

"Not much of a choice," Deena said, her fingertips touching her head. "Ow."

"Getting a headache, thief?" Nikke asked. "Don't worry, soon you won't have a head."

"Silence," Soroe said, firing a harsh look at the taller Finder. "If she becomes shaky, make sure she does not fall down. Trust me, this is important."

"Approach, Soroe," the voice continued. "Do not make me ask a second time. I am becoming impatient."

"Very well," Soroe said as she strode through the ranks of insane followers of this horrific demon.

The ranks closed behind them as they strode into the remains of a once proud and noble structure.

The robed figure stood before the flickering flames within the monstrous furnace. The one hidden beneath the cowl twitched slightly as they halted several feet before the towering idol.

"You were clever," the voice said, the sounds echoing throughout the plains. "That path was not known to me until great Moloch sent me a vision. I could have given you to my followers, but I did not. I will even let you leave my lands in peace."

"Why?" Soroe asked as Deena reeled slightly, supported by Nikke.

"Because you have something Moloch wishes as a gift," the cowled figure answered. "Your scepter, the Soul of Soroe. Hand it to me and I shall grant you free passage."

Soroe flicked her fingers in the air and the Soul of Soroe appeared in her outstretched hand. She extended the jeweled rod towards the hood person, stepping nearer and covering the distance between them.

"No, Soroe, don't!" Deena said. "He's lying!"

A soft, pudgy hand emerged from the oversized sleeve, its sausage-shaped fingers rippling and grasping the air. The hooded person stepped closer, closing the last remaining inches.

"I know," Soroe said, as the scepter vanished from view again.

Stepping back, the Queen-elect of Atlantis produced the object in her left hand. A beam of golden light emerged from the shimmering jewel, striking the hooded individual, freezing him in place.

Screams and howls erupted from the masses at the rear, and they cowered backward, their hands held over their shrieking faces. As the savage bodies collided, battles broke out, with the crazed followers of the demon lord falling upon each other while fleeing the powerful glow of the ancient artifact.

"Who are you?" Soroe asked as the leader of this tribe shook in place, frozen beneath the power of the gem.

The cowled figure straightened and lowered the hood, revealing a wide skull and flowing locks. No words emerged from the puffy lips, but none were needed.

"You?" Soroe asked. "It cannot be!"

CHAPTER LVI

"Two days travel by horseback," Argall said as they walked out of the city gates of Ceqir. "Yet, you two refused any animal! It will take a week on foot!"

"It will take me half a day by air," Macha said, "but I will not tarry and place poor animals in danger."

"Will you carry us?" the Erm-Gilt-Hermian asked. "Can you turn into a massive bird we could ride the distance?"

"Do I look like a beast a burden to you, youngling?" Macha replied, her pale cheeks flushing. "The only man who rides me will be my mate. No offense, but the idea of you and I... ugh, I may be ill..."

Jaska snorted and shook his head. "You walked into that one, Argall. The proper behavior when speaking to a shapeshifter is to wait for their invitation. If they choose to have you ride them, it is a gift they can extend."

"Well said," Macha said. "So no, Argall of the Erm-Gilt-Herm. You shall never sit upon my back."

"That still does not answer my question," Argall said, flushing at her words. "How will you and I cross the distance, Jaska?"

Macha rolled her eyes, shook her head, and said, "Is he always this slow?"

Jaska shook his head, and replied, "His people have little understanding of the world. They are probably the fiercest fighters in any land, but in certain areas, they are limited."

"Interesting," she said. "Well, show him so we can move along."

"What are you two talking about?" the Erm-Gilt-Hermian chieftain asked, feeling the anger rise in him.

"Watch," Macha said as Jaska stepped to the side of the road.

The powerfully-built gray haired warrior sorcerer crouched low, the sinews across his arm and back rippling. There were several cracks and snaps from his torso as he bent lower, hands upon the ground. His legs shook, shot backwards and quivered.

"What?" Argall asked. "What is happening?"

Jaska's head bent low as thick gray fur exploded from his body. His torso thickened, growing wider and lower with each passing second. A moment later, his hands had vanished, replaced by enormous paws better suited for one of the titanic cave bears of the northern wastes.

A wolf now stood where Jaska had once knelt, though it was no average beast. This creature's head was larger than a man's torso and he stood taller than the Atlantean warhorse the nobles of that city rode into battle. The thick fur was a deep gray, and the eyes were the same ice blue that always indicated a degree of inhumanity within the Pohjolan.

"Do you think," Jaska asked in his normal voice, "I was known as the Gray Wolf because of my hair?"

"Um... ah...," Argall said, "Um..."

"Close your mouth, youngling," Macha said. "You'll attract flies."

"We can continue this discussion later," Jaska said as he lowered his haunches. "Climb aboard and hold tight to my fur. Oh, and you may wish to cover your ears in a moment."

Macha smiled and her body transformed into a black cloud of black feathered birds. The murder of crows circled overhead, and a powerful raucous cry emerged from their sharp beaks. At the same time, the titanic lupine head of Jaska the Grey Wolf rose and rippling, howl emerged from the fang-filled snout.

The screams of these beasts shook the very air and Argall winced at the power of the exclamations. Answering howls and roars chorused through the land as Jaska charged off the paved road and into the Kurga Plains.

The massive wolf moved with a light, swift step, vaulting fallen trees with apparent ease. His pace, like that of the crows overhead, was faster than any horse, a speed only possible by a being as inhuman as this pair.

Argall held tight to the thick fur, elated by the uncanny haste. The lands around him were a mere blur as the oversized wolf and the flying crows covered a distance that the Erm-Gilt-Hermian would not consider possible.

Hours later, the grasses across the land grew sparser, with small rocky rises replacing the gentle green mounds they covered before. At the summit of such a rise, Macha appeared, seating herself upon a small boulder. Jaska stopped several feet away, depositing Argall on his rear and transforming a few seconds later.

"Ahhh," the Pohjolan said, sighing and stretching his arms. "That felt good. I haven't had a run like that in over a century."

"Why didn't you change when you were a prisoner?" Argall asked, rising, and rubbing his slightly bruised rear.

"If I had, the Dalaketnon would have killed me immediately," he said. "They wanted a gladiator, not an antediluvian wolf. In that form, I am fast and lethal, but limited."

"We may turn into impressive beasts, youngling," Macha said, "but we only are capable of what that animal could do if it had a human mind. My cousin, who turns into a fish, cannot take a walk on land when he's changed."

Argall nodded, stretched his back, and asked, "How far did we travel?"

"The Scarlet Hills are just ahead, about a mile off," Macha said. "Best to approach it with some caution. After all, something very powerful lives in those lands."

"You don't know?" Argall asked. "Also, I still don't have a weapon. We left before I could find a sword."

"I have an axe I can lend you," Macha said. "It is a fair blade, but limited. Are you trained in that art?"

"Yes," the Erm-Gilt-Hermian said. "Among my people, the axe is the weapon you learn first. Then, if you prove skillful enough, they teach you the sword."

Macha raised an arm above her head, spoke a few words and a long handled, single-bladed war axe appeared in her hand. She handed the weapon to Argall, who tested the weight and balance.

"A fine weapon," he said.

"A tool," she said with a sniff. "Axes are limited in war."

"I prefer them," Jaska said as they strode down the slope.

"Because you lived your life in those frigid steppes. Unless you intend a return to that life, you'd best expand your horizons," she said. "Do you desire a home in the land of your birth?"

Jaska shook his head, "No, never again. Pohjola has their queen, and her people chose the safety of her magic over freedom. It shall be their choice if they oppose her rule."

Macha nodded and smiled but did not comment. She walked at his side as they climbed the next hill, a taller rise that prevented their view of the lands ahead.

"Ah," Jaska said. "That wasn't there before."

"Yes," Macha said, "though the last time I walked among these crags was twenty years ago."

A marshy lake stretched across the distance leading to the rocky, reddish brown, Scarlet Hills. The hills themselves were jagged mounds jutting from the ground and resembled pieces of a mountain disassembled and tossed in every direction. There were no signs of vegetation or life among the various ridges, not even the sounds of insects or birds.

"I would fly over," Macha said, "but I suspect that may be as dangerous as a walk through the shallows."

"Oddly," Argall said. "I agree with you. Everything in the world tells me that there's something very wrong here. Even in my lands, every body of water has some life."

"Be on your guard," Jaska said, "and do not lose your weapon."

They walked down the slope, stepping gingerly into the shallows. The brackish water sloshed beneath their feet as they circled the edge of the small lake. Their movements slowed even further as the muck and mud gripped their boots tightly with each step.

A movement about Argall's feet frozen him in position. He glanced about, realizing the other pair were similarly suspicious, their keen eyes sliding over the opaque glassine surface of the lake.

Argall gripped his borrowed axe tightly, frowned and continued forward. He took two more steps when something frigid, slimy, and strong brushed across his ankles. He opened his mouth, intent on warning his companions, when a mass of tentacles exploded from the water, encircling his legs and torso. Jaska and Macha were similarly entangled, the former of whom was already hacking away with a small, thick blade.

Argall snarled a war cry, raising his axe and chopping the nearest appendage in twain. Black ichor sprayed across the lake as the tentacles about his torso tightened, pulling him towards the deeper water...

CHAPTER LVII

Padhoum, the curly-haired, ochre-skinned eunuch majordomo who had dwelled in the palace of Atlantis for years, smiled broadly. His tiny, white teeth flashed in the light of the Soul of Soroe, his true feelings revealed at last.

"You are surprised, I see," he said, giggling for several seconds. "Oh, joy of joys! I wondered how long I could keep the deception a secret! I managed it for over a decade without anyone realizing the truth!"

"What truth?" Soroe asked, feeling Deena and Nikke pressing closer to her.

"That we have entered the last days of Atlantis," Padhoum replied. "The end of life shall arrive soon. The great dragon shall arrive and consume the life of any not sanctified in his name."

"Um, lady?" Deena asked, "can you hurry this up? These maniacs are getting closer, and a few are starting to look our way."

"The great dragon? You mean Apophis?" Soroe asked, ignoring the interruption.

The eunuch cackled and shook his head, his curly locks bouncing.

"No, of course not. Apophis is a mere underling of the great dragon. The one I speak of is the creator of life, the only true divine being. He is everything and nothing, madness and joy, a being beyond our paltry imagination. The dragon shall cleanse Atlantis of life, toss the land into the ocean and an ancient, sunken city of corpses shall rise from the depths in its place."

"But you will die with us!" the Queen-elect said. "If what you say is true, you and your insane followers will die in the maelstrom."

"Not I," Padhoum said. "I am one of his children's followers. I fed hundreds of lives to Moloch's never-ending hunger. I shall survive, but you will not. My children shall soon feast upon your flesh."

"I think not," Soroe said, lifting her scepter and adding, "Remember the hallway, Nikke."

Nikke and Deena ducked their heads, turned their bodies away, and closed their eyes. The luminescent, pulsating, power of the Soul of Soroe rose, the multi-faceted illumination growing with each passing second.

The powerful flash of pure white light burst forth from the crystalline cavity, spreading in a vast circular wave across the plains. Padhoum and his maddened fol-lowers shrieked in agony, with many of the screaming, insane beings fleeing into the grasslands. The few that remained lay upon the ground, moaning, and clawing their eyes, sending bloody trails across their filthy faces.

"Gold and Iron," Deena said. "That is one powerful toy you have there, lady."

Soroe flicked her hand, sending the scepter away.

"It will be of little use for some time. I used much of its power with that pulse."

"I think it worked," Nikke said, blinking her eyes rapidly. "The screaming crazy bastards are gone, or lay-ing on the ground crying."

"But I am not," Padhoum said, smiling. "I knew what you planned, little fool, and covered my eyes as well. Now I shall gift my master with your souls and secure the return of his father."

"You think so?" Deena asked, pulling a knife free from her back.

Padhoum did not reply. Instead, he opened his arms wide, his grinning face never flickering as the young oracle aimed and threw her blade into his eye.

The dagger struck, clicked loudly, and clattered to the ground. A crossbow bolt struck him the chest, snapping upon contact with his robed body.

"I am above such mundane weapons, fools. My master granted me protection from any harm. This was how I cowed the insane tribes to obey my will. There are hundreds of them, many carrying terrible diseases that shall ravage the lands. With you dead, I shall send them out and watch as they destroy every city," he said, reaching down and picking up the dagger near his feet.

Padhoum gripping Deena's knife blade in one hand, grinned their direction, and crushed the weapon with one flex of his fingers. He opened his soft hand slowly, dropping the pieces to the ground. The flesh was unmarred by the jagged metal edges.

"Now," he said, "I will start with you, Soroe, Queen of Atlantis, high priestess of the Temple of Light. My master shall enjoy your soul. You two may flee, if you like. In the end, it won't matter."

He dashed forward, his body a blur as he covered the distance between himself and Soroe in an instant. Padhoum's hand closed about her narrow neck, and he lifted her from the ground.

"Into the fires of Moloch with you," he said, raising her slowly above his head. "You may scream now if you can manage it."

Soroe struggled in vain against the iron grip of the majordomo. She gagged as the fingers gripped tighter and the heat of the titanic furnace grew hotter as he stepped towards the terrible idol.

CHAPTER LVIII

Argall was knee-deep seconds later, having sliced free of three more twining appendages, with two thick ones remaining. The warrior felt the desire to simply release the icy rage within him and embrace the bestial fury of the berserker. Yet, he knew this was futile, that his mind was the only weapon that could save them from this creature.

Even the snow snail has a head, he thought, his eyes casting left and right across the water.

Slowly, inexorably Argall found himself pulled deeper into towards the icy depths. The tentacles, despite their violent thrashing, were heading to the right of where he stood now. The Erm-Gilt-Hermian resisted the pull for a moment, chopping at the thickest part of the appendage and causing little damage. It felt as if he were in the grip of a vast serpent, one whose thick hide resisted his strongest blows.

Then he spotted a movement ahead, a sickly green mound that bobbed several inches above the water before vanishing. Argall thought he saw a circular yellow ooze that may represent an eye of some type. The sickly furuncle bobbed to the surface again and the Erm-Gilt-Hermian spotted the same disgusting secretion of yellow and pale white for a few seconds.

The tentacles lugged him in that direction, and a plan came into his mind. Feigning resistance for a moment, he waited until the ropy limb pulled harder and leaped forward. Then, raising the axe high above his head, Argall brought the keen edge down upon the bobbing mound.

The axe sunk deep into the rubbery flesh, rebounding from a thick plate beneath the surface of the green flesh.

Immediately, the water roiled, with the tentacles thrashing violently in every direction. The Erm-Gilt-Hermian warrior swung downward again, penetrating deeply but feeling the same resistance. The roping appendages tightened painfully, and he cried out as he struggled, raising the heavy axe for one final swing. Aiming momentarily, Argall swung the axe downward, striking deeply into his original cut.

The hard plate beneath the rubbery surface snapped under the impact and he felt a softer layer beneath. The tentacles about his body tightened even harder for an instant, before slackening, shuddering, and falling away.

Not trusting his good fortune, Argall ripped the blade free, sending sprays of foul-smelling black ichor and viscous yellow fluid and flesh in every direction. Raising the weapon above his head like a woodsman splitting a log, he swung the axe downward, penetrating even deeper. The nearby appendages shook from the impact but did not rise again.

"Nicely done, youngling," Macha said from behind his position. "Not many can survive such a beast."

Argall stepped back a little as the mound he assaulted slowly slipped beneath the surface of the water.

"What was that?" he asked, turning.

"I have no notion," she said. "I view water creatures as food or beasts I should avoid. Now, get over here and help me."

Fully facing her direction, Argall understood her meaning. Jaska knelt in the water, his head drooping forward. He probably would have collapsed into the shallow, brackish water had not Macha been supporting him from behind.

"One of the slimy buggers got around his neck. I know some bones broke before you killed the thing. Help me get him to a dry spot and I'll work on him," she said as he arrived before them.

Argall reached down and lifted his friend over one shoulder, groaning slightly at the weight on his bruised shoulder. Jaska was far from light and was thicker and heavier than Argall despite being shorter. He carried the Pohjolan sorcerer out of the small lake, laying him gently only the slightly muddy edge near the hill.

"Or you could do that," Macha said. "You are strong, Erm-Gilt-Hermian. Perhaps he's right; you do have the gifts needed for saving your kingdom."

"Jaska said that? He never said as much to me," Argall said.

Macha dropped to the unconscious man's side, pulling a copper amulet in the shape of an oval leaf. She incanted for a moment, touched the medallion with one finger, and stood upright.

"Well, he wouldn't, would he?" she said. "It might not be true. Many pits you could fall down in the future."

"What is that?" he asked, pointing at the amulet.

"A healing charm. My cousin, Dian Cécht, gave me a few as gifts before I went out looking for trouble. They've kept me alive more than a few times," she added.

"Oh," Argall said, staring at the metal leaf. "I thought you would just wave your hands, chant, and Jaska would be fine."

Macha chuckled and shook her head, her crimson curls bouncing. "Like most of your kind, you think magic is a cure to all ills. It isn't. In some ways, it can be worse. Healing magic is a delicate art, one that performed improperly could destroy lives. I have not the mind for such powers. Yon sleeping man has none of that himself. Like me, he probably knows a few roots and plants that can help, but healing magic? Rarer than a hen with teeth."

"I had no idea," Argall said.

Macha patted him on the shoulder with the same amused fondness parents use when their child makes a particularly clever remark.

"Nor should you bother with such rot. Leaving that nonsense to the likes of us. Now, head across these waters and look for a trail that leads up a high ridge. There should be a cave or some such within and you'll find who sent the demon after you. Clean the axe before you go."

"You two will follow?" Argall asked, accepting a rough cloth from her, and polishing the surface of his borrowed weapon.

"In a few hours. The magic will take some time and he'll wake needing a lot of food and water. Once himself's strength is back, we will catch up," she said, shooing him away.

Argall nodded, lifted a hand in farewell, and waded around the lake. The multi-tentacled horror was no longer in evidence, its appendages having slipped beneath the surface. Keeping his axe at the ready, he circled the muddy edges of the waters before stepping onto a rocky ridge.

The reddish rocks were broken and filled with jutting sharp edges. Despite that, climbing was easy, the boulders forming a pseudo-staircase up the hill and downward. On the other side were three jutting summits, each approximately fifty or more feet upward and laying close to each other. There were no sounds or movements ahead, with only the massive, yellow-orange sun beating down on his head with relentless force.

Staring at the rocks, Argall chose the center of the three since it appeared the most difficult of the trio for climbing. The edges of the boulders appeared slightly sharper and harsher there, giving him a sense of foreboding.

"If my enemy lays there, I shall face it now," he thought as he stepped onto the first rock.

CHAPTER LIX

Suddenly, a small sword flashed through the air, striking the obese eunuch's neck. The metal shattered upon impact, but he staggered under the force, his hand slackening slightly. Soroe wriggled free, gagged, and collapsed. She panted for breath as Padhoum turned back towards Deena and Nikke.

The latter tossed aside the broken handle of a sword, reaching for a dagger in her belt. Deena circled to the side, a pair of throwing knives in her small hands.

"Have you not learned?" Padhoum asked, licking his lips slowly. "I cannot be harmed by you. Swords, daggers, arrows, lances… I even had a boulder dropped on me. I can walk through a volcano and only my clothing shall burn away, while I remain untouched. I am better than you."

"Let's test that theory," Nikke said stepping forward and thrusting a blade into the palace majordomo's oversized belly.

The wicked weapon sliced through the encompassing robes before bouncing from the flabby flesh beneath. Padhoum giggled, spread his hands wider and did not advance.

"Please, do try again," he said. "I will give you three attacks. Then I shall beat you to death. Or you may kneel at my feet and receive the flesh of Moloch. You will join my children and live until the God accepts you into his embrace."

Nikke did not reply to these comments, but sheathed her blade, tilted her head left and right and ran forward. Her fist crashed into Padhoum's mouth and the eunuch's head snapped backwards. She followed this blow with a kneed to his stomach, sending him reeling backwards, where he tripped over a kneeling Deena.

The palace eunuch landed hard on his back, turning immediately onto his front, and pushing himself into a kneeling position.

Deena leaped to her feet, jumped into the air, and landed upon Padhoum's broad back, sending him sprawling again. She rolled off him a second before Nikke's feet crashed down on his spine. The powerful Finder stepped off his body and reached down, grabbing Padhoum by the scruff of the neck.

"You cannot harm me, fool!" he said. "Knock me down, and I shall rise again and again, and tear your limbs from your body."

Nikke did not reply but lifted Padhoum up by his neck and the rear of his robe. With a grunt, she pressed him upwards, over her head. His arms and legs flailed uselessly as Deena dragged Soroe away from the idol of Moloch.

"What are you doing? Lower me at once! I command you! Put me down!" Padhoum said, his voice rising to a screaming pitch.

"I... planned... on it..." Nikke said, panting each word as she took three staggering steps towards the burning metal chest of Moloch.

"Moloch!" Padhoum said. "Save me! My children, help me!"

Nikke grunted stepped forward with her left foot and dumped the obese eunuch into the dancing, molten hot flames of the metal Moloch statue. He shrieked as he fell, the wail growing in volume before falling, fading, and finally downing away.

A low moan emerged from the depths of the fire and a charred hand reached through the gap. Deena threw one of her knives, the handle striking the blackened, shattering the burnt flesh and blackened bones. The remains of the hand fell back into the flames, vanishing from sight.

"What just happened?" Soroe asked, rising to her feet.

"I had a vision and realized something we should have figured out," Deena said.

"Which was?" Soroe asked, watching as the flames diminished before her eyes.

"Nobody ever fed the fire. We saw the thing in that ceremony. No wood, no charcoal, nothing. It had to be some type of bad magic. While you was talking with the fat bastard, I let Nikke know. The rest was easy," she added.

"No matter how protected you are," Nikke said, pulling a waterskin out and gulping for a moment, "no matter how strong, everyone is weak on their face and held up in the air. The rest was easy. If you throw someone who is not a trained brawler down, they always turn over and push themselves up. The real trick was seeing if I could hold him over my head."

"I saw you once do that to a guy his size who tried to rob beggars. One-Lip Snurt and his trusty club. I figured unless you were growing soft, you could do it again," Deena said. "Looked like you didn't do it as easily this time, though..."

"Snurt weighed about half as much as that one, so shut your lips, thief. I handled him just fine. You were the one who was slow in getting behind him," the Finder said.

"Ha!" the young oracle replied, "I was getting bored waiting for you to get close enough to push him backwards."

"Now look…" Nikke said, her hands balling into fists.

"Before you two begin brawling again," Soroe said, "we need to search these ruins. Somewhere there's a clue as to who helped Padhoum create this religion of madness."

Deena and Nikke stared at each other for a moment before breaking out into slow smiles. They turned in Soroe's direction and relaxed, nodding at the same time.

"Can't be too hard to find," Deena said. "That pig was too sure of himself. He believed that a demon would make him impossible to kill."

"Well," Nikke said. "He was close to that."

Soroe shook her head. "Not really. You see, demons dislike people who want to extend their lives. There are always a few ways of killing their servants. Nobody can name every substance. Each and every one not mentioned will be a vulnerability."

"Huh," Deena said, "so if he never mentioned something silly like flowers, you could find a way of using them in killing him?"

"Exactly," the Queen-Elect said. "One particularly nasty witch died when a farmer, in desperation, buried her in hay. He threw so much on the pile, she couldn't breathe and died. Oh, and Nikke…?"

"Yes?" the Finder asked, turning back towards Soroe.

"Thank you for saving my life. Were it not for you and Deena, my soul would be in the possession of Moloch. If there's any way I can ever repay you…" Soroe said, her voice trailing off.

"I'm sure I can think of something... or many somethings... but right now I'm more concerned with this place. We're in a ruined temple to a demon god with crazed, blind savages everywhere. We need to search this place and get out before we end up some maniac's dinner," Nikke said.

"For once," Deena said, "I agree with her. Pick up your feet, lady. We need to be out of here soon."

CHAPTER LX

The reddish rocks were broken and filled with jutting sharp edges. Despite that, climbing was easy, the boulders forming a pseudo-staircase up the hill and downward. On the other side were three jutting summits, each approximately fifty or more feet upward and laying close to each other. There were no sounds or movements ahead, with only the massive, yellow-orange sun beating down on his head with relentless force.

Staring at the rocks, Argall chose the center of the three since it appeared the most difficult of the trio for climbing. The edges of the boulders appeared slightly sharper and harsher there, giving him a sense of foreboding.

"If my enemy lays there, I shall face it now," he thought as he stepped onto the first rock.

Testing the boulder, he rose, grasping the gentler edge of the stone overhead. The rock crumbled between his fingers sending a shower of pebbles and dirt across his face. Argall closed his eyes, shook the dirt from his face, and reached again.

The lip of the above boulder held steadily, give the Erm-Gilt-Hermian a method of pulling himself higher onto the ridge. He moved slightly to the right, choosing a less direct path up the hillock. By circling slowly upward, the trail a slow, lazy, serpentine route, the danger of the climb became minimal.

Two hours passed and the summit was in sight, yet no cave or entryway emerged across the hill's surface. Argall wondered if he made a mistake as he reached the crest and regarded the vast, open Kurgan steppes. He could see for miles, yet nothing appeared visible in the horizon.

The summit of the vast hill was a flat, plateau covered in vast semi-circular flint boulders. The rocks were covered in a thin layer of crimson dust. A warm, dry wind blew across his position, yet otherwise there was no evidence of life about the Scarlet Hills.

He was about to return, when an odd scent tickled his nose, halting him in place. At first it was a mere trace, something unpleasant that distantly plucked at his memory. Then the scent grew stronger, more distinct, a horrendous, grotesque, inhuman rot that fell away a moment later.

The he recalled it, the scent quite distinct and reminding him of where he encountered it before.

The throne room... when we were attacked by the... what did Jaska call them... the dimmer.... no, the Children of Dimme-kur... call them demons and that is enough! Their leader swore revenge upon me, he thought and knelt onto the hard surface of the hill's crest.

Nothing was in evidence, but the scent reappeared twenty or so minutes later, before vanishing once again. It took some time, but Argall discovered that the further he moved from the summit, the fewer times the terrible odor of the demon appeared.

Climbing on top of the highest boulder, he would have laughed of the sight weren't so ludicrous. The boulder's center was hollow, a circular opening leading to a dark shaft with gentle yellow light distantly below. Wriggling closer, Argall spotted several hand and foot holds that he could use for lowering himself into the gap, but the bottom appeared quite distant based on the tiny light.

No rope, he thought ruefully, *Where is fifty foot of good hemp line when you need it?*

Seeing no other option, Argall lowered himself into the gap, always keeping one hand and one foot attached to the wall. This was a lesson every child in the Erm-Gilt-Herm learned very young. The treacherous wastes were fraught with danger, but the elders of the tribes always repeated that saying as the youth joined the hunting and raiding parties.

One hand, one foot, no less, they would say. Miss one and you may lose everything.

At a young age, every boy and girl obeyed this command, but as they grew older, a sense of recklessness often entered their character. Soon someone disobeyed the oldster's words, pretending they did not hear the regular chant or openly disregarding the rule. The result was someone always fell, whether to their death or severe injury. It usually only took one plummet before the truth of the statement sunk in and disobedience ceased.

I was lucky I only broke my foot in that fall, Argall thought as his foot secured itself in the wall.

He then stopped, supported in the gap by his feet and requiring no exertion in remaining in place. Squatting downward, he gazed into the gloom, adjusting his eyes to the murk below. Closing his eyes for a full minute, Argall opened both lids slowly, viewing the darkness with greater ease.

The crawlspace he used ceased five feet below where he stood. Below lay a massive drop, at least fifty or more feet to a floor covered in jutting stalagmites. The steady drip of water broke the silence, and he spotted several long, hanging stalactites hanging from the cave's roof.

I could try and lower myself by those rocks, he thought, *but the ones back home were always brittle and slick to the touch. That might have to be my last resort.*

The dreadful odor of the Children of Dimme-kur rose to his nostrils and a loud, almost violent movement of air swish past where he hung like a vast pale bat. The odor receded seconds later followed by a quick movement of air.

It is flying around for some reason, he thought, *it's all in the timing. Like a proper sword swing."*

Argall closed his eyes and counted as the stench of the creature grew and receded two more times. Opening his eyes, he drew his blade, counted to four, and pulled his feet in, falling downward.

The Erm-Gilt-Hermian chieftain's hard, heavy body fell six feet and for an instant he wondered if he mistimed the drop. Then Argall's legs and torso slammed into a massive, bony object, knocking the window from his chest.

A high-pitched screech like that of a monstrous bat pierced the air and their bodies spiraled downward. The massive arms spread again, and their path evened out, allowing Argall a moment to entwine his legs around the demon's narrow torso. A second shriek emerged from the beast, this one dropping into a growling rumble by the end.

The Child of Dimme-Kur's flight path rose, fell, spun, dipped, and flipped, yet Argall held on. His eyes adjusted to the spinning, spiraling images before his eyes, realizing that they were moving lower with each movement.

Waiting several seconds, Argall flatted his body against the chimerical back of demon. Just as they flattened out, he plunged his dagger into the creature's neck, thrusting deep with both hands.

A gurgling squawk emerged from the monster, whose wings shuddered briefly. Seeing that he was about ten feet from the ground, Argall released his hold on the beast, fell the remaining distance and rolled upright. The Child of Dimme-kur landed several feet away, reaching behind and pulling the blade free from its neck.

Argall drew his borrowed axe, swinging hard for the monster's neck. The beast, still distracted, only looked up in time to see the edge strike its plated neck. The creature fell but rose to its knees a second later. Three swings of the blade later and the horrific head popped free, rolling several feet across the floor.

"The murderer of children, Argall of the Erm-Gilt-Herm?" a familiar voice said. "The Child of Dimme-Kur that you just destroyed was mere days-old. I guess it is true, humans are simply demons without our physical gifts."

Akhkhazu, the high priestess of Dimme-kur slithered into view, standing in a thin pool of light. Her yellow, faceted eyes blazed with an inner fury and her long prehensile tail lashed the air slowly as she strode closer.

"Your kind seek my death," Argall said. "Why should I not kill your followers?"

The Child of Dimme-kur growled briefly, her talons clicking as she extended them.

"Had that one been a week or two older," she said, stopping twenty feet from his position, "she would have had full use of her tail. Then you would be a stiffening corpse."

"How unfortunate," Argall said. "I feel simply terrible about my actions."

"Liar!" the creature said, flashing elongated fangs.

Argall smiled, "The first correct thing you said to me so far. Now, how were you able to send demons against me when you have no magic?"

"Why should I explain this to a dead man?" Akhkhazu asked.

She leaped forward and spun, her tail slicing through the air towards Argall's chest. He blocked the attack with the flat of the axe and fell back. The impact sent him stumbling backwards, his hands stinging from the metal's vibrations.

"You are fast, Argall," the Dimme-kur high priestess said, "yet you are only human. You will tire or stumble soon. If you surrender, I shall make your end a swift one."

Argall chuckled and shook his head, "I do not need Jaska's sense of smell to know you are frightened, demon. I have brought about the death of four of your kind, though the other three with help. Destroying you will cleanse the world, I believe."

Akhkhazu snarled and took to the air, vanishing into the gloom. The odor surrounding her grew and fell from moment to moment, with the harsh air movements from above only indicating her flight.

Argall kept his ears open, moving into a patch of darkness, his axe gripped tightly in each hand. He turned swiftly left and right, believing he heard the approach of the chimerical horror. Flashes of serpentine flesh shot past on the edge of his vision, disorienting him momentarily.

Then the heady scent of the creature was about him and Argall found himself thrown forward. His back burned for several seconds before turning numb. Scrambling to his feet, Argall felt warmth down his back and a pulling sensation against his spine.

Gripping the axe even tighter, he backed away from his current location, seeing the droplets of blood left in his wake. The only light from this cavern came from the opening above and a series of glowing rocks on the south side. The depth of the cave was impossible to discern from these sparse trails of illumination and Argall found himself stumbling from the slick stone floor.

Stalactites and stalagmites lined the chamber, casting a demoniac air to the stygian, dank, depths. It felt as if he was stuck in the very mouth of monstrous great beast like the terrible ice dragon that is said to sleep beneath the wastes of the Erm-Gilt-Herm. The steady drip, drip, drip, of the water from above was the only other sound beyond that of the terrible floating above.

"For all your bravery, human," Akhkhazu said, her voice echoing, "you are naught but a frightened bug here. Tearing you apart slowly shall be your payment for harming my sisters."

Laughter shook the chamber, the sound rising and falling. The malicious, sadistic notes of the merriment sent a shiver down Argall's spine.

A moment later, he cried out as a pair of taloned fingers racked across his cheek, sending him stumbling. Righting himself, Argall found himself pressed against a massive slick column that jutted from the floor and appeared to reach the very ceiling of the cave. There was a gray black wall behind the enormous tooth shaped structure, and it appeared as if there was no gap.

Smiling slightly, Argall remembered the teachings of his and Maghee's fathers, the wisdom of the icy, misty lands:

"If your eyes fail, use your nose, your ears, even your skin. Only the weak surrender when darkness falls across the land."

Closing his eyes, he waited, listening, sniffing, feeling the very surroundings of the cavern. The high priestess was a swift flier, yet her movements did appear to be in a simple pattern... that of a pair of crisscrossing circles with an occasional straight line burst of speed. This was approximate for him, but close enough based on the scent and motion of air.

I must lure her close, make her attack recklessly, he thought.

Dropping to one knee, Argall let his axe droop forward. His breathing became ragged, and he hunched his back slightly. A low, barely audible whimper of pain leaked from his lips and Argall lowered his head several inches.

The sadistic screams of laughter grew louder for several seconds before cutting off entirely. Argall heard her flight on the left of his body, and he turned slightly right, pivoting his head up and down as if searching for Akhkhazu in the dark. Her flight shifted and the demon's path turned downward, her vast claws slicing through the air.

Just as she reached his position, the Erm-Gilt-Hermian chieftain slammed his back into the stone column and swung his axe in a direct arc towards her barreling body. The high priestess of Dimme-kur shrieked with surprised, vainly shifting in mid-air.

The terrible, sharp edge of the borrowed axe crashed into her face, cutting off Akhkhazu's howl of shock. Her right wing touched the ground an instant later, snapping and sending her spiraling over and over into the stygian darkness.

The impact tore the axe from Argall's grasp, and he heard the metal weapon crashing and bouncing off into the gloom. Akhkhazu rose to her feet, piteous sounds escaping from her mouth as she limped towards the north side of the cavern. Argall followed, looking for the axe as he shadowed her past the glowing stones and into a sub-cave off to the left.

Following the Child of Dimme-kur was simplicity now, her whines, the terrible odor, the coppery scent of her vitae as if spilled across the stone, and now the bizarre sound that resembled that of leather being scraped across stone. Akhkhazu was gravely injured, which was good, but that did not mean she was helpless.

A wounded animal fights fiercer, Argall thought, *and I am weaponless and hurt.*

He followed at a close distance, searching for a means of attacking his enemy. The few loose stones he found were mere pebbles and wound barely bruise him let alone a dangerous demon. He balled his hands in tight fists both out of a desire to destroy his enemy as well as a need to keep ready.

The cavern suddenly opened into a small chamber, one better lit than the one they just left. Golden beams of light peaked out from every angle, adding a bizarre kaleidoscopic affect to the gaping cave. In the center of the chamber lay a red stone circle, one that was of a darker hue than the rocks upon the hills outside.

Akhkhazu stumbled to the far end of the circle, touched the side, and performed that action three times to other points of the oval. Her whines and moans increased in volume and Argall realized that the demon was speaking in her own language. The sounds were a bizarre combination of clicks and sounds that were remarkably similar to that of human speech, but just distinct enough to remain quite inhuman.

A light glimmered upon the edges of the scarlet circle, a pulsing green illumination that dazzled for a moment before vanishing. The four points Akhkhazu touched moments ago burst into green flames, each exuding a bizarre rune while growing in intensity.

The Child of Dimme-kur sighed loudly, relief within the exhalation. Several seconds later a green triangle appeared between Argall and Akhkhazu, the center a wavering mass of energy resembling water. The injured demon shuffled forward and stepped through the vast object, vanishing from view.

No, Argall thought. *This one must not escape!*

Without thinking, he dashed forward, diving the last few feet as the odd triangle diminished before his eyes. His body felt suddenly engulfed by a cold, liquid, unlit, void and he was momentarily blinded and disoriented by the lack of sensations.

Then Argall fell, landing in a heap on a vast pile of shattered, broken bones. A stench like that of a vast abattoir overwhelmed his nostrils and he viewed several gore-stained brown rats scurrying near his fallen form.

"Argall, son of Argall," a sweet, gentle voice said, "heir to the legacy of the corrupt land of Atlantis. Welcome to my home… I am she to whom you shall serve… I am Dimme-kur…"

Argall rolled over just as a vast shape fell over his body. His eyes widened at the sight and he knew the true danger had arrived.

CHAPTER LXI

"I have no idea what we are searching for," said Soroe. "Forgive me, I am still shaken by the idea that Padhoum was so... so... twisted..."

"The bastard was a eunuch," Deena said. "Just having that done to you has to twist your mind. I mean... they cut off his... you know... forcing someone to do that would mess any man up..."

Soroe shook her head as they moved away from the cool metal statue of the bovine demon god.

"No," she said, "that is a voluntary choice. Only one who begs for the procedure is allowed to submit to it. Once that occurs, they gain powerful positions in Atlantis. The government is run by eunuchs and Padhoum was one of the most important."

"One of," Nikke said, "yeah, I've met that type. Having someone above them twists their minds and they start acting crazy. Want to bet gold that was his reason?"

Soroe and Deena shook their heads, with the latter frowning as she turned in a slow circle.

"This Padhoum," she said, "he was the one who pretended he didn't know about the secret doors and all that?"

"Yes," Soroe said, "why?"

"You'll see, if stop interrupting me," Deena said. "He liked to dress nice? Wears expensive robes and smell nice?"

"Yes," Soroe repeated.

"Really fussy about everything and it had to be done right," the former thief said, turning in a circle, "would get angry if a knife didn't shine on the dining table?"

"Yes," Soroe said a third time, not hiding her exasperation.

Deena scanned to the left and right and pointed to the right of where Nikke stood. A small wall lay behind the Finder and there was a slight overhand above that area.

"Look over there," she said, "tap the wall for a false door."

Nikke looked quizzical for a moment, shrugged, and led them to the ten-foot square space. There were four stones remaining upon the wall as well as a single circular piece that appeared to once be a statue's plinth.

The Finder pulled a dagger from her belt and tapped the stones in the wall. The first and second sections of wall sounded solid, a hard tap that did not yield. The third echoed lightly, a hollow noise quite distinct from the previous.

Deena pushed in next to Nikke, felt around for several seconds, smiled, and depressed the stone with two fingers. A small paneling swung open, a square space about two feet wide and high.

"There's a wooden box inside," Deena said, "but I'll bet there's a pressure sensor. Give me a few seconds... Ah-ha, there it is!"

She touched another section of the wall followed by a second and removed a plain box made from light wood. She studied the container for several seconds, shrugged and handed it over to Soroe.

"No traps," she said.

"OK," Nikke said, "what just happened? You were a street thief who robbed fruit stands. How did you become so knowledgeable about traps and locks?"

"A valid question," Soroe said. "You are a puzzle, Deena."

"Long story," Deena said, shrugging. "One that we don't have time to go into now. My story isn't as simple as I pretend sometimes. Now, open the damn box."

Soroe opened the lid, reached within, and pulled out a single yellow jewel and a copper pendant connected to a simple leather thong. The jewel was the size of a man's fingernail with rude, crude facets that looked quite ugly even in the sparse light.

"That looks like glass," Nikke said. "Not worth anything."

"Then why would he hide it so carefully?" Deena asked. "It must have some use."

"Who knows what a eunuch that worships devils thinks? Maybe he used it as a toy?" Nikke said.

"I think," Soroe said, returning the jewel to the box, "that it has some mystical use. But I do not know what, and would need time and a safe location to find out. Look at this item."

She opened her hand, revealing the amulet in the center of her palm. It was teardrop-shaped and carefully etched; the design detailed yet quite easy discerned. The face of a beautiful woman lay upon the upper portion, her face angular yet lovely in an alien style.

Below her lay a bloated figure, an eight-legged monstrosity that appeared attached to the attractive lady who smiled widely from above. Several light letters lay across the edge, though they were of a lined script quite different from Atlantean.

"What is that?" Nikke said.

"It's a prayer pendant," Deena said and rolled her eyes at their astonished faces. "I stole a few from some pilgrims. Gold and Iron temple ones were the easiest you could sell. Never saw one of these before."

"Neither have I," Soroe said. "However, I recognize the meaning and the word. It is the name of a weaving goddess known as Lady Tsuchigumo."

"I'm afraid to ask this, but I will," Deena said, closing her eyes for a moment, "what does that mean?"

"Tsuchigumo translates literally as Earth-Spider. She is the goddess of spiders who is said to weave a monstrous web that will one day engulf the universe," Soroe said. "This is worse than I feared."

"Keep going," Nikke said. "We need to get out of here before the crazy cannibals return. Where are we heading?"

"Two places," Soroe said. "First, to an infamous, dangerous land known as the Forest of the Jorogumo..."

Nikke, who had led them back to the trail, whirled her direction, her eyes wild.

"Are you insane? Those woods are haunted by demon women with spiders for bodies! They eat anything they catch!" she said.

"Yes, I know. However, they also possess wisdom that could keep us alive in an even deadlier location," Soroe said.

"Gold and Iron," Deena said from behind, her voice a near wail, "you don't mean...?"

Soroe sighed and replied, "Yes. The answer to saving Atlantis from these demons lays in the most dangerous place in the world... the Isle of Spiders..."

"I should have stayed a guard for beggars," Nikke said as the plunged deeper into the plains of Lamb'Ha.

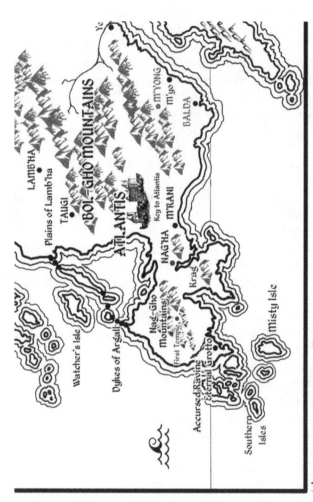

CHAPTER LXII

The being calling itself Dimme-kur was a sight that had the brave Argall scrambling backwards, seeking a means of reaching his feet. Twelve feet tall or more, she possessed a massive, bloated body that was ostensibly human in shape. Massive pendulous breasts hung low across a round, fleshy paunch and her flesh rippled like waves when she moved. Her skin was an emerald green stained with brown and crimson gore that fell away in flakes when she stepped. Her arms and legs were short for her size, as round as barrels and flapped like green wings as she moved.

These were secondary factors in Argall's mind, ones he recognized but did not focus upon at this moment. It was her head, the conical dome that lay atop her broad shoulders.

The object was dome shaped, a sickly yellow-green hue and covered in dozens, possibly hundreds of tiny pus-leaking pustules. The protrusions moved of their own accord, wriggling in various stages of agitation. It was only after a second look that the Erm-Gilt-Hermian warrior realized a fact that nearly shattered his sanity.

Within each of the jiggling abscesses lay a tiny figure, a near microscope lifeform. Argall's sharp vision comprehended the implications... These were the children of Dimme-kur. The monstrous reptile demon women he battled were born in this horror's head!

The image was horrific, nauseating, and frightening to the eye. Argall's mind shrieked with fear, yet his inner fury grew with greater intensity. Thews tensing and exploding a primeval killing rage overtook him and he snarled a challenge at the demon.

"Oh dear," Dimme-kur said, her voice dripping with sarcastic amusement, "I do believe I have upset you. Come here, human child... Mother will sooth your fears... Come to me..."

A heady musk exuded from her bloated body, wafting from her upon invisible trails of scent that tickled the nose. Argall found himself overcome by the powerful odor, his head reeling as if he were intoxicated.

"Come to me, child," Dimme-kur said, her voice a sensual whisper.

Argall stepped forward, his arms raising against his will. He took a second step towards Dimme-kur as her flabby arms spread wide for a grotesque embrace. The fat across her naked stomach then rippled, the motion becoming violent as the Erm-Gilt-Hermian slowly strode closer towards her demoniac embrace.

A split appeared in the horror's paunch, a wide, upward, semi-circle that spread for the length and breadth of terrible torso. The slice expanded, grew wider and a long red tongue slithered through the opening, spittle spreading across the chamber.

A vast cavernous mouth appeared upon Dimme-kur's body, ivory incisors in the shape of tiny daggers filling the gaping maw. A gurgling sound of amused triumph emerged from the unseen depths and the sausage shaped fingers began flexing as the Erm-Gilt-Hermian chieftain closed the distance.

Argall fought against the pungent scent, knowing it would mean his death. His mind screamed and he found himself growling from the depths of his chest. This was not the bestial snarl he heard from Jaska earlier, but a primeval human sound…a savage, ancient, rage that lingered within his race.

"What?" Dimme-kur asked, halting in her waddling tracks, "You resist? This is unheard of… Your race is too easily led by your sexual urges."

Argall crouched low, gazing about the chamber for the first time. He stood in a massive single room; a well-lit chamber illuminated by various pale jewels issue a soft, white light. Bones littered the floor in heaps, most shattered and spread haphazardly across the floor. A towering opening leading to a larger space, one in which a golden, glimmering light emerged.

Unwilling to stand in this death chamber, Argall scooped up several random remains and hurled them into the open mouth across the body of Dimme-kur. The jaws closed and crunched down upon the bones, spitting them out in disgust as the Erm-Gilt-Hermian chieftain ran for the next chamber. The heavy thud of the demon's fleshy feet followed, but her pace was far slower than his based on the trailing echoes.

The next room was one that nearly halted his step, momentarily forgetting the hungry horror at his rear. The room was gigantic, a palace sized space whose ceilings were hundreds of feet above his head. The floor of the chamber was made from alternating metals, gold, silver, platinum, and other precious metals. The walls were covered in precious tapestries, works of art so lovely they must be beyond the skills of humans. Beautiful statues stood upon high plinths, some so tall he could not view the summit.

And everywhere else lay treasure. Sparkling jewels in every color, soaring piles of coins made from metal, armor and weapons with deep jewel encrusted etchings, silken clothing that appeared both sublimely lovely and practical...there appeared to be no end to the inconceivable wealth.

"Thief!" Dimme-kur said, her shriek echoing and carrying every direction, "To me, my daughters! Come to me, a thief comes to rob your mother of her treasures!"

Shrieking cries sounded in the distance, ones that Argall recognized immediately. They were the shrieks of the Children of Dimme-kur... Monsters that nearly killed him when he was armed and ready for a battle. Right now, he was injured, unarmed, and had their massive mother seeking his death too.

One of these weapons and helms had best be practical as well as pretty, he thought and ran for a pile that lay to his left.

CHAPTER LXIII

"Hello females," the Lamb'Hai chieftain said as they broke free of the tall grasses into the bright sunlight. "I see you survived!"

"Did we?" Soroe asked. "I wasn't sure."

The bandit leader laughed, stroked his golden eagle and nodded, "Humor. A sign that you're alive. The *idugan* sensed your triumph and sent me here to bring you back. She said you shall need food and healing. She offers both and the freedom of our camp."

"We thank her, male," Nikke said, placing a hand over her heart and bowing her head. "You shall abide by the ways of your tribe and guard you while we remain among your people."

The chieftain nodded, grinned, released his hunting bird and pulled out his pipe.

"You are well-learned in the ways, hunting female. Should you wish a place in our band, you are welcome," he said. "We brought no mounts since the *idugan* moved our camp on the other side of the hill. A short walk for you. Me, I go and hunt. The giggling savages are wandering freely this day and we shall cull their numbers."

He wheeled his horse to the left and plunged into the grasses, a host of twenty or more of his fellow Lamb'Hai following. They were armed with bows, lances, spears and swords, a fearsome sight made all the more frightening by the massive circling eagles overhead.

"A cull?" Deena asked,."With the death of the fat bastard, could those poor people be saved?"

Soroe shook her head. "Doubtful. Remember when we met, and you told me that the cannibals giggle all the time? How they seem insane? That is not because of some spell, it's a disease. When you eat brains, you may catch a sickness called the Laughing Death. It afflicted Atlantis when the priests of the Temple of Gold and Iron ate the bodies of those sacrificed to Apophis. The first Argall and Soroe banned the eating of other humans for that reason."

"OK," Nikke said, "How do you know this... More to the point, *why* do you know this?"

The high priestess of the Temple of Light shrugged. "When we returned from finding the Soul gem, I had some free time. I used it to research the cannibals of the Plains of Lamb'Ha since that disturbed me greatly. I found the answer and discovered that even the healing magic of the light cannot cure that disease."

"You have weird reading habits, lady," Deena said, and they shared a laugh while entering the camp.

An elderly man whose wobbling step indicated either a lifetime in the saddle or being born with bowlegs, waved them to a small tent near that of the *idugan.* A gray-haired man dressed in a furred hooded cape followed them inside. He examined their cuts, scrapes, and injuries with a brusque clinical manner and hard, leathery fingers.

To each injury he applied a poultice made from roots, a wooden bandage, and a wooden cup filled with a noxious smelling brew. He never spoke but urged them with hurrying-up motions while pointing to their lips.

Deena sniffed the concoction, recoiled, her face demonstrating her revulsion.

"What is this, some type of poison? Or one of those drinks that help you puke all over the place? My mother gave that to me once as a punishment for eating the last piece of bread."

Nikke shook her head. "It's a drink called *ayrag*. It tastes bad, but it can be pretty potent if made right. Drink it. It'll help us sleep."

She downed hers, handed back the cup and bowed to the unspeaking man. Soroe and Deena copied her actions, with the latter appearing revolted and turning slightly pale at the deeply sour taste and odd, bitter chunks within the brew.

The medicine man nodded once and swept out just as three children appeared holding bowls of food. They giggled, bowed, ran to the center of the empty tent, and busily lit a small fire in the pit in the center. With a second bow, they ran out, leaving the three women alone.

As they busily ate, weariness crept over them, and their talk grew softer. Finally, they finished their food and lay down upon the small, furred palettes set out for them near the fire.

Just as sleep began to overtake them, Deena asked in a soft, almost slurring tone, "By the way... what is *ayrag*?"

"Fermented mare's milk," Nikke replied. "The favored alcohol of the Lamb'Hai"

"I hate you," Deena said, her voice trailing away as she fell asleep.

CHAPTER LXIV

One of these weapons and helms had best be practical as well as pretty, Argall thought and ran for a pile that lay to his left.

Sadly, that was not the case in the set of weapons before him now. The sword was a long blade, as narrow as a toothpick with a sharp point and no edge. It would serve well as a stabbing weapon, but he doubted it would piece the thick hides of the Children of Dimme-kur. The helm was interesting, a wide car with horns protruding from the crest like some monstrous bull. A leather chinstrap was attached to the metal side, but he dropped it softly to the ground after a quick examination.

If someone hit the horn, he thought, *the blow might snap your neck. Useless.*

Another pile lay about ten feet away to his left and Argall immediately strode in that direction. A figure shuffled into his path, and he stepped back, recognizing the creature immediately.

Akhkhazu looked no better than earlier, her face still twisted from the impact delivered by the lost axe. Her wing appeared quite broken, bloody, and twisted. She angrily lashed the air with her ivory tail, sending showers of precious items spilling every direction. She hissed, but the sound was more of a sloppy spitting noise than that of an angry beast.

Argall ducked her tail, diving to his right and rolling up and onto his feet. Lunging forward, he extended his arm, the thin blade still in his fist. The tiny sharp point entered her single visible eye and a bubbling warble emerged from her lips. Her chimerical body fell back, ripping the sword from his grasp.

Not sparing a second glance, the Erm-Gilt-Hermian ran to the next set of weapons. The first was a vast, oversized spear that looked quite serviceable. An oversized war hammer with a small handle lay next to this weapon as was a long sword with a thick blade.

Preferring swords, he lifted the weapon and found himself impressed by the balance. This was a war weapon, a little too long for his preference, but useful. A tightly fitting helm with some runic script also appeared serviceable, covering his head and face but permitting easy vision.

A little more comfortable now, Argall stalked forward, seeking his enemies. It did not take long, with one of the Children of Dimme-kur alighting near his location.

"Clothing yourself with the weapons of dead warriors will not save you, human," she said. "Surrender and I shall make your end gentle."

"No," Argall shouted, swinging the sword between them. "I've killed your kind before. You die as easily as anyone else."

The demon woman snarled, leaping forward, her claws extended. Argall, prepared for such an attack, threw himself backward, swinging the sword towards the monster's body. The Child of Dimme-kur, like her sister Akhkhazu, screamed as the blade sank deep into her skull. She crashed to the ground near Argall, thrashing madly and snapping the sword in twain.

The Erm-Gilt-Hermian sighed, annoyed by the loss of another weapon. Picking up the long spear, he raised the weapon above his head and plunged the leaf shaped blade through the monster's convulsing back. The point pinned her to the ground and the Child of Dimme-kur quivered like a fly trapped in a spider's weapon.

Snatching up the hammer, Argall brought the maul down on the skull, shattering the bones and spreading black ichor across his body. Two swings later, the handle cracked, but the demon stopped moving.

Retrieving the spear, he glanced about, knowing his luck could not continue. So far, the pair he faced were foolish in their attacks, the first being enraged, the second underestimating his strength. The others would not be so foolish.

There has to be a truly useful weapon here, one like the sword my ancestor wielded, he thought, seeing, and rejecting sever more piles of weapons.

"Here!" a voice said from above. "He is here! The human murdered two of our sisters!"

Argall spotted a Child of Dimme-kur ten feet above his head. Raising his borrowed spear, he cast the weapon upwards, piercing the wing and sending the chimerical monsters spiraling down to the floor below.

Curse me for a fool, he thought as more forms appeared in the air, *I should have used the spear and held them off.*

That was his last thought as his back was suddenly aflame with pain. His body fell forward, crashing into a pile of gems that fell in a heap over his arms, legs, and torso. The noxious odor of another of those monsters appeared and he screamed in pain as one of the demon women sank her talons deep into his chest and propelled him across the room.

Vicious mocking laughter rang in his ears as he bounced down a pile of coins and collapsed in a heap. A pair of hard, scale-covered fists grabbed him by the legs, swung him in a circle and sent him spiraling through several stacks of treasure.

"Play with him, my daughters," Dimme-Kur said, her voice distant and off to the right. "But do not kill him. I want him alive to deliver unto him a lifetime of pain for his crimes he committed against your mother."

Argall, his vision wavering, pushed himself onto his hands and knees. He scrabbled about for a handhold, a means of rising, but the mound of coins about him merely shifted like water. His hand sank beneath the surface for a moment and a hard, circular object fell into his palm. Frowning, Argall tightened his grip, feeling warmth across his palm and arm.

I'm bleeding there too, he thought as he drew the item upwards. *I hope this is a scepter or a club… Something I can hit with at least."*

The warm sensation ran through his arm, spreading across his body. It was as if he had fallen into a gentle warm pool, a soothing bath that relaxed his muscles and removed a bit of the pain across his ailing body.

The terrible smell of the Children of Dimme-kur returned and he slowly turned, using his body's weight for the final yank. A shower of coins rained across his arm and chest and a brilliant yellow light flared through the air. A wailing shriek filled the air, and he smelled the scent of charred beef as well as the sound of two heavy objects striking the floor to his right.

Argall blinked several times, clearing his vision. Then his mouth dropped open at the sight before his eyes.

Clutched in his hand was a sword, an Atlantean blade in the style of the weapon he inherited from his father. This blade was older, with greater care and workmanship; however its hilt and grip were well-worn from use. An ancient sword, but one still very serviceable. Oh, and it was also on fire.

A yellow and blue flame danced along the blade's edge, exuding a powerful heat that simply warmed Argall. He smiled at the sword rising easily now as he spotted the two halves of a dead Child of Dimme-kur to his right. Apparently, the sword blade slice one as he pulled it free of the treasure horde.

Clapping the fallen helmet back on his head, Argall raised his weapon above his head and yelled out his war cry.

"For Atlantis!" he shouted, his words drowning out the terrified shrieks of the Children of Dimme-kur.

CHAPTER LXV

Once again, the trio sat in the wide tent of the Lamb'Hai *idugan*, though this time was quite a bit less terrifying than before. The shaman, a tiny woman with a soft, round face and eyes that appeared too ancient for her youthful countenance, sat across from them sipping away at a gourd filled with the juices of crushed fruit. This brew was sweet though a little cloying after a few swallows.

"You slept a full day," she said, "and I was surprised your rest was not longer. Your battle was short, but terrible. Very clever, kill the priest with his own power. I would not have thought of such a way."

"Deena had a vision of it," Nikke said. "Then we just used an old hunting trick to remove his strength."

"Why did Padhoum turn to that demon god?" Soroe asked.

The *idugan* lifted the pendant that handed her upon arriving in her tent. She tapped the image with one tiny finger.

"This is the one who knows. Tsuchigumo is no friend of our kind, but not an enemy. She simply *is…* and concerns herself with her people and her plans. If you find out how to survive her island, she will know the reason *Kerey Han*, whom you call Moloch the defiler, and the other children of Erlik pollutes the land."

"Others?" Soroe asked, tensing.

The shaman nodded her head sadly and slowly, "Yes, Queen in waiting. Across the lands, the children of the Great Darkness enter our world. Some are invited, others have slept here and have awakened. You weak-

269

ened the way fort this one, but he still seeks entry. Another battles to the north against your beloved. A third was invited in by evil witches and he is the worst of those foul beasts."

"I still don't know why the fat bastard had that pendant," Deena said. "If that spider lady is the enemy of his god, why would he want her things?"

The *idugan* chuckled and shook her head, "Who knows? Maybe the Defiler wanted to try and enslave the Earth-Spider. Maybe he planned on attacking her or weakening her power before arriving. Trying to understand the *tngri* is the way of madness. He had his reasons, and you will see if she will help or at least not hinder your battle. The more of Erlik's children are swept from the world, the better chance we have of surviving the battle."

"Wait, wait, wait," Deena said. "I thought if we stop Moloch and the one Argall is fighting, we keep Apophis or whatever you call him from coming!"

The shaman laughed, clapped her hands, and wiped tears from her eyes.

"Child," she said, "you are believing the tales humans use to hide from the *tngri.* We make up stories of one person or weapon that will destroy any evil from the lands. The truth is less enjoyable."

She leaned forward her face suddenly serious.

"Evil and good, black and white, night and day, life and death, front and back, up and down," she said, "they exist together. Both are always in the world and cannot be cleansed. Erlik, or whatever name we call him, is coming. Whether it is today, tomorrow, or one hundred years from now, we shall never know until he arrives. I believe he will come very soon. If we send back his children, he shall not be all-powerful. Whether he prevails or not is a question none may answer. Not even you, who sees the future."

"I think I understand," Soroe said. "Do you have any other advice?"

The *idugan* shrugged, handed back the amulet and said, "Try and survive. If you do, and a war begins, you will have the tribes of the Lamb'Hai at your side."

"Thank you," Soroe said while rising and bowing. "We had best get onto the road."

"My people will guide you," the shaman said, "and we shall give you food, water, and some money. The rest, you must do on your own. I would suggest avoiding the sea. The spirits are very unhappy there and storms are growing across the waters."

They made their thanks and within an hour were back on the road they left a short time ago with the Lamb'Hai. A long caravan of mules and oxen carts were ahead of them as well as a troop of armed mercenaries who stared their direction with hostile gazes.

"Ignore them," Nikke said. "They're part of a company I once met while fighting against some M'Yong rebels. They're prefer showy displays to actual battle."

"Sounds intelligent," Deena said. "Who would actually enjoy fighting in a war?"

"What do you mean by that, thief?" Nikke asked.

"I would explain it," Deena said, "but I'd have to stop and draw pictures in the dirt so you could understand the big words..."

Soroe sighed as the bickering commenced, though she was hiding a smile. At least, her trip into another land of danger would have some entertainment.

CHAPTER LXVI

A Child of Dimme-kur wing smoked and sizzled as the now dead owner fell in three pieces before his feet. The few remaining demon women had taken flight, screaming in terror after he butchered four of their number with single swings of the flaming sword.

"You dare?" Dimme-kur asked, her massive form somehow larger as she approached. "You murder my children, and you steal my treasures? You are a bug, Argall of Atlantis! A barbarian insect beneath my feet! I shall consume you and your soul shall feed my new young!"

The horrific, uncanny creature now stood twenty feet tall or more. Her body appeared leaner than before and the monstrous, razor fanged maw was larger and wider than Argall. Her enormous hands flexed slowly as she stopped about ten feet from the Erm-Gilt-Hermian warrior.

"How did you find that sword, you filthy unevolved ape? I buried the Sword of Argall beneath tons of metals and jewels over five centuries ago!" the demon woman said, her voice shaking with rage.

"We have two sayings amongst the Erm-Gilt-Herm that may apply to this puzzle," Argall replied. "The first is this, things that shall never stay buried are bad news, good gossip, and perfect weapons."

"And the second?" Dimme-kur asked, her hand slowly lifting.

"Oh, that?" Argall said. "Just this, shut up and fight!"

With that, he leaped forward, his blade held high, the flames crackling as he passed through the air. The demon goddess however was ready, snatching a massive marble statue from a nearby pedestal and hurling it at the Erm-Gilt-Hermian chieftain.

Argall sliced the statue in twain, sending the shards spiraling left and right. He landed in a crouch, only to find himself launched across the chamber by a back-handed slap by Dimme-kur. Bouncing end over end, the Gilt-Hermian landed on his back, exhaling loudly before regripping his sword. A happy smile crossed his face, and he leaped forward again.

Dimme-kur moved with incredible speed, her body a blur of motion. Yet to Argall she appeared almost slow. He grinned wider, flipped to the side, and brought his blade down in a chopping arc. The demon goddess moved aside in time, or at least most of her did. The flaming sword sliced through her arm, removing the massive appendage from the elbow.

Dimme-kur shrieked in agony and rage, swinging swiftly towards Argall, who ducked under her first blow and dived and rolled away from her second attack. Just as he rolled upwards, her foot lashed out, kicking him in the chest... or at least partially...

A second earlier, Argall raised his sword, the edge between him and Dimme-kur. The kick sliced the enor-mous appendage in half, with both pieces striking him in the chest. He felt several ribs break under the impact and a pair of shooting pains appearing like vast blades of ice stabbing into his sides. His breathing grew ragged, yet he rose again, weapon in hand.

Dimme-kur howled loudly, fell sideways, and then laughed. A loud ringing shriek of merriment shook the very walls of the enormous cave. She rose again, her body completely healed again.

"I am not some mere human or even as weak as my children," she said. "I am Dimme-kur, daughter of darkness. I am also known as *Shyngay Han*, the spirit of chaos, child of great Erlik. You think some mere blade can destroy me? Me? I am eternal, you pathetic bug! I am the mother of demons, and nothing can kill me!" she said.

Argall laughed and said, "Then I have nothing to lose!"

He ran forward, diving over her swinging arm, rolling to his feet, and slicing off her lolling tongue. The massive mouth opened wide in a sustained scream and the Erm-Gilt-Hermian dove forward, his blade raking across the lover row of sword shaped incisors. Falling flat, he rolled forward, his sword above his head.

The flaming blade sliced the right foot from Dimme-Kur, sending her sprawling forward. Rising, he removed the right foot and ran back several steps.

"I will kill you, human," Dimme-kur said as skin began forming around both feet.

Knowing this was so, Argall chuckled stepped to the right and swung his sword in a swift arc. He ran back three steps, placing his hands on the platform above where he swung and pushed. The pedestal did not yield for a moment, but then cracked, crumbled, and topped forward. An enormous statue of a man with a fish tail fell on top of the fallen demon goddess, pinning her beneath the tons of rubble.

Argall fell backwards, the impact shaking the floor and sending columns of treasure flying every direction. An avalanche of gold and jewels fell over her form, with only her horrific head visible as the dust cleared.

"You think this will hold me, insect? I am immortal! If it takes me a thousand years, I shall crawl from this wreckage and destroy your race," she said.

"Possibly," Argall said, his voice weak. "Though I think I will use a little advice my friend Jaska taught me. Nothing in the world can live without a head."

The Dimme-kur shrieked, her weak voice almost a whine that did not register in his hearing. Within a few seconds, the tone of her screams changed, the language bizarre and repulsive.

"*Ia... Father... Achamoth... Erlik... save me... help... mother... Shupnikkurat... n'gha'ghaa, bugg-shoggog...*" she said, her voice becoming a gurgling cry.

Revolted, Argall raised his sword high, screamed, "For Atlantis!"

He swung downwards, knowing this was the last of his strength. The globular head popped free, rolling across the mounds of precious treasure before coming to a rest. The weeping pustules shivered briefly before stilling and drooping. A moment later, the entire structure fell inwards, the form transforming into a foul-smelling yellow paste that disappeared after dripping onto the stone floor.

Sighing, Argall fell to his knees. He had no notion of where he was, nor the location of Jaska or Macha. Also, he had no food or water and his entire body ached terribly.

"I did find the sword and more wealth than anyone could want in ten lifetimes," he said to himself and laughed, wincing as the movement made his body ache.

Pushing himself upright, he limped several steps and picked up a gold encrusted lance. Using this once-precious item as a crutch, he stumbled towards the distant exit. His quest was not yet over, he suspected.

CHAPTER XLVII

"You are a most uninquisitive slave, Yerra," Hiisi said as he tossed a flesh-free femur before her kneeling form.

Yerra, who was both clean and dressed in clothing similar to that of her former royal robes, knelt before the terrible demon, her head lowered.

"I am a slave, master. A slave does not question, they obey."

The demon called Hiisi laughed, a pleasant sound that was oddly soothing upon the nerves. He laughed often, delighted by every experience. When he killed an entire village of farmers, eating them before their families, he laughed. When he stepped on a newly-formed beehive whose queen was birthing her young, he laughed. When he caused demon cults to kill each other for his amusement, he laughed. Every act of malice brought joy to this being.

"I see those silly northern witches have taught you well, little Yerra. However, this renders your conversation very dull to me. I shall allow you to ask me any question. If I do not like the inquiry, I shall tell you. If you ask the same ever again, I shall beat you. Otherwise, you may learn much at my feet. Here is a way for you to begin. Prince Hiisi is not my true name. I took that as an identity to enslave the Pohjolans. Now, ask me your question," he said.

Yerra did not raise her head, still frightened by the twisted form of this being. Shivering, she chose the proper phrasing of her question.

"What is the name you wish to be known by, master?"

The laugh came again, a delighted sound followed by a gentle pat upon her head.

"Good girl! You knew better than to fall for my trap and ask my true name. That would be very offensive if you learned it, and it would grant you power over me. The question you did ask was quite good. The answer is, I have thousands of names. Certain tribes of humans call me Yabash Han, the god of defeat; others use the name Caishen, or Pazuzu. I prefer a simpler name, one that expresses my true purpose..."

The horrific creature rose, laughed again, and said, "My name, my dear slave, is Azazel, and I shall bring about the end of this pathetic world and all its useless inhabitants."

"Yes, master," Yerra said, her eyes filling with tears as she knelt before her master.

NOW READ ON FOR A PREVIEW OF
MARGHAEL OF ATLANTIS
by Jean-Marc & Randy Lofficier

A novel taking place hundreds of years before this trilogy, in which you will discover the origins of the Brotherhood of the Axe, the secrets of the Wyrm, and more...

CHAPTER I

"Why this meeting, Leychert?"

The man who asked this question was wearing the traditional garb of a scribe of the Temple of Light: a white tunic, adorned with a single gold medal in the shape of an owl.

"It's something important, Benar. Anyway, that's what the Chief Scribe told me. You and I know that the scribes are always the last to be informed of such things."

The man who had just answered him was older than his companion; he, too, was dressed like a scribe, but his clothes looked more worn, frayed at the edges. After a short period of reflection, he continued:

"My guess is that we're going to hear some kind of statement from our new Commander. Also, perhaps, another speech from young Marghael."

Surprised, his companion looked up.

"Marghael?"

"Yes, Benar, I know, another one. It will be, what? His fifth speech this year? But, after all, it is his right. He is our oracle."

"I know, I know," sighed the other scribe. "But I never quite understood why the High Priest deemed it useful to appoint him at that post. For my part, I still can't see the point of having an oracle. We would be better off relying on the path of the stars, as our ancestors always did."

"I quite agree, but it's still a hotly debated topic. And Marghael is quite good at his job, wouldn't you say? Besides, he had the right to choose his position within the Temple, and that is what he did. You're familiar with the custom?"

"He aced all the rituals, didn't he?"

"Yes, he was... is a particularly gifted young man. It is even rumored that our last High Priest..."

"Sorry to cut you off, but I wasn't in Ceqir at the time. I was still in Atlantis. I've only been here six years. Is Marghael from this town, or did he come from the Eastern Isle to the South?"

"Neither, my dear Benar. He is a foundling."

"A foundling!"

"Now you understand my somewhat grudging admiration. Yes, he was found as a child, abandoned in the Scarlet Hills, north of here, in an area left untouched since the War of the Axe began. His parents were probably victims of an attack by the Brotherhood of the Axe. The boy survived by eating worms."

"That's extraordinary, Leychert! I did not know that."

"Our then-High Priest didn't want to turn him into a case, especially since he was doing so well in the Temple. Too well, in fact, considering his past. Old Fougax thought the boy was enchanted. Myself, I considered for a time another hypothesis..."

"Yes ? Which one?"

"That somehow his parent had been enchanted by the Dalaketnon, and somehow escaped."

"That's very improbable, Leychert. If the Dalaketnon exist at all, it's on the far side of the Bol-Gho... No survivors could have traveled all the way from there to the Scarlet Hills. In fact, except for a few isolated groups of resisters who've managed to survive, the entire area around Boulder Hills is still a vast, toxic wasteland inhabited by foul creatures too awful to even be named."

"But do we know this for a fact, Benar? Our knowledge comes mostly from the Warrior Caste."

"This discussion is pointless, Leychert! As a scribe, you should know that the Warriors are worthy of high praise for everything they do for us. I'm surprised you lend an ear to such malicious gossip."

"Don't be too severe with me, Benar! At my age, it is good to be less dogmatic and I do love to study our history... Did you know, for example, that Queen Yerra is rumored to have come from the North..."

The old scribe began a long and tedious monologue that his colleague had heard many times before. Meanwhile, they arrived at the Temple of Light. Outdoors, a busy host of people from various castes milled about: scribes in white tunic, brown-garbed farmers, traders in opulent costumes, and, more rarely, warriors in red leather garb.

The Temple itself was a large, grey building of three stories with ornately decorated doors and windows that stood in the center of a small park with four fountains. The temperature and ambient light contributed to the sense of joy and relaxation of this beautiful spring day.

Benar interrupted Leychert's lengthy exposé as they entered the Temple.

"If you wish, we will continue this interesting conversation another day, my dear Leychert..."

Once inside, the older man looked around.

"It's funny, I don't see Marghael."

"He must be late."

"I don't think so. It's not like him. He's very peculiar about it."

"You say this as a compliment."

"But it is one, Benar!"

They climbed a flight of stone steps and arrived in a spacious amphitheater. A man also wearing a white tunic came to welcome them.

"Good day, Leychert! Glad to see you, Benar. Glad you could come. We have some unexpected surprises in store today."

As the Chief Scribe walked away to greet other arrivals, Benar dropped sarcastically:

"Our good Mallon put on his great owl today!"

Leychert thought that remark was a rather petty comment. The Chief Scribe had opted to wear the great insignia of his office, traditionally worn only for the noblest of ceremonies, but so what?

His train of thoughts was interrupted by the arrival of a bulky individual wearing the red leather armor of the Warriors. Although of medium height, the man exuded a sense of strength and power. His head was shaved, and one could see his muscles roll under his tunic.

The High Priest stepped onto the dais and invited the participants to sit. Then he introduced the newcomer:

"My dear colleagues," he said in a stentorian voice, "I have the honor of introducing you today to Kalzan, our new Commander of the Warriors, who has an important message to communicate... A message of the utmost importance... from Grand Marshal Tark himself. Commander Kalzan..."

At the mention of almost legendary name of the leader of the Warriors, the room fell silent. On the dais, the High Priest yielded his place to the man in red. Murmurs of wonder now traveled through the audience.

Priests, scribes, seers, all were attentive to what the new Commander was about to say.

The man looked at his public for a few seconds, then began to speak:

"Noble Lords, I would first like to thank your High Priest for allowing me, sooner than I had expected, to make you aware of the serious events that I was dispatched here to reveal..."

Kalzan stared silently at the audience for a minute.

"Hitherto, you have lived on the outer margins of the war that pit us against the Brotherhood of the Axe. Some of you may not even be aware of the course of the war. This relative peace was because you were many leagues away from combat zones. This, alas, is no longer the case!"

A deep silence fell over the room, as palpable as a living entity. The Commander took a few steps and, walking back and fro, in a solemn tone, continued:

"The Brothers of the Axe have gained much power in the East recently. The slowly increase their domain every day. Some believe it is because they worship a foul deity they call the Wyrm; others think that the strength of their cult comes from some new drug, extracted from the fabled black lotus... It could be both... In any event, the Temples have joined forces in Atlantis, and Queen Yerra herself has declared a war of extermination upon them... This war has lasted too long already, and shows no signs of abating. New efforts are required; more resources are direly needed to combat the Brothers of the Axe... We Warriors have done our best, but as much as it pains me to admit it, it is not enough"

The Commander went on to paint scenes of ruthless battles. Men in red fighting with giants armored in dark steel holding heavy battle-axes, seemingly insensitive to blows, yet fierce enough to fight to the death.

"…This is what we are fighting to prevent," continued the Commander in a powerful voice. "The total and definitive enslavement of all our continent! You think you're safe? Think again! As I have said just now, Ceqir is no longer in the backwaters of the war. The front has moved north, and soon, you will be at the heart of the battle. That's why I was sent here, to enlist men, collect food, make weapons… All necessary for your protection!"

The last sentence was almost shouted. The faces in the audience now expressed impotence and fear.

Suddenly, another voice broke the silence:

"I do offer a better choice!"

The audience turned around, stunned. The voice belonged to a young man, tall, thin, with grey eyes and short brown hair, dressed in a simple blue tunic.

The newcomer walked to the dais clearly feeling nervous. Under his arm he held a scroll.

"I have found the means to defeat the Brothers of the Axe once and for all!"

The High Priest recovered his composure. His voice was dry as he observed:

"Marghael, you have not been summoned to speak—yet."

The young man made a gesture that could pass for an apology.

"Please, I beg you to let me explain, my lord."

CPSIA information can be obtained
at www.ICGtesting.com
Printed in the USA
BVHW040950220622
640410BV00001B/21